Books by Dane McCaslin

The Proverbial Crime Mysteries
A Bird in the Hand
When the Cat's Away
You Can Lead a Horse to Water

The 2 Sisters Pet Valet Mysteries
Doggone Dead*
Cat's Meow*
Playing Possum*

*Published by Kensington Publishing Corp.

Playing Possum

Dane McCaslin

LYRICAL UNDERGROUND
Kensington Publishing Corp.
www.kensingtonbooks.com

LYRICAL PRESS BOOKS are published by

Kensington Publishing Corp.
119 West 40th Street
New York, NY 10018

All Kensington titles, imprints, and distributed lines are available at special quantity discounts for bulk purchases for sales promotion, premiums, fund-raising, educational, or institutional use.

Special book excerpts or customized printings can also be created to fit specific needs. For details, write or phone the office of the Kensington Sales Manager: Kensington Publishing Corp., 119 West 40th Street, New York, NY 10018. Attn. Sales Department. Phone: 1-800-221-2647.

Lyrical Press and Lyrical Press logo Reg. U.S. Pat. & TM Off.

First Electronic Edition: October 2021
ISBN: 978-1-5161-1016-2 (ebook)

First Print Edition: October 2021
ISBN: 978-1-5161-1019-3

Printed in the United States of America

For my sister. She'll know why.

Chapter 1

"What. The. Heck." Nora Goldstein, my best friend, sat frozen in her living room, one manicured hand holding out a letter as if it had bitten her.

We'd just arrived back at her apartment after a grueling hour spent chasing a runaway dog, and all I wanted to do was sit quietly without any drama. I liked running a business with Nora, I really did, but some days made me wish I'd stuck with my original plan of doing absolutely nothing following my early retirement from teaching.

Still, 2 Sisters Pet Valet Services kept me in pocket money for those occasional shopping excursions to the local Goodwill, and now that my allergies were in check, spending time with animals kept my blood pressure down.

Except for days like today, of course.

Glancing now at Nora and the object she dangled from her fingers, I could see *her* blood pressure was on the rise. Something had her slacks in a swivel, as my granny liked to say, although "slacks" was the furthest thing I could ever imagine on Nora.

Today she was dressed, as usual, in black yoga pants, a tight neon-green top, and ankle-breaking stiletto heels. Compared to my faded denim capris and occasional skirts, billowy shirts, and comfy Birkenstocks, Nora looked like a tropical bird. The two of us couldn't have been any more different, and I liked to think that was the glue that had kept us together since our kindergarten days.

Watching her now as she sat staring at the letter, her eyes opened as wide as they could go, I knew my wish for a drama-less afternoon was kaput.

"I guess you'd better tell me what's up before you blow a gasket." I struggled to sit up as I motioned to the letter. "Care to share, or should I read it to myself?"

"I'm not sure I believe what I'm seeing, Sis." She waved the letter in my direction. "You'd better read it and tell me what you think it says."

With a slight groan, I pushed myself up and shuffled over to where Nora sat, plopping down on the other end of the overstuffed sofa.

"I swear to goodness." I leaned down and rubbed my legs with both hands and wiggled my toes, wincing as I did. Our first pet client of the day had really done me in. Running in Birkenstocks as we chased the little darling was not the smartest idea I'd ever had. "Not only are my dogs barking, my calves are mooing as well." I glanced at Nora, my mouth twisted in a grimace. "Take my advice and drop that maniac animal from our client list. I'm in no shape to chase that thing again, no matter how much his owner offers us."

"Already done." She leaned back against plump cushions and thrust the letter in my direction. "Read, please."

I opened it and carefully smoothed out the stationery with one hand, noting the address embossed at the top of the page. "Is this from your lawyer?"

Nora shook her head against the pillows. "Nope. It's from the lawyer that my ex used."

"Which ex?"

That wasn't a facetious question. Nora, bless her little romantic heart, had quite a collection of men who carried the label of "ex-husband." It was thanks to these exes and their various divorce settlements that she'd become a millionaire in her own right.

"Number three. The one I like to call the 'Bottomless Pitt.'"

"As in Hades?" I lifted one eyebrow in question. "That bottomless pit?"

Nora's short-lived marriages were often so brief in duration that I missed them completely during the years when we weren't in as frequent contact. I wasn't familiar with this particular nickname.

"Of course, and the fact that his last name is Pitt. And because he managed to hide more money than he admitted to having."

I looked back at the letter and quickly skimmed the information. The brief paragraph inserted between the greeting and the closing made my eyes widen, and I could see why Nora had reacted the way she did. Clearing my throat, I held the letter up and began to read aloud.

"'Dear Mrs. Pitt.'" I looked over at Nora. "'Mrs. Pitt'? When did you ever use that name?"

She chuckled. "I never did. I was always Nora Goldstein, just as I am now." She paused, head tilted. "Maybe that's why none of the marriages lasted."

I grunted, looking back at the letter. "Maybe it was because all five of them were absolute stinkers. Except, possibly, the Bottomless Pitt, it would seem. Why in the world did he appoint you as his executor? Had you seen him recently?"

"No, not since the divorce." She held up one hand, counting silently on her fingers. "Let's see. It's been at least fourteen, fifteen years. I've seen his kids Merry and Martin more than I ever saw him."

"That's bizarre. Maybe he thought you were the most honest person in his life and could be trusted to handle this." I handed the letter back to her.

Nora gave a short laugh. "That's a pretty sad commentary on his family, I'd say. Although," she added with a small hitch of one shoulder, "I might agree with him. Both of his offspring were absolutely despicable as kids, at least the way I recall those two brats. I can only imagine what type of adults they've turned out to be."

We sat silently for a few moments. I debated getting up and making coffee, but a twinge in my right leg changed my mind. Maybe I should give Brent a call. He'd be glad to come over and help. Actually, Brent would be glad to come over and escape his younger brother. I was about to make the suggestion when Nora abruptly headed for the desk she kept in one corner of the living room. It was tucked discreetly behind a folding Japanese screen, and its shiny top held a state-of-the-art computer and printer.

I sat with my head leaning back against the cushions as I listened to Nora rummaging in the various desk drawers. What I really needed was a good long soak in Epsom salts. Herc, my black-and-white rescue dog, would have to be content to use the doggie door to do his business.

I'd almost drifted off to sleep when a loud noise brought me straight up, my heart pounding as loudly as the bass drums in the high school marching band. Had someone broken in and targeted Nora? An extreme reaction, I know, but with all the murders we'd been involved with lately, anything unusual could make me as jumpy as a frog in a hot skillet.

"That rat. That unbelievable, absolutely despicable, downright irritating rat!"

Another loud bang told me exactly what had startled me. Nora was slamming desk drawers as loudly as she could.

"If you don't want your neighbors to think you're being attacked, I'd advise you to bring it down a notch or two."

My best friend marched from behind the screen, two bright spots of red on her cheeks.

"And to which rat are you referring? Marcus? Or the Bottomless Pitt?"

She glared at me as she shoved her cell phone into her top, currently doubling as her carrying case, and kept marching past the sofa and down the hallway. A loud slam told me she'd gone into her room and closed the door.

Marcus Avery was Nora's on-again, off-again boyfriend, a private detective whose reputation as the local Lothario sometimes got him into hot water with her. I could never figure out why he was so attractive to the ladies, to be honest. His physique was on the rotund end of the scale, and his thinning hair topped a round face that had seen better days. Apparently, he had a charm I couldn't detect. As long as he kept my friend happy, though, I was content to leave it at that.

My own taste in men tended to run toward retired dentists with laugh lines and a wonderful smile. Particularly one named Roger Smithson, owner of two aging golden retrievers named Max and Doc, and lately, I had to admit, of my heart. Just thinking about him gave my pulse a little jump, and I was grinning like a loon when Nora banged out of her room and stomped back to the sofa, where she sat down.

She gave me another glare. "What's got you so tickled, Sis? You think dealing with the Bottomless Pitt is funny?"

I came back to earth from the cloud on which I'd been floating, landing with a thud beside one very irate Nora. Something had put her panties into one king-sized twist. Maybe this last order from beyond the grave had her reliving the problems from her marriage to the occupier of said grave.

I stared back at her, my eyebrows riding near my hairline. "Funny? Apparently not."

Leaning over, I gently touched one arm. She was trembling, almost vibrating, under my hand, and I was instantly on guard. This wasn't like Nora, not at all. If I didn't get to the bottom of the issue soon, I was afraid she'd make herself sick.

"Nora?" I spoke quietly as I scooted closer, placing my arm around her thin shoulders. "You need to tell me what's wrong, okay?"

At first, she sat there stiffly, acting as if she hadn't heard a word I'd said. I was tempted to shake her and make her talk, but I wasn't sure how she'd react in her present mood. Besides, we'd only had a handful of real disagreements over decades of friendship, and I didn't want to chance one now.

Finally, she gave a deep sigh and leaned back against me. The crisis, as my role model Miss Marple would say, had passed. She'd tell me in her own time.

"Hey, you." I gave her shoulders a little squeeze and stood. "I'm going to get us some coffee, okay? Then we can talk about this."

She nodded but said nothing. I got the coffee made in record time and carried the steaming mugs back into the living room. Handing her one, I took the other and reseated myself on the other end of the sofa.

"I'm not well-versed in law and wills and that sort of stuff." I took a cautious sip of coffee and winced. It was still too hot to drink, but the aroma of the smooth Ethiopian blend was delicious. "Do you have to abide by your ex's request?"

Nora gave a half-hearted shrug. "I'm pretty sure it's binding, especially since he used a lawyer." She took a small drink of coffee. "Knowing him like I do, that man didn't leave any loose ends. And that's not what's bothering me, if that's what you're getting at."

"Ah." I looked at her, scrutinizing her face for any hint of what had made her so angry. When none was forthcoming, I decided to switch tactics. Whether she liked it or not, I'd get it out of her eventually. "If I were you, I'd make an appointment with the lawyer and get the scoop on what your role really is." I kept my tone neutral, still observing her closely.

"Oh, believe you me, Sis, I intend to do just that." Nora's lips were a firm line of annoyance. "I wouldn't put it past him to get in one last dig, you know? He never got over the settlement I got after our divorce." She gave a short, unamused laugh. "What a piece of work."

I gave her an uneasy look. She was beginning to sound cynical, something that wasn't like Nora. She could be sarcastic, certainly, but cynicism wasn't in her style book.

"What? Do I have something on my face?" Nora attempted a smile, but I wasn't fooled.

"You make that appointment, and I'll go with you." I lifted my coffee mug in a salute. "One for all and all for one, right?"

She snorted. "Yep, that's us, Sis. The Two Musketeers."

I was glad to hear her sense of humor beginning to resurrect itself. "Then let's get this show on the road." I glanced at my cell phone. "It's early enough to cancel tomorrow morning's pet-sitting assignments. You can let the lawyer's office know we can be there first thing tomorrow."

"No need." Nora's tone became brisk, businesslike. "Between Brent and Rachel, they can handle the jobs."

"If you say so." I frowned slightly as I mentally counted off the jobs. "I think we might need to hire another dog walker and free up Rachel to take on more of the pet-sitting assignments."

"Have anyone in mind?" Nora gave me a mischievous grin. "Maybe a certain gent who happens to like dogs?"

I wanted to stick out my tongue. Instead, I lifted my chin haughtily. "I don't know what you're talking about."

"And the Bottomless Pitt was the sweetest man on the face of this earth." Nora shook her head in wry amusement. "You call Roger and ask if he'll help us out. I'll get busy calling this lawyer."

Talking on the phone was never my favorite thing to do, and the advent of text in place of actually speaking to a faceless voice had made my life easier. I never minded a face-to-face exchange, but there was something inherently awkward about carrying on a conversation with someone I couldn't see.

Still, texting Roger instead of calling him seemed somehow discourteous, as if he wasn't important enough for a call. I opened my contact list and found his name.

He answered on the first ring, and his cheerful voice made me smile. "Gwen! How nice to hear from you."

I could hear the muted sounds of a television in the background.

"How are you today? Anything new and exciting?"

"Not unless you call getting a letter from an ex-husband exciting."

There was a momentary silence from his end of the line. "An ex-husband, you said? I thought you've never been married."

I chuckled, imagining the expression on his face as he tried to figure this out. "Not *my* ex. One of Nora's."

At this, my best friend turned to stare at me, one eyebrow lifted.

I waggled mine in return. "Apparently one of them made her the executor of his will, and now she's got to talk to the lawyer. I said I'd go with her."

"Aha. That makes more sense." The sound of canned laughter rose in the background. "Give me a sec, would you? I need to shut this thing off."

"Sounds like you're watching *All in a Day's Work*. Those candid camera shows can get really silly."

"Indeed they can." There was silence as he clicked off the television. "Now, where were we?"

"I was calling to see if you could lend a hand tomorrow with the pet business." I shifted around on the couch, trying to find a more comfortable way to sit that didn't make my legs ache more. "Rachel and Brent will be here, of course, but with Nora and me at the lawyer's office, I'm afraid they won't be able to handle it all."

"Not a problem. I'd be happy to walk a few dogs for you."

"Oh, that's great." I gave Nora a thumbs-up. "I'm sure there'll only be one, maybe two at the most."

"That's fine. What time would you like me to be there? I'm assuming I'll start off at Nora's place, right?"

I paused, trying to think through the list of appointments. "Hang on a moment, Roger. I need to check before I give you the wrong information."

Nora disappeared behind the silk screen that hid her desk, and her polished fingernails tapped an impatient tattoo on its shiny surface. "They've got me on hold, if you can believe it. *And* I'm stuck listening to some God-awful pop song that sounds like a cat getting its tail pulled." She shook her head in disgust. "What was wrong with good ol' elevator music, I ask you? At least I didn't have to hear 'ooh baby baby' over and over."

I distractedly waved her complaints away. "Listen, Roger said he'll be glad to help tomorrow. I just need to know if he should come over here in the morning or go straight to the client's house."

"Whatever you think." Nora's continuous fingernail tapping was getting on my nerves. "It might be easier to send him a text with the client's information. Everything's already opened on my iPad." She pointed with her chin to the desk, where the tablet lay. "The list for tomorrow is right there on the first page." Her fingers paused in mid-tap as she listened to something on the other end of the line. "And it's about time, too. Do you have any idea how appalling your hold music is?"

I shook my head, smiling to myself as I grabbed the iPad from her desk. A sassy Nora was a normal Nora. And if that lawyer had any sense about him, he'd better be ready with all barrels locked and loaded, or at least with some answers.

My job would be to get answers from Nora, including what it was that had suddenly set her off. Was the Ghost of Rotten Husbands Past about to make a visit? If so, it had better be warned: no one messed with my best friend, and I'd do everything in my power to see they didn't, no matter if they were dead or alive.

Chapter 2

The next morning's sunrise outside my bedroom window was feeble, the rays battling a growing bank of dark clouds as they attempted to get through. My brain was in feeble mode as well, and as I slowly shuffled toward the kitchen in search of life-restoring caffeine, I began to regret my promise to go with Nora to see her ex-husband's lawyer.

I'd had a restless night, despite the lavender chamomile tea I'd sipped as I re-read Agatha Christie's *They Do It with Mirrors*. There was something about the friendship between Miss Marple and her American pals that had colored my dreams, and I'd awoken with a sense of anxiety. I had no explanation for feeling that way, and I chalked it up to Nora's upcoming appointment.

However, once the caffeine hit my system and I'd had a shower, I began to feel much more like my commonsensical self. Maybe I needed to change my bedtime reading to something more soothing, such as *Good Night, Moon*.

Whatever the reason, I was back on an even keel by the time I arrived at Nora's. I'd left my rescue dog, a black-and-white mixed breed I'd named Hercule, sound asleep on the living room rug. The doggy door I'd installed a few months before would let him out to do his business, and I'd left ample water. This, at least, was one less thing for me to worry about as Nora and I stood outside her apartment building waiting for our Uber.

I'd only visited this part of Portland a few times in my life. For such a small town, it had some amazingly hidden recesses that seemed to appear from nowhere, an American version of Brigadoon. After waving goodbye to our (thankfully) taciturn driver, Nora and I headed toward the building that housed her ex-husband's lawyer.

The name emblazoned on the opaque glass door reinforced my highland musings. "I. MacWhirter, Esquire" was picked out in a gilt script that mimicked cursive, an art that was rapidly disappearing in our schools, much to my sorrow.

"Ready to rock 'n' roll?"

Nora's question shook me out of my reverie on the demise of cursive.

I reached over and gave her arm a brief pat, smiling my encouragement. "You betcha, girlie. Let's do this."

Despite the elegance of the front door's presentation, the reception area looked as if a rainbow had exploded in the room. A lipstick-red sofa sat against one wall, its ends bracketed with a pair of mustard-yellow arm chairs. Pillows in green and blue added to the mix, and the teak coffee table that perched sedately on top of the multi-hued rug looked like the third wheel on a romantic date.

"Who decorated this place, Bozo the Clown?" Nora's muttered comment made me smile. "Marcus would love it."

I chuckled as I took in the busy room. "All that's missing is a plaid jacket or two."

"Plaid jacket? Sounds like my type of man."

The voice behind us made us jump. We spun around, my hand clutching Nora's arm.

A pair of green eyes twinkled above a wide grin, and the tight red curls that covered her head gave the woman a Brillo pad appearance. She thrusted out a freckled hand. "Ione MacWhirter at your service."

"You're the lawyer? My ex-husband used a woman lawyer?" Nora's mouth gaped in a most unbecoming manner, and I was tempted to shut it for her. "The Bottomless Pitt hated women. Hence the 'ex' in front of 'husband.'"

It was difficult to tell if Ione MacWhirter was flushing. Her freckles seemed to have multiplied in the few moments since we'd met her, and her narrowed eyes had lost their friendly welcome. "If you'll give me a few minutes to review your case, I'll be happy to speak with you."

Turning around, she headed for the bright yellow door behind a low teak desk. I exchanged a shrug with Nora. Clearly, something had upset the lawyer, and ten to one it was my best friend's choice of words.

"Let's sit down." I motioned to the colorful seating arrangement. "I've got a feeling her 'few moments' might stretch out a bit longer."

"Oh, more than likely." Nora gave her thin shoulders another hitch and followed me over to the sofa. "She's got to prove a point, right?"

I stared at Nora, my eyebrows lifting in mock confusion. "And why's that, pray tell?" I knew the answer already, having been a witness in the past to my pal's verbal skirmishes, but hearing Nora say it would be much more satisfying.

"Oh, don't play stupid, Sis." Nora didn't look at me, turning instead and giving an assessing gaze to the small reception area. "I got up her nose. She got up mine."

I let her words go without comment. The visual was enough.

"Speaking of playing stupid," I said, "what was up with you earlier? You were acting like a toddler in a tantrum."

Nora lifted one shoulder. "That's because I was. Give you three guesses what it was about, and the first two don't count."

"Surely not Marcus." I stared at her, trying to catch her train of thought. Nora could change topics as swiftly as that runaway puppy we'd chased, and I was having a tough time following. "I thought this was about the Bottomless Pitt."

"Got it in one. That was a monthly statement from my accountant, and he's not happy. Wants me to discontinue my support of that so-called detective agency Marcus claims to be running. I'm telling you, Sis. Marcus and my ex should be tied together and tossed in the nearest lake." Nora pointed at the opening door. "And it looks like the show's about to begin."

Ione MacWhirter silently led us down a surprisingly colorless hallway, pausing in front of the only open door I could see. She motioned us in ahead of her and then followed, closing the door behind her with a smart snap.

I chanced a quick glance at Nora, and she'd assumed her "high and mighty" posture, chin held high and eyes narrowed. She looked ready for battle. Sighing, I sank into a visitor's chair farthest from the desk. It would behoove me to stay out of the line of fire.

Nora perched on the edge of the other chair, her rigid back mirrored in Ione's as she sat facing us from behind her desk. They reminded me of the bantam roosters my granny had raised, feathers ruffled and heads lowered whenever they felt challenged. I hid a sudden smile behind one hand, unable to wipe the image from my mind.

With a suspicious glance in my direction, Ione cleared her throat and began the meeting. "As you mentioned in your call, Mrs. Pitt—"

"Mrs. Goldstein. Please."

"Mrs. Goldstein." Ione nodded to show she understood, the beginnings of premature jowls appearing along her jawline. "When you called earlier about Mr. Pitt's will, I found myself in a unique position."

Nora returned the nod, hers a regal movement that kept her own flawless chin on display. "Unique in what way, if I many ask?"

Instead of answering immediately, Ione clasped her hands on top of a buff folder and stared at them intently. She was either trying to gather her thoughts or was deciding what to say. Neither boded well for Nora.

"Mr. Pitt did indeed file his will with our office. He did that with my father, Ian MacWhirter, while I was still in law school." She grinned suddenly, causing a light network of wrinkles to appear around her eyes. "I had to call Dad this morning to get the scoop, to be honest."

"The scoop? You mean on how he…he passed?" I sounded as confused as Nora looked. "Why would you need to do that?"

"I'm sorry." Nora spoke up, gesturing in my direction. "This is my friend Miss Gwen Franklin. Anything that needs to be said today can certainly be said in front of her."

"Because you'll end up telling her anyway?" Ione's tone was sardonic, but her smile seemed genuine.

"You've got it." I smiled back. "But, back to the Bottomless…to Mr. Pitt," I corrected myself. "You said you needed to speak with your father."

Ione shrugged. "Yes, I did. I've never had a case quite like this one."

Beside me, Nora let out a groan. "Oh, don't tell me the old coot managed to add something crazy to the instructions like making me join a chess club or something in order to execute his will. If that's the case, you can count me out."

Ione and I both laughed at the absurdity of her comment.

"Nothing as crazy as that," Ione assured her. "In fact, we don't know for sure if he's actually dead."

"You're kidding me, right?" Nora's eyes were opened as wide as they could go, and her thin eyebrows almost disappeared into her tight blond curls. "Then why did I get the letter?"

"Because the police want to find out as much as they can." Ione hitched up one shoulder in an apologetic shrug. "And because they'll be here in a few minutes."

"Nothing doing. Sis," Nora turned to me as she stood, "we're off like a dirty shirt."

"Like a *what*?" I stood as well, waiting for her to move ahead of me before I started walking. "Is that a Marcus-ism?"

I didn't get a chance to hear her response. The office door opened to the arrival of two detectives. One, unfortunately, looked very familiar.

"Oh, not Rachel's dad," groaned Nora. "What else can go wrong?"

"Detective." I spoke with as much dignity as I could, while trying to keep Nora from bolting. "I'd ask to what do we owe this delightful meeting, but Ms. MacWhirter has just informed us."

"Imagine my surprise when I saw your name on the list of people to speak with." Rachel's dad, an athletically built man with the same dark eyes as Rachel, moved past us and into the office. "I've got a good mind to tell my daughter she can't be seen with you anymore."

"And I've got a good mind to call her right now and remind her she's well over eighteen." Clearly Nora had recovered enough of her aplomb to respond with her usual sass.

I groaned inwardly, waiting for the fireworks.

I was relieved when he laughed and held out one hand.

"Let's start over. I'm Rachel's dad, Detective Joe Day."

Nora took his hand, her head tilted as she smiled at him. "Day, huh? Sis, did you know that?"

"No. I've never thought to ask, believe it or not."

"Wait a minute." Detective Day looked from me to Nora, a quizzical expression on his face. "Do you mean to tell me that you've employed my daughter for the past few months and you've never known her full name?"

Nora and I looked at one another and shrugged in unison.

"Since I don't pay her myself, Detective, I let that info slide into my mind and right out again. I've got more important things to worry about than someone's last name." Nora's eyes narrowed. This wasn't going well at all.

"What Nora means," I jumped in, "is she stays very busy with not only the pet valet business, but she also gives her time to different charities. Because of that, we use a payroll company to handle all paychecks and paperwork."

"And it's a legit payroll company. I'm not paying your daughter under the table, if that's what you're insinuating." Nora's chin was now jutting forward in a very unfriendly manner. Detective or not, Joe Day needed to watch himself around her.

"Well, now that we've all been introduced and are getting along so brilliantly, I'd say it's time to get down to brass tacks." Ione motioned for us to be seated. "And feel free to join us, ladies."

"With pleasure," Nora said.

I walked behind her as she commandeered one of the chairs. I hesitated a moment and then took the other, leaving the two detectives to stand behind us.

Ione sat behind her desk, her hands clasped and her expression somber as she looked out at the four of us. I almost felt sorry for her until I remembered the rather hefty fee she was most likely earning for her time.

Clearing her throat, she met Nora's gaze. "Mrs. Goldstein, as I've already said, your ex-husband appointed you to be the executor of his will. Unfortunately, he was reported missing nearly four years ago by his children. They're now requesting that a court declare him dead, which can happen as soon as next month. Your part as executor is to decide if there's a need for probate or for selling any property."

Nora shook her head, with a baffled expression. "So what I'm hearing you say is no one knows if he's really dead or not, but the kids are anxious to get their sticky hands on his property. Is that about right?"

From behind me, I thought I heard one of the officers muffle a laugh.

Ione, to her credit, managed to keep her expression neutral. "That sums it up." Reaching for the folder that lay in front of her, she opened it and slipped out a single sheet of paper. "This is a copy of what was filed with the court. I've made this copy for you, so feel free to peruse it at your leisure."

Nora took the paper and gave her a scowl in return. "Since you requested my time, which is at a premium, by the way, I'll read it now. You can take your fee from my ex-stepmonsters."

This time I was certain I heard a chuckle from one of the detectives. I looked at my hands and smiled to myself. Nora in a snit could be funny as well as dangerous. It didn't take a genius to see which way this conversation was headed.

Ione, it appeared, had a temper of her own. She bit her lip in a clear struggle to keep in the words that were practically flashing in neon above her head: I do not get paid enough to deal with idiots like this one. Professionalism conquered all, however, and she gave a tiny smile as she nodded her acquiescence. I liked the way she kept it going under pressure. She would have made a great high school teacher.

"Okay, I've read it." Nora folded it before tucking it inside the velvet fanny pack she'd recently begun wearing. Only Nora could get away with such a goofy, in my opinion, fashion accessory. You certainly wouldn't catch me wearing one of those, even if I could find one to comfortably fit my girth.

"Do you have any questions for me?" The lines on Ione's forehead smoothed out slightly as she spoke. Perhaps she thought this ordeal was coming to a close. I wasn't as optimistic.

"As a matter of fact, I do." Nora leaned back and gave her bottom a wiggle as she readjusted her posture. Crossing one Lycra-encased leg over the other, she stared straight at Ione.

The worry lines on the lawyer's forehead reappeared in full force and seemed to have invited a friend to the party. Poor woman. I should've told her Nora was all bark and very little bite, but I wanted to see how this would play out. Not many folks were able to withstand the onslaught of my best friend's, shall we say, *forceful* personality. I wondered if the two detectives were taking notes for future encounters.

"Please. Go ahead." Ione gestured for Nora to continue. "If I can't answer all of your questions, I'm sure these officers can provide further information."

"Wait a sec." Nora turned around and gave each man the once-over before turning back to Ione. "I thought they were here to ask *me* questions, not give answers."

Nora crossed her arms over her chest and began to slowly tap one foot as the silence grew thicker. Her signals were as loud and clear as the wail of a tornado warning, and I mentally crossed my fingers, toes, and eyes that this would not end with Nora getting arrested for assault of a peace officer or a lawyer. Or both.

I was pretty sure Ione would refuse to handle her case.

Chapter 3

The silence in the lawyer's office was as thick as my granny's morning oatmeal. I wanted to jump up or shout or something to break it, but this was Nora's show. If she wanted information, she'd get it one way or another.

Finally, she gave a small sigh and slid to the edge of her chair. "Ms. MacWhirter, is there any evidence whatsoever that my ex-husband is dead?" When Ione began to protest again that it wasn't her call, Nora held up one hand to stop her. "I have a good reason for asking, believe me. That man has always had an issue with the truth, and it wouldn't surprise me one iota if he's only faking it to give us all fits."

The officers shuffled behind me at her words, and I was tempted to turn and give them the ol' teacher stare, guaranteed to quell a small riot. My attention, however, was caught by the expression on Ione's face: one part suspicion, two parts curiosity. I had a feeling she'd never dealt with anyone quite like Nora in her short legal career.

"I do have some information, Mrs. Goldstein, but it might not help in the way you want it to." Ione reached across her desk and grabbed a stack of papers. Her bottom lip was caught between her teeth, transforming her appearance into something that wouldn't be out of place in *A Wind in the Willows*.

An image of the water rat flashed into my mind, and I had to transfer a laugh into a cough. Ione looked at me, a sharp expression in her eyes, and I had a feeling she'd read my mind. Giving her a half-smile and waving off the water bottle Nora offered to me, I settled back into my chair and waited to hear what information Ione might have.

"All right, Mrs. Goldstein. According to the information from your stepchildren—"

"*Ex*-stepchildren, if you please." Nora earned a replica of the same sharp stare I'd gotten from Ione.

"Fine." Now Ione's tone was tighter, all pretense at affability gone. I imagined I could see a large clock ticking above her head as she calculated Nora's bill to the nanosecond. "Your *ex*-stepchildren, Martin and Merry Pitt, recently filed paperwork indicating they wish a certificate of presumptive death to be filed on behalf of their father." She glanced over our heads at the detectives. "And I presume you already have copies of this?" She looked down at her desk and plucked an official-looking paper from a precarious stack, waving it in the air and causing a small snowstorm on her desk as the rest of the papers scattered.

Beside me, Nora slumped backward in defeat. I'm not sure how she expected the Bottomless Pitt's children to act, especially with a sizable estate on the line. Still, it was a shock to hear how swiftly they'd filed their own paperwork, and I confess my own mouth dropped open in surprise before I quickly clamped it shut. I could almost hear my granny's voice reminding me not to gape like that.

"Girls catch men, not flies, Gwennie. Be a honeypot, not a flytrap."

Was that what Roger Smithson thought I was? A honeypot?

I honestly tried not to analyze my feelings for the retired dentist. It was a new thing for me, having a romantic relationship and being part of a couple. I liked his company, his sense of humor, and his dogs.

"It's a lame dentist's joke," he'd explained one day when we'd been at the Portland Pooch Park. "I was a tooth doctor, and I took care of many a maxilla."

"And my Herc is really Hercule, after the Belgian detective created by Agatha Christie." I'd reached down to give my rescue dog a rub between his ears. "When I saw his black coat and white front and paws, it reminded me so much of a tuxedo, and that, in turn, made me think of Hercule Poirot." I'd shrugged shyly, hoping I didn't sound like a nitwit.

If Roger's approving smile had been any indication, however, I wasn't a nitwit in his eyes. A honeypot? Probably not. But at least I wasn't a goofball.

I jumped as a hand snapped impatient fingers in front of my face.

"Earth to Gwen. Come in, Gwen."

I pushed Nora's hand away and smiled apologetically around the room. I must have missed something aimed in my direction while I was busy with my Roger-tinged daydream.

"You don't need to shout, Nora. I heard you."

My very best friend in the whole world gave me a first-class eye roll.

"And I'd ask you to repeat it, but I don't have all day. This little confab is going to be expensive enough as it is." She glanced quickly at the two detectives before turning back to me. "How do you feel about a little trip up north? I think I need to confront those two idiots face-to-face and find out why they're in such an almighty hurry to get their mitts on the money."

"I'd like to remind you, Mrs. Goldstein, that you're not a detective. You're not even remotely qualified." I wanted to laugh as Rachel's dad unhooked his badge from his belt and held it up for Nora to see. "That's why I wear this little jewel and you don't."

"And where were you when we uncovered who killed that reporter, I'd like to know? Or found out who killed that woman I discovered in my kitchen, of all places?"

Nora was working up a good head of self-righteous steam, but she did have a point. She and I had become involved in two previous murders and had lived to tell the tales. Still, Detective Day had a point as well, and he was making it for all he was worth. I decided to step in and defuse the situation before it got out of hand and we both got arrested.

"Listen, you two." I turned around in my chair so I could see the two combatants. "Nora has the absolute right to take a trip to see her ex-husband's children. She also has the right, as the will's executor, to find out the particulars of his disappearance."

Detective Day began to protest, but I ignored him. It was all about choosing the hill on which to die, I always maintained. Getting into a side argument would slow the entire process.

"And, Nora, he's correct when he says you're not a detective. You aren't."

Nora spluttered, and I held up one hand.

"Now listen. You and I can take a trip, as you put it, to figure things out on the will end of things. Let's leave the legalities behind his death to the police, all right?" I gave the entire room a stern look and rose. "Why don't we go on home and make a plan. Besides, you know we think better with coffee and a snack."

Ione surged to her feet as well, nearly toppling over the desk in her haste to clear her office. "I think that's a marvelous idea. Why don't you call me when you've discovered whatever it is you think you need to know, Mrs. Goldstein, and we'll get this wrapped up. I'm here to help see this through to the end, that's for sure."

Her facial expression, however, didn't match the comment. I would never claim to be a body language reader, but this woman's nonverbal communication was screaming, "Get me off this crazy ride," as surely as if she'd said it out loud.

Nora's jaw tightened, but she followed me out of the office without saying anything. I really was ready for some coffee, and just talking about a snack had my stomach already anticipating something sweet.

Maybe a quick stop at Voodoo Doughnuts would take the edge off both my sweet tooth and my growing irritation at the Detective Day and Nora Goldstein show. At any rate, if I didn't get something in me quickly, I was going to begin snapping at everyone as well.

* * * *

The ride back to Nora's place after our doughnut foray wasn't as quiet as the ride to Ione's had been. Our driver, a young woman with multi-colored braids all over her head and more piercings in her ears than I could count, kept up a steady stream of chatter, talking about the most recent Portland Trail Blazers game with the enthusiasm of a true basketball fan.

"It was unbelievable, I swear. When Curry grabbed the ball from Carmelo's hands, I thought it was gonna go down right there." She gave a laugh that didn't sound the least bit upset. "I swear, sometimes I think those guys are complete egomaniacs, thinking they can get away with sh—oops, I mean crap...right in front of the ref." She gave another chuckle as she flipped on the turn indicator and pulled up neatly in front of Nora's luxury apartment building. "I guess they don't care about fines and all that kinda stuff with all the dough they make. Unlike me," she added with a wink over her shoulder at me. "I'd appreciate any tip you can leave, ma'am."

I pointed at Nora. "This is the lady you need to speak with. She's paying for the ride." I reached up and patted her shoulder. "I can give you a tip, though, from a retired teacher's perspective: remember that an education will help you get along in life, and you won't need to drive crazy old ladies around any longer."

To my surprise, our driver tossed her head back and laughed as loudly as if I'd told her the best joke. My back stiffened. I was unsure how to react to this obvious disdain for my suggestion. Education, in my opinion, was nothing to sniff at.

"Oh, ma'am." She wiped her eyes on her sleeves and turned a face rosy with laughter toward me. "I'm not laughing at you, but I just finished a PhD in macroeconomics. I'm leaving town next week for a teaching position at Boston College." She glanced at Nora as she sat with one finger poised over her cell phone, her mouth hanging open as she listened to this exchange.

"Tips are still appreciated, though. I won't be getting a paycheck for a few weeks, hence the Uber gig."

I was stunned into silence, more from my own assumptions than anything else, and I was certain my face was as pink as the driver's, only mine was from embarrassment. I'd just done exactly what I'd always encouraged my students not to do—assume. I was glad Brent wasn't there to see me in action.

Nora slid a mischievous glance my way, undoubtedly aware of exactly what I was feeling. With a final tap on her cell phone, she slid it back into her top and smiled broadly as she gave me a push toward the car's door. "Well, missy, I hope the tip I added helps you get settled in Boston. That place costs as much as Portland when it comes to housing. You'd think everyone was rolling in riches from the prices they charge."

"I'm sure it's perfect, ma'am. And thanks from the bottom of my heart, seriously." The driver shook her head and set colorful braids swinging. "It's been really sh—oops, I mean crappy...living on instant noodles and frozen burritos."

"Sounds like typical teacher rations," I muttered, ignoring a sharp poke on my arm, courtesy of my best friend. I firmly believed in telling the truth, and I sincerely hoped this young woman knew exactly what she was getting into. Most teachers I knew didn't go into the profession for the big bucks. "I wish you all the best." I stepped out of the car.

I didn't wish her luck. She'd have to learn to make her own. This world could be a cruel place.

And folks like me didn't make it any easier. I could have kicked myself for letting an assumption color my conversation with a very decent young woman. My best pal, as usual, didn't hold back.

"Yeesh, Sis. Judgy much?"

The elevator ride to Nora's floor was silent, except for the muted noises emitted by the various pulleys and wires holding the steel cage on its tracks. Nora, I had a feeling, had moved on from my transgression and was busy cooking up an excuse for contacting Marcus Avery.

Nothing like having Portland's plaid-clad Romeo hanging about while I tried to keep Nora focused on the task at hand. And traveling with two people billing and cooing wasn't my idea of time well spent, no matter who it was. Unless, of course, I was part of the "bill and coo" duo.

Visions of Roger sent a sudden wave of heat from my neck to my crown, and Nora's sharp eyes missed nothing.

"I thought all that nonsense was over and done with, Sis." Her stare was as pointed as her nails, one of which she shoved painfully into my non-cushioned chest. "Or is there something you're not telling me?"

"Like what?" I pushed her hand away in irritation, trying to edge past her and into the cooler confines of the hallway. "I have no idea what you're babbling about."

"You know." Nora didn't give up easily, particularly when there might be a tidbit of juicy gossip within reach. "Your own personal summer. The change. Losing your marbles."

I stopped abruptly, staring at her in astonishment. "'Losing your marbles'? What in the world does that have to do with menopause?"

"Oh, you should talk to my mom, Miss F. I'll bet she can tell you all about old ladies losing their marbles. Like my grammy and all that, you know?"

Nora and I turned as one, gaping at the sight that was Brent Mayfair. His mop of dirty blond hair was hidden underneath the hood of his oversized sweatshirt, and in his arms was a small white dog with big ears and an even bigger bark, which she promptly demonstrated for us.

"Can't you keep that mutt quiet? And get that hood off, young man. You look like a hoodlum." Nora's words were negated by her smile, and she reached out to give Aggie's soft fur a pat.

"That's a good one, Mrs. G." Brent yanked back his hood with his free hand, grinning from ear to ear. "Hoodlum and hood—get it?"

I turned away from him so he couldn't see my expression. Brent, one of my past students, was still such a child in many ways. His brand of humor was definitely juvenile, and I imagined him telling this to his girlfriend Rachel's police detective father. Detective Day probably wouldn't chuckle as Nora was doing at the moment. Hoodlums weren't the stuff of humor in his line of work.

"Come on in, folks." Nora unlocked the apartment door and motioned with her chin for us to follow.

Aggie, stubby tail wagging furiously, struggled to get out of Brent's grasp, nearly diving headlong onto the floor.

"She's sure happy to be here, Mrs. G. I'll bet she thinks you've got some snacks or something for her." Brent's gaze moved across the room toward the kitchen. "Or maybe leftovers, like from lunch."

Brent's preoccupation with food was second to nothing, not even Aggie or Rachel. I didn't think I'd like playing second fiddle to a hamburger.

"Let's take a look, kid. And you'd better make sure that dog doesn't leave me a present, like she did last time." Nora scowled at Brent, her hands resting on her narrow hips. "You keep telling me she's house-trained, but I haven't seen proof of it yet."

"Aw, she's only a baby, Mrs. G. You gotta cut her some slack." Brent's eyes widened as he looked at Nora and then at the dog, who seemed intent on chewing a hole in one of Nora's house slippers. "Besides, she don't understand what 'potty' or 'go outside' means."

"She *doesn't* understand," I corrected him as I leaned over to rescue the somewhat-tattered slipper. "That's why it's called 'training,' Brent. You've got to train her."

"Like teaching her to do a trick?" Brent's forehead furrowed, staring at Aggie as she began sniffing the carpet, circling one particular spot until she found the perfect spot. As she began to squat, he quickly scooped her up, holding her to his chest, giving us a lopsided grin. "Aw, don't get mad, Mrs. G. Aggie's just playing possum. She wouldn't really whizz on your floor."

I had to bite my lip to stifle an automatic smile as a dark patch began to track its way down the front of Brent's shirt.

"Aaaand point proven." Shaking her head, but with most of her irritation fading, Nora held out her hands for Aggie. "Kid, get yourself down the hall to the bathroom and wash the front of that shirt. And hand me that bundle of trouble. I'll get her outside." She shot me a sardonic grin. "You'd think we didn't have a clue about handling pets, right?"

"I'll go with you, Mrs. G." Brent reached out and took Aggie from Nora, dropping an affectionate kiss on the pooch's head. "You never know who you'll run into, like muggers and stuff."

I smiled to myself as I listened to Brent's awkward explanation. Nora, however, seemed not to notice and started for the door, Brent trailing her with a squirming Aggie in his arms.

"I'll go with you." I reached over and gave Aggie's ears a scratch. "We need to come up with a plan."

"Plan? For what?" Nora seemed to have forgotten all about the morning spent in the lawyer's office. Or perhaps this was the first sign of senility.

"The will? Your ex-husband? Ring any bells?" I leaned forward, enunciating my words and watching carefully through narrowed eyes to see that she understood.

Nora reared back, staring at me as though I'd grown a horn in the middle of my forehead. "Are you okay? You're squinting like you've got something in your eyes, Sis. Here." She fished into her shirt and pulled out a folded piece of tissue. "Use this."

I wrinkled my nose and pushed the tissue away. Knowing where it had been gave me the willies. Why a grown woman felt the need to store things in her bra was beyond me. What was wrong with tucking a tissue in a sleeve, like my granny had done? I told Nora as much, and we were still bickering over tissue storage when we left the elevator and stepped into the building's plush lobby.

Tissues, however, were the least of my concerns when I saw who was sitting there, a smug expression on his wide face. Marcus Avery, Man About Town and Nora's on-again, off-again boyfriend, was wedged into a chair, one plaid-encased leg crossed over the other, hand lifted in greeting.

"Well, if it isn't Prince Charming," Nora drawled, arms crossed over her chest. "Care to explain where you've been hiding out?"

Before Marcus could sputter an answer, I offered a cheery greeting. "Always a pleasure to see you, Marcus." I glanced at his trousers. "Of course, I couldn't miss you in that getup. Been raiding the local upholstery shop?"

Marcus gave a sniff and reached out one hand to brush an imaginary speck from one leg. How in the world he could see anything against the loud pattern was beyond me.

"I've been busy." He shifted his bulk to the edge of the chair and gave a grunt as he stood. I had to admire the man, his choice of clothing notwithstanding. His shoes, clearly old and slightly worn on the toes, shone with a recent polishing, and the shirt collar that peeked out of his jacket was snowy and starched. This was a man who took his outward appearance seriously. "I do run a detective agency, in case you've forgotten."

Beside me, Nora snorted. "My accountant won't let me forget. In fact, he reminds me of it on a regular basis. Let's just say we might need to talk soon about your spending habits."

Marcus tossed his head, a parody of an irritated teenager being in a stand-off with his parents. I hid my amusement behind a quick cough. Men, in my opinion, could regress at the snap of a finger.

"Hey, Mrs. G. Are you going to talk to me about my habits too?" Brent's earnest tone as he glanced from Marcus to Nora caused me to chuckle.

We didn't need an audience at the moment, though.

I gave him a tiny push. "Why don't you take Aggie outside, all right?" I looked pointedly at his wet shirt. "Before she adds to the mess."

"Aw, Miss F. I wanna hear—"

"Go, Brent. Now." I pushed him again, and this time I put some elbow grease behind it. To my relief, he left, muttering sulkily into Aggie's fur.

Nora smiled and held out one hand to her pouting beau. "We can talk about it later. We're on our way to The Friendly Bean, if you'd care to join us."

Marcus's eyes lit up at the thought of a free coffee and maybe a gooey pastry or two.

"I hope you've got your wallet, pal. This is on you."

He gave a shrug and mumbled something, watching his shoes as if they were suddenly the most interesting things in the world.

"I'm sorry. I didn't catch that."

"I said, 'I forgot my wallet.'" He looked up and glared at Nora. "Happy?"

"Let's go back in to your place, Nora." I gave her arm a gentle poke. "I'm sure you've got coffee and a muffin or two there."

"Fine." Nora sounded anything but hospitable. "You're lucky I don't take this out of your paycheck, Marcus."

He opened his mouth to protest, but I slid a warning glance in his direction. He shut his mouth with an audible snap.

Without another word, Nora marched ahead of us to the elevator. It was a silent ride to her floor, and when she unlocked her apartment door and went straight to the kitchen, Marcus and I followed, both as quiet as two rather uncomfortable mice. I sat at the round kitchen table, silently motioning for Marcus to do the same.

Together, we watched Nora prepare a pot of rather weak coffee for the three of us and fish a partially eaten package of lemon sandwich cookies out of her pantry. Tossing it on the table, she slid into an empty chair and aimed a glare at the portly detective in plaid.

We ate and drank in silence for a few minutes before Nora spoke. "I know you didn't come here to pass the time of day." She took one of the cookies and broke it open, using her teeth to scrape the lemon filling into her mouth. "Spill it already."

"I got an interesting phone call yesterday." One finger pressed into the pile of cookie crumbs on his plate, popping them into his mouth. "I'd say it's on the curious end of things." He stared across at Nora, his small eyes narrowed.

I decided not to mention the dusting of crumbs at the corners of his mouth.

"Do you know someone called Merry?"

My thoughts turned from cookie crumbs to names from my past. It wasn't ringing any immediate bells with me.

Before I could say anything, though, Nora sat up straighter and glared at Marcus. "She's one of my ex-stepkids. What's she done now?"

Chapter 4

Marcus's laugh came out as a bark, causing me to jump and Nora to frown, pressing her lips together in a tight line, as if she was keeping words from getting out into the open.

"Seems like she's accusing *you* of 'doing something.'" His pudgy fingers looked almost comical as they formed air quotes around the words. "She's asked me to find out what your game is in regard to her dad's will."

"I'd like to ask her the same thing." Nora's tone was indignant. "And what made her call you, of all people? Last I heard, she was living north of here, in the Seattle area."

Marcus's shoulders rose in an expansive shrug, his tone irritatingly unctuous. "I put it down to my stellar reputation. Folks around here know I can get things done."

I jumped in before Nora could respond to this lavish personal assessment. Besides wanting to keep things semi-peaceful, I was curious to hear what his explanation would be.

"Let's give you the benefit of the doubt and agree that the agency is building a solid local following."

Nora shifted in her chair and muttered something under her breath.

I ignored her. "What I want to know is this: Why would someone from another city, not to mention another state, call you for help?"

Now Marcus's expression morphed into something almost pious. I fully expected him to fold his hands and offer a prayer for guidance.

When he spoke, the words rolled out in a tone so thick with syrup I was amazed they didn't stick to the roof of his mouth. "We've reached out to people in many areas of this great state, in many walks of life." He paused, one bushy eyebrow raised, as Nora made a gagging sound. "If you're going to be sick, might I suggest heading for the nearest bathroom?"

Ignoring his comment, Nora leaned forward and gave Marcus a hard stare. "Well, *we* don't believe you. And who's this 'we' anyhow?" She crooked her fingers in air quotes, mimicking his earlier action, and Marcus flushed. "I don't recall hearing anything about hiring another *detective*."

She'd given that last word just enough emphasis to unveil her contempt for his commentary, and the red that slowly flooded Marcus's face showed me he understood it as well.

"Well, I'll have you know, Mrs. Goldstein, that my reputation has grown far past the confines of this town."

I flinched when he said "Mrs. Goldstein." That was as bad as throwing down the proverbial gauntlet. I'd never heard him call her that before, although it was far better than the sappy drivel of "honey buns" or "sugar bear" I usually heard being tossed between them.

Nora was really good at picking her battles, though. She didn't respond to Marcus's snide use of her name, and I slowly let out my breath. Maybe she was going to let this argument die before it got any bigger. That was a false hope, of course. Nothing was ever that simple with Nora, especially when it came to men.

What she did have to say was even deadlier. "Reputation? I'll give you 'reputation,' you snake in the grass!" She stuck one manicured hand inside her top and withdrew her cell phone. Tapping quickly on the phone's tiny screen until she found what she was looking for, she turned it around and held it out for a clearly bewildered Marcus to see. "I wasn't aware you knew Merry this well, *Mr. Avery*."

I cringed at the venom in her voice when she said his name. Marcus was in for the lambasting of his life.

"Could this be the 'we' you've been referring to?"

I craned my neck so I could see the picture displayed on her phone, and when I did, my mouth fell open. Marcus was in a serious clinch with a blonde, her ruby lips puckered as they aimed for his grinning mouth. How in the world did the man find the time to do these kinds of things and still get some work accomplished? And more importantly, at least to me, how did he find the women willing to snuggle with him?

Marcus, his eyes darting around the room as though looking for an emergency exit, stuck out his tongue and licked his lips. I'd read somewhere that when a person felt cornered or was going to tell a lie, a surge of adrenaline caused the mouth to feel dry. Judging from the amount of lip licking I was witnessing, Marcus was getting ready to tell Nora a class-A whopper.

One look at Nora, however, told me she was going to let him have it with both barrels if he gave her even the tiniest of fibs. If I were Marcus, I'd keep my mouth firmly zipped.

"Where'd you get that picture?" he managed to squeak out in a voice that sounded as parched as the Sahara.

At least it wasn't a lie. Before I could relax, though, Nora's jaw clenched in anger, so it might have been better for him to try a little subterfuge first. At least she'd expect that from him. Practically admitting to whatever was happening in that picture was tantamount to getting the boot from Nora. My best friend wasn't big on forgiveness, especially when it came to all things family.

Or ex-family, as the case might be.

With a dramatic sweep of her arm, as good as any I'd ever seen in a Shakespearean play, Nora pointed in the direction of her oaken front door. "*Out.*"

I mentally added "damned spot" to her words. She would have made the perfect Lady Macbeth. Nora and I watched in silence as a subdued Marcus shuffled his way to the door and left.

I waited a few minutes as Nora's breath slowed and her anger ebbed away. For whatever reason, Marcus Avery had some kind of hold over her emotional state, no matter how many gals he got caught kissing.

"I think we could use a walk and some stronger caffeine," I suggested when I thought she was ready to talk.

We sat across from each other in The Friendly Bean, both of us cradling a mug of hot coffee between our hands. There was no froufrou froth on these drinks: I'd ordered for us this time and had gotten the Bean's "Foglifter" blend. Nora needed to focus, and I needed the caffeine.

The silence lengthened, and I quietly sighed. Nora in a blue funk could be a tough cookie to handle. If we were going to get a grip on the will and the problem it had created, though, we both needed a clear mind.

I stood abruptly. She needed sugar, particularly the chocolate variety. Heading toward the clear-glass counter, my gaze zeroed in on a round Danish pastry, its top drizzled with twin streams of caramel and chocolate.

"Hey, Miss Franklin. What can I do ya for?" The young man behind the counter gave me a cheeky grin, one round cheek displaying a deep dimple. "D'ya remember me? I took your English class." He stopped talking and guffawed. "Took it twice, as a matter of fact."

I did. It was difficult to forget a repeat offender such as Caleb Greene.

"Oh, I remember you all right, Caleb. It's good to see you so occupied."
If I could have predicted his future, it wouldn't have included anything
like having a job or doing something that required effort. I pointed to the
Danish. "How about heating that up for me? And I need two forks, please."

"Two forks, huh?" He flashed the lone dimple again as he reached
into the display case, withdrew the pastry, and slid it onto a waiting plate.
"On a hot date?"

I gave him my best withering stare. I wasn't going to start discussing
my private life, what there was of it, with this kiddo. It was bad enough
dealing with Brent on a regular basis. "Two forks, Caleb."

He gave a shrug and handed the plate to me with a flourish. "Don't
do anything I wouldn't do." An added exaggerated wink aimed at me
made the two teen girls standing behind me giggle. Caleb winked again,
this time at them.

Sighing, I turned from the counter and began to thread my way back
between the tables toward Nora. I was beginning to remember exactly
why I'd retired. I reached the table where I'd left Nora, noting she hadn't
moved an inch since I'd left. She sat with one hand bunched under her
sharp chin, looking as gloomy as a toddler who'd been caught writing on
a freshly painted wall.

Sliding the warm plate under her nose, I held out one of the forks. "Eat.
You need sugar."

She rolled her eyes toward me and back to the Danish, wrinkling her
nose. "I'm not hungry."

"I didn't ask you if you were hungry. I said you need sugar." I took the
fork from her and used it to cut a piece of chocolatey pastry. "Open wide."

"Oh, good grief, Sis." She snatched the utensil from my fingers and
shoved the bite into her mouth. "There. Happy?"

I ignored her, using my own fork to slice off a piece for myself. "When
you've finished that one, take another bite." As she started to protest, I held
up one hand to stop her. "Look, earlier we agreed we needed to make a plan
for dealing with the will and your stepchildren. The last time I checked,
a functioning brain was a requirement."

"*Ex*-stepkids." She took a bite, then another. And another.

"Hey." I battled her fork with mine. "I got this for us to share,
not just for you."

"You should've said so." She gave me a sassy grin and neatly forked
up the last piece of Danish, popping it into her mouth.

At least she hadn't said one word about Merry Pitt and Marcus Avery.
I knew she hadn't forgotten about it, though, and it would be up to me to

help her channel her well-deserved anger toward Marcus into something useful. She still had a will to execute, not her almost-ex boyfriend.

After another round of warm pastry—her treat this time—Nora and I agreed to call it a day and regroup the next morning.

"Not before ten, though." She shot me a quick smile, ducking her head in that way she had whenever she didn't want to go into detail. "And you should bring Herc with you. I haven't seen that dog in a while."

I was curious about the timing but decided not to ask. If it had anything to do with a man, ignorance was bliss.

Back at her building and waving goodbye as the elevator door slid closed, I leaned back against the mirrored wall and closed my eyes. I was tired after the emotional afternoon, not to mention the busy morning, and I was looking forward to a quiet evening on my couch, book in hand, hot tea within reach.

* * * *

I believe it was Robert Burns who said something about "the best laid plans going awry." He could have been speaking directly to me.

I heard the visitors long before I saw them. A cacophony of noise emanated from my small backyard, and I could clearly make out Brent's voice over Aggie and Herc's barks, his words loud enough for the rest of Portland to hear.

I sighed as I unlocked my front door and dropped my bag on the easy chair that sat angled toward the couch. It would take more energy than I currently had to get rid of the boy and his fluffy dog.

A happy thought struck me, and I felt a surge of hope. Maybe Rachel was here as well. She had enough common sense for the two of them, and I knew I could rely on her to round up Brent and Aggie and leave at a decent hour. Shaking my head and wondering, not for the first time, how Brent had managed to hook such a great girlfriend, I crossed my small kitchen, unlocking the back door and stepping outside.

Brent was sitting cross-legged on my small patch of grass, and both dogs were doing their best to get into his lap.

"Hey, Miss F. Me an' Aggie came over to see Herc. And you, of course." He smiled at me from his seat on the ground. "I'm just waiting for Rachel to get here." He held up the can of Diet Coke that sat beside him, miraculously still upright despite the bundles of fur trying to climb into his lap. "Hope you don't mind me raidin' your fridge."

"Of course not." I stopped mid-stride.

I looked at him, perplexed. How in the world had he gotten into my house? Surely, I hadn't lost my mind and had given him a key? Or had I forgotten to lock my doors? I let my mind race back over my arrival, noting that the front door was locked and I'd had to turn the dead bolt to open the back door. I asked him as much and was surprised to see him beam with pride.

"Me an' Aggie used the doggie door, of course." He pointed to it as if I'd never seen it before. "If I go in feet first and then hunch my shoulders, it's a piece of cake." He ran his fingers over my dog's furry back. "And Herc here didn't even bark or anything."

I sighed deeply. Of course he didn't. Trust me to have the only canine welcoming committee on the block. I was just getting ready to grab one of my lawn chairs (from the local Goodwill, of course) when another thought struck me.

"Brent, if you got in through the doggie door, how did you get back out?" I kept seeing the dead bolt in my mind. I'd had to turn it to unlock the door, and it needed a key to relock it.

He gave another laugh. "The same way, Miss F."

Of course he did. He probably hadn't even considered opening the door in the traditional manner.

I let myself collapse backward into the chair and leaned my head back, closing my eyes against the glare of the late-afternoon sun. Between the circus named Brent and Nora's current mess, I was worn out. Beginning my day with a runaway dog hadn't helped either.

After Rachel finally showed up, apologizing for leaving Brent at my house for so long, I decided to take a warm bath and attempt to relax away the knots that had developed between my shoulder blades. Between a good, long soak in the tub and a few chapters of Agatha Christie's book *They Do It with Mirrors*, I hoped I'd be able to sleep.

My intention was to sleep soundly that night, but like all good plans, my night went as smoothly as a flat tire on a gravel road. I lay there in the dark, Herc snuffling quietly on the floor beside my bed, and replayed the entire day over and over in my mind.

First off, how in heaven's name did Nora get hold of that incriminating photograph of Marcus and Merry? Someone had to have sent it to her, especially since I couldn't imagine her witnessing a romantic clinch such as that and not reacting immediately. And I couldn't imagine Marcus would be able to talk, much less walk, after being caught in such a compromising situation.

The only answer I could surmise was that Nora had hired a private detective to spy on Marcus. Surely the money thing hadn't warranted hiring an outside agency. I'd never known her to do anything this drastic before, and it was common knowledge, at least to us, that Marcus wasn't the most dependable man in the world. Something must have occurred to make her react the way she had.

What would Miss Jane Marple have thought of this situation? What would she have done? From what I'd read in Agatha Christie's books, she'd never hesitated to investigate things on her own. Hiring someone would never have been a Miss Marple choice.

I was still turning this thought over and getting no closer to a solution when I finally dropped off to sleep.

My sleep that night was restless, and what dreams I did have were a mishmash of a grinning Marcus inching his way through a very large doggie door and Brent and Aggie chasing one another around my kitchen table as Nora took picture after picture with a bright pink cell phone. I woke up as a very weak sun struggled to pierce an almost-perpetual cloud cover, thankful none of that was real.

What *was* real, however, was a pale Nora stretched out on my couch, one arm flung over her eyes, open mouth slack with sleep. Good grief. Did everyone know how to avail themselves of my house? What happened to being able to sleep safely without needing to worry about intruders, known or otherwise?

My guard dog was still asleep on the floor of my bedroom, of course, nose buried between his front paws. Knowing he wouldn't wake up during the night for a trip outside, I'd placed a kitchen chair in front of the doggy door and had pushed the table up against it as well, hoping that no one would be able to access it without a lot of noise.

Glancing over my shoulder, I saw that the table and chair didn't appear to have moved in the slightest and that the flap on the kitchen door's doggy entrance was still in place. It seemed Nora hadn't come in that way, at least. Perhaps I really *had* left the front door unlocked this time.

I should have known better, of course. Leaning over my slumbering friend, I saw the small silver item that had fallen from her hand and recognized it immediately.

Nora, bless her devious heart, had used a lock pick to enter my house.

I reached down and gave Nora's shoulder a quick shake, tempted to pull the pillow from underneath her bleached-blond curls. It was a favorite of mine, a souvenir from Multnomah Falls, and one I kept to display rather than use. "Hope you're not expecting a kiss, Sleeping Beauty."

Paws clicked against the bare hardwood floor, and Herc made a beeline for our guest. With a joyous yelp, he leapt forward and planted his front paws on her enhanced chest, giving the entire side of her face a thorough washing with his tongue.

"You have got to be the world's worst kisser, Sis." She struggled to sit up, pushing a wriggling Herc away with one hand. "*And* you've got a bad case of dog breath."

"Oh, hardee har." I wrinkled my nose in response and dropped into the easy chair, pulling my bare feet underneath me with a grunt. I wasn't built for compact seating, but I didn't want to leave my feet on the cold floor. "Since you're awake, how about some coffee?"

"That sounds fabulous." Nora, finally upright, patted the sofa cushion, inviting Herc to join her.

With a happy bark, he jumped up beside her, resting his head on her lap and rolling his eyes upward to look at her with something akin to adoration. Traitor.

"I'll take mine black, please. My brain still hasn't engaged."

I snorted. "I'm not offering to make it. I'm suggesting we get some on our way to your place. After I get showered and dressed, that is. And, since you're such great pals, you can take Herc out to do his business."

"Gee, thanks, Sis." Nora poked out her tongue in response, but I could see she wasn't mad.

It took a great deal to make her upset—like a picture of Marcus and Merry—and it was uncommon for her to remain angry. I was definitely interested in hearing what she had to say about Marcus this morning.

I was also interested to hear why she'd slept on my Goodwill couch instead of on her top-of-the-line king-sized bed. That could keep for the moment, though. I needed a plan for the day and a shower, not necessarily in that order.

Chapter 5

After a quick but restorative shower, I fed Herc and filled the indoor as well as the outdoor water bowls. Nora, I was pleased to see, looked more awake, one long manicured nail busily tapping away on her cell phone. Did the woman sleep with the thing?

I sat beside her, giving her arm a friendly jab with one elbow. "Heard from Portland's Romeo this morning? Or are you still not speaking?"

She briefly lifted her gaze from the small screen, glaring at me. "Not only are we not speaking, I'm considering closing down his entire operation."

"The detective agency? Surely not." I'd seen her angry at him before, but never had she threatened to take away his livelihood. Granted, the entire business ran on her dollars most of the time, but it had helped us out in the past as well. "What would happen to Marcus?"

She shrugged. "No idea, and I don't particularly care this morning, to be completely honest." She gave one final tap at the screen and tucked the cell phone back inside her top. "As soon as I clean up, we can hit the road. I need caffeine by the gallon right now."

"Care to share why you ended up here?" I held up the lock pick, head tilted as I surveyed my best friend. Her eyes, usually snapping with sass, looked dull, and even her blond curls seemed to droop. "I'm ready to listen if you want to talk."

Again the shrug. "Just didn't want to stay by myself, that's all."

And I've got seafront property in Idaho for sale.

Surely it couldn't all be Marcus and his latest woman connection. We'd dealt with that scenario before. My guess was the intrusion of the Pitt family. It would bother me as well if I thought I'd gotten rid of an ex and then he'd turned up again. Well, maybe coffee would help bring it out into the open.

I reached over and patted her shoulder, nodding toward the bathroom. "You get ready, and I'll call Brent for a ride to The Friendly Bean."

Nora snorted, shaking her head as she got to her feet. "Not on your life, girlfriend. I'd rather walk."

And it was a nice morning for a walk, at least by Portland standards. Although the sun was weak and the sky was filled with clouds, there was a welcome warm undertone to the breeze that lent the morning a summerlike feeling.

"Did you happen to see how many jobs we have lined up for next week?" I tucked one arm through Nora's as we strolled, my Birkenstocks slapping comfortably in time with her three-inch-heeled shoes. "Hopefully, there'll be enough to keep the Boy Wonder and his amazing girlfriend busy."

"There're more than enough. In fact, I've been thinking we need to hire another helper, at least part-time." She gave me a sideways glance. "Know of any other students who are looking for a job?"

I shuddered inwardly. I wasn't sure if I could handle working alongside any more of my students. Brent Mayfair, gangling pied piper of animals and constant clown, was more than anyone should have to deal with. Rachel Day was a saint in the making, in my opinion. "Maybe. I'll give Shelby a shout and see what she says."

Shelby Tucker, a former student and now a topnotch journalist for a Portland newspaper, had proven helpful before. Nora and I had returned the favor as well, helping to uncover the real killer in a case in which Shelby had been wrongly accused of the crime.

The Friendly Bean was busy as usual, and the small café was filled with the aroma of brewing coffee and quiet conversations. A quick glance behind the counter assured me Caleb Greene wasn't there (thank the coffee gods), and I relaxed my prematurely tense shoulders, giving the barista a dazzling smile. Two years of trying to teach the kiddo how to write a decent essay had been adequate torture.

My smile, however, wasn't returned. Nora's earlier grumpiness seemed to be spreading. With a swipe at suspiciously wet eyes, the barista took our order. Nora had gone to snag an empty table, so I stood alone at the counter, staring at the girl's woebegone face as she reached into the glass display case and plated the large slice of zucchini bread I'd requested.

My two decades plus of teaching in a high school setting had fine-tuned my counseling radar, and without another thought, I leaned over the counter and asked quietly, "Is there anything I can help you with, my dear?" I almost missed the nod, it was so tiny, but I didn't miss the tears that ran down her cheeks and onto the front of her apron.

"It's Ca-Caleb. Caleb Greene." She glanced around quickly as if expecting to see him. "You know. He was in your class." Her voice was soft, almost a whisper. "He's not working here anymore, and I don't know how to get hold of him."

And that's a bad thing? I wanted to say, but instead, I reached out and patted the hand not holding my zucchini bread. It was the last piece, and I didn't want it on the floor instead of in my stomach. "Yes, I know Caleb." I made a quick decision. "Can you take a break? You'd be welcome to join me if you'd like to talk more about this."

She glanced over at the woman working an array of coffee machines and nodded again. "Yeah. It's my break time right now anyways." She looked at the plate in her hand. "Let me get your order together, and I'll bring it out to you."

Moving so I could see better, I squinted at the name tag pinned askew on her apron. "That's sounds like a deal, Hannah. I'll see you in a few minutes."

I wound my way among the various tall tables as I made my way to where Nora was sitting. She'd managed to snag one of the few regular tables and was sitting with her hand on one empty chair and her feet on another. At least I wouldn't have to beg, borrow, or steal a chair for Hannah to use.

"We're going to have company, so please be on your best behavior." I gently pushed her feet off the chair and slid into it, grimacing as my bare toes collided with the table leg. "It's the barista who took our order, and she's upset."

Nora sniffed, crossing her Lycra-covered legs and looking down to admire the effect. So did the two men at the table next to ours. "Lots of that going around right now, I'd say."

"And it's over a young man, so I'd say you two might have something in common."

She gave another sniff, but I could see the edges of a smile appearing. If there was one thing I knew about my best friend, it was that she had an ability to empathize with others. I almost said as much but stopped as Hannah arrived, carrying a tray with our coffees, my zucchini bread, and a plate of small blueberry scones I hadn't ordered.

"Hannah, this is my friend Mrs. Goldstein. And I'm Miss Franklin, by the way." I gestured to the empty chair between Nora and me. "Please, have a seat."

"I know." Hannah smiled shyly at me as she slid into the chair. "Caleb was talking about you the other day."

I pretended not to see Nora's amused expression. Instead, I returned Hannah's smile as I took my coffee and bread from the tray. "I hope he had good things to say."

"Oh, yes, he sure did." Hannah bobbed her head earnestly. "He said you were the only teacher who actually made him work for his grade and that you told him he could do anything he set his mind to." To my dismay, the tears from earlier were making another appearance. "And that's why he left, Miss Franklin. He's gonna work for someone else."

And with that, she bent over and rested her head on crossed arms, shoulders shaking, as she quietly cried. I looked across at Nora, my eyebrows raised in alarm as I signaled for some help. She gave a quick nod and scooted her chair closer to Hannah and put an arm around the girl's shoulders.

"Hannah, trust me when I say that all men have to follow their dreams." She leaned in closer, her voice lowered. "If he doesn't, he'll be a pain in the neck."

Hannah looked up, twin rivulets of black coursing down her face. "But it's more like a nightmare, Mrs. Goldstein." She picked up a paper napkin form the tray and swiped at her cheeks, smearing the mascara down to her chin. "He's gonna work for some guy who's been in jail before!"

Her voice rose, and I reached over to pat her shoulder, sending Nora another silent SOS. I had no desire to be the center of attention at The Friendly Bean.

Nora, however, was used to being the focus and ignored the various faces that turned in our direction. Instead, she gave Hannah a hug and removed the rest of the smeared mascara from the girl's face with her own napkin. "Did he tell you that, or is that something you got from reading between the lines?"

"He told me." Hannah's voice was indignant, and I shot Nora a warning glance. There was no need to add fuel to the fire, especially since I'd spotted the shift manager casting several glances in our direction.

"Okay. Let's say he did." When Hannah started to protest, Nora lifted a finger. "Just play along with me, all right?"

Hannah lifted one shoulder in a tiny shrug, and I let go the anxious breath I'd been holding.

"Can you remember where this job was? Here in Portland? Out of state?"

The girl's forehead wrinkled in thought. "I think he said," she began slowly, "that he'd be going out of town. Yes, that's what he said. 'Out of town.'" She peered anxiously at Nora. "That doesn't really help much, does it?"

"Of course it does, Hannah." I jumped in, without giving Nora a chance to respond. "Did he give you an idea of where that might be? Eugene, maybe, or across the river?"

"Across the river" was Portlandian shorthand for "in Washington," our neighbor that was just a hop, skip, and a jump on the other side of the majestic Columbia River.

Nora and I waited.

Finally, Hannah's eyes widened, and she grinned broadly. "I remember now! He said he was going to be working at some laundry business in Seattle. He called it a 'front,' if that helps."

I remembered just in time not to let my mouth hang open in astonishment. It would never do to be seen looking like a flycatcher waiting for prey, but Nora had no such compunction.

"Seattle? You've gotta be kidding." The words leapt from her gaping mouth as though shot from a cannon, and the screech at the end was enough to bring the manager scurrying from behind the counter, headed straight for us.

"Is everything all right over here?" She gave Hannah a questioning look, and the girl looked down, cheeks reddening.

"Yeah. Sorry, Donna. We were just talking about Caleb and you know…" Her voice trailed off as she shrugged.

"Well, I could certainly think of better topics." The frown on Donna's face was dark, and Hannah jumped up, a guilty expression in her eyes.

"Sorry. I'll get back to work. Nice to've met you two." And with that, Hannah made a beeline for the counter.

I was happy to see she'd left behind the plate of scones, though, and reached for one as Donna retraced her steps and headed back to work. I pushed the plate toward Nora and reached for my mug of cooled coffee. Something about the way the girl had said "Seattle" had jiggled loose a recent memory.

"I'd say that's a sign from the universe, Sis." Nora picked up two of the mini blueberry scones and popped one in her mouth, her cheeks as round and full as those of a squirrel gathering nuts for the winter.

"What is?"

She held up that one finger again, and I waited for her to swallow the scone.

"Two people mentioned Seattle, that's what." When I didn't respond immediately, she added, "Don't you think so?"

"Nora, we live nearly next door to that city." It was my turn to hold up the verbal stop sign as she began to speak. "We probably hear things about Seattle every day."

"Not directly." She smiled triumphantly, scooping another scone from the plate. "And not twice in a row."

I rolled my eyes at her comment. "That's hardly consecutive," I pointed out as I snagged the last scone from under her hand. "If you're speaking of the visit to Ione's office and the conversation just now, that's certainly not 'in a row.'"

"It is to me." She could be as stubborn as a mule at times, and now was clearly one of those times. Nothing I said would be able to change her mindset, not when she was in this mood.

"Fine." I sighed deeply, blowing a trail of crumbs across the table. "We'll call it twice. So why Seattle? What's the importance?"

"It's the criminal angle." She gestured wildly with one hand, nearly knocking a full mug of coffee from the hands of the person seated at the next table. She ignored the irritated mutter, and I smiled at the man in what I hoped was an apologetic manner.

"Seattle seems to be the place where crooks end up, with apologies to the Emerald City and all that jazz."

I had made a similar connection, but I wasn't about to admit it. Still, I couldn't help asking, "And how does that connect to your ex-stepchildren and their father's will?"

She raised both shoulders in a shrug, with a sassy grin. "My ex made his money in the dry-cleaning business, and my gut is telling me it's connected, and if I'm wrong I'll wear those horrible sandals for one week straight." She jabbed a finger in the direction of my feet, a derisive eyebrow lifted. "And you can take that to the bank, Sis."

"And what's wrong with my shoes?" I looked at the stilettos on her feet and wrinkled my nose. "Just don't expect me to return the favor."

The walk to Nora's apartment building was as pleasant as the stroll to the café had been. The breeze was still rustling the branches of the tall pines that lined the street, and the remaining pine needles that had held on over the winter loosened their grasp and fell at our feet. It was the perfect day for a walk at the Portland Pooch Park, but I'd left Herc at home. Still, it wouldn't hurt to go over there and watch the antics of the various dogs that came to the park every day. And maybe, just maybe, a certain pair of golden retrievers might make an appearance.

"Hey, you. Did you even hear a word I said?" Nora snapped her fingers near my face, and I jumped backward, almost colliding with a young mother and the toddler holding her hand. "And you've got that goofy grin on your face again." She bent her arm and jabbed my side. "Betcha a certain doc is floating around in that head of yours."

"He is not floating around in my head." I scowled at my best friend and rubbed the spot where her pointy elbow had nearly pierced the skin. "I was only thinking about his dogs, so there."

Nora's shout of laughter was loud enough to scare a flock of pigeons from the top of a streetlight. The toddler behind us clapped his hands and shrieked with delight. I was not amused.

"I can always tell when you've got Roger on the brain." She reached over and tucked her arm through mine. "Now, how about a stroll by the river?" She patted her flat stomach with her free hand. "I need to walk off all those scones."

I didn't bother telling her my scones (and zucchini bread) had already made themselves at home on my hips and thighs. With a pat on my own midsection, I smiled in agreement.

Besides, I needed more time to get my mind around the Seattle connection. Despite my earlier skepticism, I was starting to think Nora's gut feeling was right. Something—or someone—was askew in the beautiful Emerald City. There was nothing to do but pay a visit to our neighbor to the north.

* * * *

Once we'd revised the pet-sitting and -walking schedule and let Rachel and Brent know, Nora and I headed for Seattle. My old car, rarely driven since my early retirement, had been taken out and filled with gas. The tires were aired up to the suggested poundage, and I'd even added a gas treatment to the tank. With both hands gripping the steering wheel as tightly as a novice driver would, I pulled away from the curb in front of Nora's building and joined the traffic headed north.

"I've made reservations at an Airbnb," Nora announced. "According to the description, it's a 'charming bungalow set within sight of Puget Sound.'" She wrinkled her nose as she tucked her cell back into her tight top. "Makes it sound like an exclusive bed and breakfast. I'll bet it's full of mold and worn linoleum."

"If there's mold, we can sue." I spoke in a dry, joking manner, but Nora took it at face value.

"Oh, you bet we will." She laughed, a short sound that seemed to lack humor. "That'll give Ione some real work to do."

I chanced a quick glance at her, curious at her words. "Are you saying the will isn't legitimate work?"

"Oh, that's all her dad, and you can bet your life on it." Again the laugh that wasn't quite humorous. Nora was slipping into a funk as dark as the clouds that had begun to gather overhead. "She's still learning the ropes, and I'll bet her old man was speed-dialed as soon as we left that office."

I looked into the rearview mirror and then leaned forward slightly to check the side mirror before changing lanes. "Your ex wouldn't have allowed a woman to handle the legal paperwork." It was a statement, not a question.

"Absolutely not." Nora's snort was contemptuous. "That man thought women were good for three things: cooking, cleaning, and making babies." Now the chuckle was genuine. "And since I did none of those, it's no wonder the marriage didn't last."

I shook my head, eyes still on the traffic ahead of me. I wondered how Roger felt about those things. The thought made my face warm, and I knew I was blushing. Nora, however, seemed miles away now, her own thoughts keeping her busy. I left her to it, content to concentrate on my rusty driving. Mold or not, I wanted to arrive at the bungalow in one piece.

Chapter 6

The bungalow was situated on a narrow, winding road lined closely with a gauntlet of tall pines. The promised view of Puget Sound occurred only sporadically whenever one of the branches moved in the wind, but the house itself was as charming as the description. Pulling the car to a stop in front of the house and cutting the engine, I took in the scene with curiosity. I'd never been much farther away from Portland than the occasional trip to Multnomah Falls, and while the topography here seemed familiar, it still had the exhilaration of being a Trip with a capital T.

"Well? Don't just sit there, Sis." Nora flung open the passenger door and was walking toward the front door almost before her stilettos had hit the pine-needle-strewn ground, her mouth set in a purposeful line. "We've got places to go, people to interrogate."

A woman on a mission to single-handedly save the environment couldn't have looked more determined. I shot her an exasperated look as she made her way up the path. I needed a few minutes of personal buffer time before I moved on to the next activity.

The home's owner was a young woman with blond dreadlocks and a large nose stud in the shape of a frog. I tried not to stare at it, all the while thinking how it must get in the way of blowing her nose.

"I've always wondered about those things." Nora motioned to her own nose and our hostess, rather than being offended, only laughed. "Did it hurt?"

"Not at all. It was over in a sec." She gave Nora a cheerful grin. "If you're thinking of getting one, I can give you the address of the place I went. And I'm Fern, by the way."

"I'm Nora, and I'll let you know." Nora's answering grin included me as well, widening in glee probably from my shocked expression.

"Actually, I'm asking for my friend." And with a teasing thump on my shoulder, she followed the waving dreadlocks as they led the way to our room. I followed, rubbing my shoulder, tempted to poke out my tongue at my best friend's back.

Despite a careful scan of the assigned bedroom and adjoining bathroom, no mold was in sight. The linoleum was cracked, certainly, but a flotilla of braided rugs covered the worn areas like a fleet of colorful boats. I wasn't sure what I'd been expecting, having never stayed at an Airbnb before, but it was almost like staying at a friend's house.

"If you'd like the bed closest to the bathroom, I can take this one by the window." I hefted my overnight bag onto the aforementioned twin bed as Nora closed the closet door. "Do I have time for a quick wash?"

"Why wouldn't you?"

"You made it sound like we've got to rush off to meet someone." I sounded cross, but my back was sore from sitting and driving from Portland to Seattle. "And I'm going to freshen up first." I marched into the bathroom and firmly closed the door behind me.

"Be my guest." I could hear her through the door. "I'm going to make a call and then check to see what time we're expected to be in tonight."

I felt much more myself after a change of clothes and a quick scrub at the old-fashioned pedestal sink. I blamed the unaccustomed drive to my current mood, and I determined I'd be pleasant company the rest of the day. I was in the middle of performing a series of stretches for my back when Nora breezed in, her cell still held to one ear.

"We'll be there as soon as we can." She paused a moment. "That will be fine. If we get lost, we'll give you a shout."

"If we get lost going where?" I gave my lower back a twist, lifting both arms straight into the air to maximize the stretch. "I'm not crazy about driving around this place, to be honest."

"Oh, don't stress, Sis." Nora waved her cell at me. "I'm getting us an Uber."

The driver, much to my relief, was a middle-aged man who greeted us with a short nod and a reminder to buckle up. My past experiences with Brent's driving had almost convinced me all Uber drivers were college students needing money for frozen burritos and tuition. Aside from confirming the address that Nora had given him, he drove silently, both hands fixed at exactly ten and two on the steering wheel. Brent could certainly learn a few things from him.

"Martin said he'd meet us at one of his businesses." Nora was busy tapping away on her cell phone's screen. "Apparently my ex-stepkid Martin

Pitt has made something of himself, despite being his father's son. Owns a chain of dry cleaners and laundromats."

"Really. That's very interesting." I recalled Hannah's comment about Caleb moving to Washington and working at a laundromat. It was probably a coincidence, but I'd be keeping my eyes open for a certain past student. "Very, very interesting, especially since Caleb has moved to Seattle to work for a laundry business that's a 'front,' as Hannah put it."

"I thought the same thing, but really, isn't that too much of a coincidence?"

"Hercule Poirot said 'three motifs repeated cannot be a coincidence,' or something to that effect." I wrinkled my forehead as I tried to recall the exact quote in Agatha Christie's *The ABC Murders.* "Of course, there've only been two incidents concerning a laundry business in Seattle And I'm referring to laundering money, not clothes. I know there's no evidence, but…" I let my words trail off along with my thoughts on the matter. Were the two actually connected?

"That would make my day—if Martin and Merry were into something criminal." Nora's tone seemed optimistic, her face arranged in a hopeful expression. "Maybe that would make the Bottomless Pitt's money mine, not theirs."

Our driver slowed to make a right turn, pulling up smoothly in front of a store whose sign, PITT'S FAMILY CLEANERS, was displayed in large letters over the smaller declaration, "We want your dirt." Curious and ironic, especially if Hannah's words were true.

"Here you are, ladies." He looked over his shoulder. "If you need a ride back, just give me a call."

Nora gave a quick nod. "Will do. Thanks for the ride here." She opened the door and stepped out, one foot in its high heel placed carefully on the curb. "Gwen, let's do this."

The inside of the cleaner's was humid and close, and I imagined my hair was frizzing into a style resembling a Chia Pet, those nutty-looking clay vases filled with tiny green leaves. We waited for a young woman with three small children attached to various points on her body to take the hanging dress shirts from the man behind the counter and stagger her way out the door.

"Makes me glad I never had kids," Nora murmured in my ear. "Did you see her shoes?"

Typical Nora, always with an eye for fashion or, in this case, the lack thereof.

All of Nora's ex-husbands could have been described as typical as well: tall and broad and overbearing, at least according to her descriptions. The man standing behind the counter was short, however, and skinny. He had a pointy face that reminded me of a squirrel, sporting a thin ponytail that could've doubled as a rat's tail.

Martin must've taken after his mother.

"I'm looking for Martin Pitt," Nora announced, and I smiled inwardly. So the man wasn't her ex-stepson. "I have an appointment."

"He's, uh, taking care of something at the moment." Glancing over his shoulder with a curious indecision, he started to walk away but then seemed to think again, turning back toward us. "His office is back this way, if you want to follow me."

Not only did this man look like a rodent, he was acting as shifty as a rat in a pantry. I wouldn't have trusted this man as far as I could throw him, which wouldn't have been all that far, despite his thinness.

We followed his scurrying gait down a dim hall that smelled damp, exchanging glances. Nora's eyebrows were raised, and I could see she was picking up on this character's caginess too. As irritating as Caleb could be, I sincerely hoped he hadn't come here. I didn't care for the underground feeling of the place.

Our guide paused in front of a partially open door, using his knuckles to rap a quick tattoo on the door frame. "Your visitors are here, Mr. Pitt." A bell sounded from somewhere in the cleaners. Without another word, or even a look in our direction, the man hurried away.

Nora looked at me and shrugged before pushing the door fully open and walking in. I followed her, careful to leave the door ajar. I wanted a clear path to the hall in case we needed a quick escape.

Martin was sitting at a large desk, a slim cell phone held to one ear, and the scarred top of the desk was filled with uneven stacks of paperwork. He held up a finger and then used it to point at the two empty chairs that seemed to lean against the wall. With another lift of her shoulders, Nora sat. I hesitated only a moment before taking the other chair for myself.

"I need that package, Benny. And I need it tomorrow, if you get my drift." Martin's voice was as rough as his appearance. His cheeks reddened, dark eyebrows drawn together in annoyance. "You better get it here. That's all I've got to say." With a jabbing motion of his finger, he disconnected the call.

Although he hadn't stood yet, I could see he was a tall man with the wide physique Nora had attributed to his dad. I imagined the man at the counter felt intimidated beside him. That most likely explained the quick departure, not just the bell.

"Well, well, well. If it isn't Stepmommy Dearest." He turned in his chair so he was staring straight at Nora, with an unamused smile. "Come to talk about Dad's will?"

"Oh, trust me, Marty. This isn't fun for me either, so let's get this over and done with before I lose my lunch."

Angry color rose again in his face. He hadn't cared for the nickname, and Nora knew it. Watching these two made me want to keep score: Who would get in the most verbal zingers?

Tossing his phone on the desk, he held up both hands in mock surrender, both his tone and words underscored with a definite sneer. "Oh, yes, ma'am. It's always gotta be your way, doesn't it?"

Nora didn't bother responding to the goad. Instead, she leaned forward and spoke in a conversational tone, almost as if she was having a friendly visit with a pal. "As you say. I'm only here to find out why you and your sister think your father is dead."

Now it was Martin's turn to lift his eyebrows. "The man's been gone for over three years, and we haven't heard squat from him in all that time." His broad shoulders rose and fell. "In case you don't remember, he liked to keep in touch, even if it was only a few hours since we'd seen him. He was a family man."

Nora snorted derisively. "He was a *what*? Surely you meant '*fancy* man,' Marty. The only thing I can recall about that man is his continuous lineup of women." The italics in her voice were as clear as if she'd written the words on a piece of paper.

They continued to glare at one another across the desk, and I sighed, shaking my head at them. Time to put on the referee's stripes before things got any uglier.

Leaning forward, I placed both hands flat on the desk and stood. "Listen, folks. I didn't drive all this way here to watch you two engage in a pissing contest."

Nora's lips curved in amusement, but Martin's eyebrows only drew together more tightly, his mouth opening.

I didn't give him a chance to speak. "I'm serious. You," I pointed at Martin, "need to answer Mrs. Goldstein's question now." When Nora's smile widened, I looked at her. "And you need to stop antagonizing him." It was her turn to sputter, but I simply held up one hand, staring straight at Martin. "For whatever reason, your father asked that she be the executor of his will. You might not like it, but it's all been done legally. So, can you two work together and get this taken care of?" I reached around and rubbed the small of my back as though I could still feel the soreness from the drive. "I don't plan on making this trip again anytime soon."

For a moment, they both sat looking at me without speaking, and then Martin glanced at Nora, his expression a mixture of irritation and calculation.

"Fine by me. And before you say anything else, it's more Merry than me that wants this thing handled."

I shuddered inwardly at his grammar. It was like listening to Brent, only without the naïve charm. Something about Martin was unsettling, and it wasn't only his size.

"She's the one who kept saying we needed to declare him dead. If you ask me, someone should investigate *her*." Martin's expression added a silent "so there" as he glowered at Nora.

"Still getting along with your sister, are we?" Nora shook her head, a look of distaste on her face. "You two made me crazy with all your bickering."

"She was always starting something." Martin's voice was sulky. I fully expected to see his lower lip jut out in a full-fledged pout. "And you never took my side."

Nora rolled her eyes. "Oh, grow up." She looked away from him and at me, adding in a conversational tone, "I think I'm beginning to see exactly why his dad made me the executor."

Martin stood up abruptly, nearly toppling over his chair. I was right: the man was tall. I drew back from this display, but Nora only rotated one finger on the side of her head as she rose.

"Let's go, Sis. I think we should be talking to Merry, not this nutcase."

"I'd be careful who I called a nutcase." The tone of Martin's voice had changed from petulant to threatening, and when I stood, my knees were trembling.

I was glad I'd left the door slightly open.

"Dad might not be the only one who disappears."

Nora grew still and stared into Martin's angry eyes, her back as straight as an arrow. "Is that a threat, Marty?" Her voice was as quiet as the moment before an explosion.

"No, Stepmama." His voice grew colder, and he leaned closer, eyes narrowing. "That was a promise."

The light outside seemed almost too bright, despite the overcast Seattle sky, and the air was sharp in comparison to the dense dampness inside the dry cleaners. Nora's ability to move quickly in her stilettos had always amazed me, and she nearly ran over me in our haste to get out of Martin's office. Loud laughter had followed us down the hall like a trail of smoke, and the look the thin man in the outer lobby shot in our direction was full of pity, a "better you than me" expression on his face.

I didn't stop to argue. With my heart beating like a drum in a rock band, I crowded in close to Nora and tried to catch my breath. She'd already tugged her cell phone from its convenient carrying case, aka her bra, and opened the Uber app with one manicured nail.

"I'm getting a car back here pronto, Sis, and we're gettin' the heck outta Dodge." Her hand was shaking, and I put one arm around her shoulders. "That kid is as crazy as his dad was, or is, or whatever." She entered our address for pickup and shoved the phone back into her top. "And I'm taking that will back to Ione's office, and she can deal with it."

"I'm not sure you can do that." I gave her shoulders a little squeeze before releasing her. "I'm not a lawyer, but I'm pretty sure something like that is binding."

"Whatever. I'll just pretend I didn't know about it."

I laughed, shaking my head in amusement. "And what'll you tell Rachel's dad and his partner? I think they'll remember being in Ione's office."

"Then I'll fake amnesia. I'll bet that's what the Bottomless Pitt is doing this very moment. He's playing possum, that's all."

I was spared having to answer that piece of nonsense as our Uber driver returned, sliding smoothly to a stop in front of the curb. I needed coffee and a nap more than we needed answers about Nora's ex-husband's whereabouts, and the sooner I got those, the better. Otherwise, I might get as cranky as Martin had been.

* * * *

"I've left a bottle of chardonnay chilling in the fridge," Fern called out from the kitchen as we stepped inside the bungalow's cheerful entryway. "Feel free to have a glass before dinner." She stuck her head around the kitchen door, dreadlocks bundled on top of her head, smiling broadly. "Hope you like white bean and ham soup. It's my mom's recipe and absolutely amazing."

I glanced at Nora, and she seemed as surprised as I was. I didn't know Airbnb hosts offered food or drink, but I wasn't one to turn down an offer, especially if it was free.

"You don't need to put yourself out for us." Nora hooked one arm in mine and began walking away. "And we might be going out again this evening. We can grab something to eat then."

"Oh." Fern's smile drooped slightly. "I've made a huge pot of the stuff. You'll save me from eating the same thing for days." She gave a little shrug. "I'm from a big family, and I've never learned how to cook for one." "It does smell wonderful." I smiled at Fern as I gave Nora a surreptitious poke in the side. "I'm sure we've got time to join you. Only to save you from leftovers, of course."

We left Fern at the stove, whistling tunelessly, and made our way to our room. Nora hadn't said anything else and showed every sign of being deep in thought. Probably the encounter with Martin had troubled her more than she'd admitted. If I was honest, his parting words were bothering me as well.

"I think I'm going to lie down for a bit." I sat on the edge of my bed and slipped my feet out of my Birkenstock sandals. "My back is still tight from the drive here." I yawned and stretched my arms over my head, trying to release some of the tension in my lower back. "We need to decide what to do about Martin."

"Uh huh." Nora was already tapping away at her cell phone, a frown between her eyebrows as she concentrated on whatever was on the small screen. "That's good, Sis."

"Did you even hear a word I said?" I fell back against the pillows and closed my eyes. I was more tired than I'd thought. Maybe a power nap would help.

"What was that?"

"Nothing," I murmured sleepily, feeling myself drift off. "We can talk later."

The last thing I remembered was the sound of the bedroom door closing behind Nora as she left.

Chapter 7

I awoke to Nora's hand on my shoulder, gently shaking me.

"Wake up, sleepyhead. Fern's dishing up dinner."

I turned over and lifted one hand to rub my eyes, mouth open in a wide yawn. I felt almost drugged, as though I could sleep straight through to the next morning. Through the open doorway, I could smell the soup and something else that might have been freshly baked bread, and my stomach growled.

"Well, at least part of you is awake." Nora chuckled, putting out a hand to help me sit up. "We'd better feed that monster before it decides to get any louder."

I wrinkled my nose in response, but I allowed her to pull me to my feet. Food sounded good, and a glass of chardonnay sounded even better.

"So, what brings you ladies here to Seattle?" Fern passed the basket of rolls to Nora. "Doing any sightseeing?"

"We don't have time, unfortunately." Nora took a roll and then added another to the small plate that sat to the side of her soup bowl. "It's family business. Sort of." She tore off a piece of bread and popped it into her mouth, chewing with her eyes half closed. "This is so good, Fern. Another family recipe?"

Fern chuckled and shook her head, sending her dreadlocks bouncing. "Nope. Just frozen dough I had in the freezer. Something I picked up at the grocery store."

I took a small sip from my wineglass. The buttery flavor brought back memories of last fall's Clear the Shelter event. It had been held at Coopers Hall Winery and Taproom, a wonderful venue forever coupled in my mind with a crazed killer. I set the glass down and smiled at Fern, making an effort to wipe that event from my mind.

"Seattle is quite the city. I'd love to see more of it if we ever visit again." I hesitated a moment, carefully planning my words before I spoke. "Have you heard of Pitt's Family Cleaners?"

Nora's quick intake of breath was unmistakable, but I kept my gaze fixed on Fern as I lifted a spoonful of soup to my mouth. If we weren't going to have any more time for investigating Martin, the least I could do was question a local resident about him. If he was as shady as my gut was telling me he was, surely someone would have heard something.

"Maybe." Fern's forehead wrinkled briefly. "Are you talking about that dry cleaners over in the industrial part of town?"

Nora and I looked at one another and nodded in unison, a pair of wary bobbleheads.

"It backs onto an alley, right?"

"That's the one." I took another sip of wine. "Have you used it before?"

Fern gave a short laugh. "You wouldn't catch me dead down there, to tell the truth. That's one scary neighborhood."

"Well, he's one scary guy." I spoke before I thought.

Nora might not appreciate me airing her ex's dirty laundry, no pun intended.

"No kidding." Fern leaned over and topped off my glass. "Everyone knows he's an underhanded character."

"Is that so?" Nora gave me a quick glance and then looked at Fern. "Define 'underhanded.'"

Fern put a hand to her mouth, her eyes wide over it. "Oh, I'm sorry. I didn't mean to make him sound like a criminal."

Nora laughed and held her glass out for a refill. "That's all right. He's my ex-stepson. I was married briefly to his rat of a dad."

Fern smiled as she poured the remainder of the chardonnay, relief in her eyes. "That's good." When Nora's eyebrows lifted in response, she added quickly, "I don't mean it was good you were married to his dad. I just meant it's a good thing you're not still in that family. Trust me: the Pitt name is not something to brag about."

"Care to share? The more I know about him, the better." Nora sipped her wine and leaned forward, her expression somber. "I'm the executor of my ex's will, for whatever reason, and Gwen and I made the drive here to see what's up with his son."

"Hmm." Fern's lips pursed as she thoughtfully swirled the remainder of her drink around in her glass. "I can tell you Martin Pitt's partner was indicted last year for embezzlement." She lifted her glass and took the final drink. "And I don't mean embezzling the cleaners. This guy was caught dipping his sticky fingers in the city till."

"Seriously?" My mouth hung open in the most unflattering manner before I snapped it shut. "How in the world did that happen?"

Fern shrugged. "He was moonlighting as an accountant for the city, and I guess temptation got the best of him. It was all over the news for a while, maybe two or three years ago, and I remember hearing that Pitt was interviewed by the police too." She gave another slight lift of her shoulders. "Guess he was clean, or at least they weren't able to pin anything on him."

"Why would they be looking at him?" Nora broke off another bite from a roll. "It was his partner who was working in the city's offices and not Martin, right?"

Fern's eyes lit up, and she held up one finger. "Ah, but listen to this. The dry-cleaning business had filed for bankruptcy only a few weeks before the partner took on that accounting job, and then suddenly it withdrew the petition." Before Nora or I could comment, Fern added, her tone disgusted, "And then Pitt was seen driving a brand-new Tesla around town, and you know how much *those* things cost."

"Well, good grief." I couldn't think of anything else to say. I'd been an English teacher, not a mathematician, but I could add two and two together and get four. "So were they able to find a connection between this sudden windfall and the embezzling?"

"Nope." Fern's hair swung wildly from side to side, uneven blond ropes whipping around her head. "And that's the kicker. All of us here in Seattle just *knew* he'd gotten some of that embezzled money, but even the cops couldn't prove it."

She snorted, an angry sound that made me think of Martin's threatening demeanor. I shivered inwardly, wondering how we'd gone from a missing ex's will to criminal activity in such a short amount of time. Were they connected? Had Nora's Bottomless Pitt been a part of something that made it convenient to stage a disappearance? Maybe the ex was funding his son's lifestyle and business from the Great Beyond…or from a comfy hideaway on one of the San Juan Islands off the Washington coast.

"Sis, whaddya say to staying here one more night?" Nora looked across at Fern, who smiled her agreement. "That way we can talk to Merry and maybe see what we can find out about Martin and his miracle money."

"We need to let Brent and Rachel know. I don't think there are more jobs than they can handle themselves, and Roger might be willing to help out if they get in a bind."

That last comment had popped out of nowhere. Yes, Freud might say it had appeared from the subconscious, but it really had surprised me.

It seemed to surprise Nora as well. "Ya think?" She tilted her head sideways as she surveyed me, smiling. "Is this something you two lovebirds have talked about?"

Fern looked from Nora to me, and I saw interest in her eyes. I, however, was not about to discuss my love life, what little there was, with a relative stranger.

"Something along those lines." I kept my voice casual, willing my face not to blush, and turned to look at our hostess. "Fern, this is absolutely delicious soup. Can you share the recipe?"

The rest of the evening passed pleasantly. Fern had quite a store of knowledge of the state's most important resident, Sasquatch, and she had Nora and me in stitches as she described one particular trip with friends to "catch" the legendary monster.

"Do you remember that crazy commercial with men trying to bait a trap for Sasquatch with beef jerky? For some reason, we thought that was a great idea, so we bought out a convenience store's stock of jerky before we left." She wrinkled her nose, waving one hand in front of her face. "Let's just say that a musty men's locker room smells better than a car filled with beef jerky."

"I thought it came in plastic wrap." I took a sip of my cooling after-dinner coffee. "Surely you couldn't smell it through that."

"Oh, that's true enough." She laughed as she spoke, a sassy twinkle in her eyes. "But when someone gets the bright idea of unwrapping it all in order to save time, well, let's just say the aroma was beyond overpowering. It couldn't smell any worse if we had had a real live Bigfoot in the car with us, trust me."

"Sounds like something Brent would do." Nora smiled across at me. "Sometimes I'm amazed the kid is still alive and breathing."

"I'd say it's thanks to Rachel." I took a final sip of my coffee. "Fern, if you don't mind, I'm going to take a warm bath and then hit the hay." I glanced at my cell phone to check the time and then was hit with a horrible thought: Herc was alone. I needed to get someone over there quickly to take care of my pet. "Speaking of Brent, I need him to run by my place and take care of Herc."

"Oh, good grief, Sis." Nora lifted one hand and planted the palm on her forehead. "I totally forgot about that dog when I mentioned staying another night." She drew out her cell phone from its handy carrying case, otherwise known as her brassiere, and rapidly tapped on the screen before holding the phone to one ear. "Brent? Oh, sorry, Rachel. No, it's fine. You'll do." After a brief conversation that concluded with a satisfied smile and an excited yipping from the other end of the line (Aggie, I assumed), she disconnected the call. "All set. Brent said he has his own key and it's 'no prob.'"

She gave the last two words a set of air quotes, and I groaned. "No, he doesn't have a key. He goes through the doggy door. All I need is for one of my neighbors to see him and call the police."

Fern laughed as she stood and began collecting our empty coffee cups. "Sounds like my youngest brother. His idea of personal space is nil. *Su casa es mi casa* and all that jazz."

I had to stop and digest that last bit. "I thought it was '*mi casa es su casa*,' not the other way around."

"Not with my brother," Fern said wryly. "He's a free spirit who's okay with perpetual couch-surfing, if you get my drift."

Nora sniffed. "Sounds like he's well on his way to becoming as bad as my third husband's kids. Those two seem to think the world owes them, not the other way around."

"And that's most likely why your ex asked for you to be the will's executor. His own offspring wouldn't have a clue about how to be fiscally responsible." I stood up slowly, a little stiff, giving my lower back a massage with both hands. "Nora, I'm going to get that bath and then read for a while."

Nora, tapping away on her smartphone, looked up briefly at the mention of her name before flicking her gaze back to the small screen in her hand. I'd been dismissed by the digital world.

"Fern, thank you for letting us stay another night. To be honest, I wasn't thrilled with the idea of having to drive home tomorrow evening." I smiled warmly at our hostess as I began heading out of the room. "Just kick my friend out of here when you want to shut things down for the night. Otherwise, she might sit here until the sun comes up."

"Makes me glad I don't have one of those things."

I stopped and looked back at her.

"I use my laptop to communicate with my family, and I figure if I need to actually speak with someone, like use words, I can use my neighbor's phone." She gave a wry smile. "And it sure saves me a ton of money each month, so there is that."

"What do you do in an emergency?" Nora and I both had our cell phones with us, but I didn't like thinking of Fern's vulnerability—being unable to contact the police or fire department.

In answer, she walked over and pulled open the wide drawer slotted in the side of her coffee table. She fished around for a moment, her eyes half closed. With a triumphant grin, she withdrew her hand and waved something in my direction.

"I use this old flip phone." She let it drop into her lap, an object almost as archaic as a typewriter. "It doesn't have service on it, but I can still dial nine-one-one."

"Really? You don't need to have a cell plan to use the phone?" I was perplexed, trying to think how that might work. "I thought unused cell phones were only good for the trash."

"Oh, absolutely not." Fern sounded shocked. "I'm part of a group that collects old cells to donate to the local homeless shelter. It gives them a way to contact the police without having to pay for a phone."

"What a great idea." I paused for a moment, thinking about the cell phone I'd given to the phone company when I purchased my smartphone. They hadn't asked for it, but I hadn't known what to do with it. Fern's suggestion, though, seemed like the sensible answer to a real problem. "Who do I need to speak with to get my own collection going? It would need to be in the Portland area, obviously."

"I'll bet Rachel can help, Sis." Nora had tucked her phone away, looking up with a curious expression. "I mean, her dad works for the police department, right? You'd think he'd have the connections to get this done."

I nodded eagerly, my back, bath, and book forgotten. Instead, I was already considering how to gather used cell phones for the large homeless population in Portland. Maybe Roger could do some networking as well.

"Is this something we can ask Brent to do?" I asked Nora, my forehead wrinkled in thought. "It can't be that difficult, can it?"

Nora looked at me, one eyebrow lifted sardonically. "I'm fairly certain 'Brent' and 'not difficult' aren't synonymous, Sis. I say we keep it to Rachel and let her decide whether or not to involve the boy."

I nodded. "That's a good idea. She'll probably be a bit kinder than we would be."

Nora snorted at my comment, and Fern looked curious.

Before I could explain, my lower back gave a small twinge. I reached around and gave it a rub, smiling ruefully at Nora and Fern. "I'd love to talk about this more, but I think I need to get my hot bath." I gave a wry chuckle. "It's something to look forward to, Fern. Achy backs and achy feet"—here I stared pointedly at Nora's heels—"come with the territory."

"Speak for yourself." Nora tossed her head as if practicing for a shampoo commercial, her short curls bouncing like miniature corkscrews. After losing nearly all of her hair to a bad perm the year before, she'd finally grown enough back to replace the fake hair pieces she'd taken to wearing. "I plan on being young for a long time, so there."

"Well, you certainly sound juvenile enough." I smiled sweetly at her and then laughed outright at her disgruntled frown. "And if you keep wrinkling your mug like that, pal, you're going to have more wrinkles than that cute shar-pei puppy we took care of last month."

I tossed that last comment over my shoulder and chuckled all the way to the bathroom. I really loved a good exit line. I expected that Miss Marple would have approved.

Whether it was from the leisurely soak in the tub or the two chapters I'd managed to read before my eyes began to close, I slept like a log that night. Nora was already in bed when I came out of the bathroom, the light from a bedside lamp shining on her face. She was still absorbed by her cell phone, and I glimpsed the familiar blue text boxes of instant messaging as I walked past.

Judging by the way she curled one hand protectively around the phone, I had a feeling she was texting Portland's version of Romeo, one Marcus Avery. I could only hope she'd been giving him a piece of her mind and not her heart.

* * * *

"This was beyond nice of you, Fern." Nora patted her mouth with a cloth napkin and discreetly hid a belch behind it.

I couldn't blame her. A homemade zucchini muffin with real butter, a veggie omelet, and freshly brewed tea had me full to the brim.

"To tell the truth, I didn't expect any of this." She made a sweeping motion around the kitchen, and I saw her index finger's fake nail was missing. Good grief—had the woman texted it down to a nub? "You're talented enough to open a café."

"Oh, it's my pleasure. Really." Fern's cheeks had flushed a rosy pink at Nora's words. "I love to bake anyway, and it's nice to be able to have someone here to help me eat it." She smiled at us and patted her flat stomach. "If I'm not careful, it'll all go straight here."

Not wanting this to move into a conversation comparing diet and fitness routines, two of my least favorite subjects, I took a final sip of tea. "Nora, if we're going to catch Martin at home, we'll need to get going fairly soon."

The idea had popped into my mind and out of my mouth before thinking it through, but now that it was out, it sounded as sensible as any other plan.

I eyed the lone muffin that still sat on the hand-thrown platter and then glanced at Fern. "Would it be all right if I took that with me?"

"Oh, please do." She smiled at my words, and I hoped she was truly as sincere as she appeared to be. "The less I have around here, the better."

"Gwen's still in 'starving teacher' mode." Nora dropped one eyelid in a wink, taking the bite from her words. "You sure couldn't tell it by looking at her, though."

Okay, that last part did sting a bit, and I executed an eye roll that would have made my students proud. Fern, bless her heart, kept her mouth closed. I could only imagine what she thought of the Nora and Gwen comedy routine. Giving Nora one of my patented over-the-glasses stare (minus the glasses, of course), I pointed toward the clock hanging above Fern's stove.

"Just call it 'teacher' mode, smarty-pants. It's time to start moving."

My best friend snapped off a sassy salute, nearly knocking her plate to the floor. "Aye, aye, captain. Booking us a ride as we speak."

She maneuvered the cell phone's touch screen, bottom lip held between perfectly even teeth. I had to hand it to her. She was perfectly comfortable in this digital age, unlike me. I wasn't *that* old, for Pete's sake, just horribly incompetent when it came to technology. Give me a book any day, and I was a happy camper. Ask me to upload lesson plans or a digital receipt, and I was lost.

I had made one attempt to join the digital age a few months before. With Nora's help, I'd downloaded a food-delivery app and scrolled confidently through the local restaurant offerings.

That's where something went terribly wrong.

Finally, after I'd managed to order three extra-large pizzas without knowing how in the world it had happened, I'd turned to the local expert on all things internet and begged for a quick tutorial. I was determined to master—or at least learn to navigate—my smartphone for once and for all.

Brent hadn't even batted an eye at my request. He was a horrible driver and couldn't spell to save his life, but he knew what he was talking about when it came to technology.

And he'd eaten all three of those pizzas, anchovies included.

Chapter 8

"I'd say he's already spent a great deal of Daddy's money on this place. Either that, or he's got more going on than that dumpy dry cleaners." Nora's voice held a tinge of envy, but I wouldn't have wanted to live like this.

We stood outside the closed, locked gate of Martin's house, both staring in disbelief at the mansion that rose at the end of a tree-lined gravel drive. Overhead, mounted on a pole just inside the gate, was a security camera, trained directly on us. With an extravagant sigh, Nora reached over to punch the gate's intercom.

There was a discreet crackle, and then a voice said, "Can I help you?"

Rolling her eyes, Nora gave the security camera a one-fingered salute. "Yeah, you can help me, Marty. You can open this gate. Who do you think you are, anyway? The godfather?"

I fully expected her to be told where to go and how to get there. However, the gate began to open inward, the mechanism making almost no sound. Someone had spared no expense on security.

"Are you sure that was Martin?" I murmured, aware the intercom might still be open. "It might have been an aide or something."

"An aide." Nora gave a derisive snort, her nose wrinkling, as if she'd smelled something rotten. "That boy has always liked to play bigger than he is, so, trust me, that was him."

We began walking up the drive, Nora's stilettos sending little pieces of gravel flying and my Birkenstocks collecting them as neatly as if I was wearing a catcher's mitt on each foot.

"Hey, can you stop a second?" I begged when I couldn't take the stones under my feet any longer. "I need to lean on you while I dump the rocks out of my sandals."

"And that's exactly why you need to wear something besides those ghastly medieval shoes." She gave me her hand as I leaned over and removed each shoe and emptied it. "Not to mention that the bottom of your feet have got to be absolutely filthy from all the walking we're doing."

"I'll have you know I keep my feet clean." I hopped in place as I slipped on the newly rock-free sandals. "And better a little dirt than a herniated disc from trying to walk on stilts."

I gave her shoes a disapproving glare. Yes, they were adorable, bright pink with tiny rhinestone hearts fastened on the pointed toes. But as everyday footwear? Not in my lifetime. Certainly not on my feet.

I was saved from further fashion commentary by the appearance of Martin. He was closely followed by a short, stocky man whose physique reminded me of a compact version of The Hulk. I couldn't recall ever before seeing anyone with this many muscles. And if the unpleasant expression on his blemished face was anything to go by, he was probably as nice as a root canal without anesthetics.

"Well, would you look at what the cat dragged outside," Nora drawled, her arms crossed, one hip thrust out as she surveyed the two men. "Sis, have you ever seen anything as sweet as these two?"

I shot her a surprised glance at the description. "Sweet" was not an adjective I'd have chosen. Martin, however, must have read something entirely different into that comment. His mouth, already set in a hostile sneer, now tightened into a thin line. His pal didn't look any happier.

My heart gave a little jump, and I shivered, wondering how fast I'd be able to run back down the graveled drive. I snuck a quick look over my shoulder and saw it wouldn't matter anyway. The gate had reclosed, effectively cutting off any escape route.

Nora, however, didn't seem perturbed in the least. Maybe it was from dealing with all of her ex-husbands, or maybe it was a legacy of being Martin's stepmother. At any rate, she simply returned their stares, eyebrows lifted and lips pursed in an assessing manner.

Martin blinked first. "Whatever. Still the same charming old hag, I see." Giving an exaggerated shrug, he looked at his companion. "Zeke, take these two up to the house and stick 'em in the front room. And keep an eye on 'em, especially the skinny one."

I let out my breath, glad for once to be built on the padded end of the scale. The skinny one, though, had moved closer to Martin, her eyes narrowed in a manner I knew didn't bode well for the target.

I reached out and snagged her arm, giving her a little tug. I wasn't sure how many more proverbial bullets we could dodge, and I was still thinking about the gate. "Let's just get inside, okay? Maybe he'll have coffee."

"Don't count on it." Zeke said in a surprisingly high voice. Anabolic steroids did that to you, I'd heard. That could explain his skin condition as well. "Martin don't make coffee for nobody. He only drinks tea."

"Well, lah dee dah." Nora's sarcastic comment saved me from correcting The Hulk's poor grammar. "It's a good thing we drink tea then, isn't it?"

This didn't get a response, but the man's shoulders tightened slightly. Fantastic. Was he getting ready to use those anabolic-built muscles on us? Maybe Martin's direction to "put us in the front room" had been code for something far more sinister.

Nora needed to play a tad bit nicer, especially since we'd told Fern not to wait up for us. Had we even remembered to tell her where we'd be? I couldn't remember, but that wasn't surprising, given the amount of adrenaline now flooding my system. Soon this would start the cortisol rolling, and everyone knew cortisol made people heavier.

Great. Thanks to Nora and her sassy mouth, I was going to gain even more weight. At least Martin had said to keep an eye on the skinny one and not on me. Maybe I could blend in with the furniture. One could only hope it was of the overstuffed, old-fashioned variety and not sleekly modern. Come to think of it, that could have described me and my best friend as well. If that was the case, Nora would be able to blend in far better than I would.

Hysterical laughter was building, and I prayed silently for a distraction. Where was my rescue dog when *I* needed to be rescued?

As if my thoughts had suddenly taken form, a small dog bounded out of the house and straight toward us, its small pink tongue hanging out in a friendly fashion. Without thinking, I dropped to my knees and held out one hand, fingers loosely curled into a fist.

"Oh, what a cutie you are."

The dog, one of the more expensive breeds, thrust a curious nose at my hand and then gave it a lick. Good. At least I had one ally here.

"And get that good-for-nothin' mutt back inside." Martin's voice rose angrily from behind us. "I told her to keep it put up when I'm home."

"Can I carry him?" I looked at Zeke's impassive face, hoping to appear innocuous. "I really don't mind."

"You heard the boss." Zeke reached over and plucked the dog from my hands and tucked it, squirming wildly and barking frantically, beneath one muscle-bound arm. "Go straight through that door there and into the first room on the right while I deal with this."

"You could at least carry the poor thing correctly," I said indignantly. "Can't you see you're scaring him?"

My concern for the small animal had removed any trepidation I might have been feeling. Bullies of any size were not my favorite people. Zeke's expression was blank, but irritation was growing in his eyes. Still, I wasn't about to let him get away with terrorizing a defenseless dog, especially one as small as this one.

"Oh, give the woman the dog." A new voice, female, came from somewhere down the hallway of the house.

The three of us turned to see a young woman sway into view, her well-endowed shape barely covered by a leopard printed robe. "And tell Martin I make the rules around here, not him." She reached out a manicured finger and gave Zeke's broad chest a poke before giving the squirming dog's head a gentle rub.

"Yes, Mrs. Pitt." Zeke's voice, already high, had risen to a new register.

His face was reddening, the blotchy color only emphasizing his poor skin. The man would be wise to give up the steroids. He might get smaller, but at least he wouldn't sound like a mouse caught in a trap. Without another word, he thrust a surprised animal at me and turned on his heels, almost falling over in his haste to leave.

"I'm sorry about that, but he comes with the territory." She rolled large blue eyes, her fashionably sculpted brows lifting slightly. With one hand holding her flimsy garment together, she offered the other, a friendly smile on her face. "I'm Teresa Pitt."

Nora and I looked at each other and then back at Teresa. I didn't recall hearing about a wife, assuming that was who she was, and Nora appeared just as flummoxed.

"I'm Gwen Franklin, and this is Nora Goldstein. Or Nora Pitt. At least she was once upon a time." I lifted one shoulder in an apologetic shrug at my oldest friend.

Teresa didn't comment, only giving Nora a curious look.

"It's a pleasure to meet you. And this little cutie." I leaned down and gave the dog a quick kiss, something I wouldn't have been able to do only a few years ago. "What's his name?"

Teresa's grin was impish. "Well, that depends on who you're asking. Me? I call her Lala."

"Sorry, I meant 'her.'" I gave Lala's soft head another ruffle and returned her smile. "I'm guessing Martin calls her something different?"

Teresa chuckled, a pleasant low sound. "That's putting it mildly. I won't even begin to tell you some of the things he's called her. Let's just say that 'mutt' is probably the nicest." She gave Lala a fond look. "And trust me when I say she's no mutt."

"Nora and I have owned our own pet valet business for the past year or so, and I'm beginning to appreciate how expensive some breeds can be." My cheeks grew warm as soon as the words came out, but Teresa didn't appear offended.

"How about coffee?" Nora's suggestion covered my embarrassment.

She was timely, I had to admit. I could do without some of the sassiness, but then she wouldn't be my best friend.

"Of course. Follow me. And you can bring Lala, Gwen."

Nora and I walked behind the swishing leopard-print robe, me busily nuzzling Lala's soft ears and Nora taking in the surrounding décor. It was nothing like what I might have expected someone like Teresa to have, all glass and brass. Instead, it was heavy on the retro side, almost an anachronism of sixties kitsch and color schemes.

The kitchen was off the end of the hallway, its bright oranges and yellows accented with a touch of teal. If I hadn't known I was in a stranger's house in Seattle, I'd have sworn I'd gone back to the house of my childhood. My mother, typical of her times, had loved that particular color combo. I avoided it whenever I could.

The table, a round laminated version of Mom's secondhand oak table, was surrounded with six upright chairs, the seats covered in what looked like geometric printed vinyl. It was too shiny to be a sixties leftover, and I couldn't bring myself to consider how much the modern copies would cost. More than I would ever spend, that was for sure.

"I have a Keurig, but I love to use my percolator," Teresa said over her shoulder. "I think it makes for a better taste."

She busied herself with what surely had to be an authentic Proctor percolator, its glass knob shining above the white lid. I recalled watching my parents make coffee in much the same way in the same brand of percolator, only I had no idea what had happened to that much-used coffee maker. It would be worth a pretty penny right now, I had a feeling, and I made a mental note to scour the Goodwill when I got back home.

Nora wasn't the least bit sentimental, though.

"Do you mind if I make myself a quick cup with the Keurig? I think I might fall over if I don't get some caffeine in me." She eyed the percolator warily and shuddered. "And I seem to remember those things leaving lots of grounds in the cups. Not for me, thanks."

"Go right ahead." Teresa motioned toward a gleaming steel machine with her chin. "The pods are in the drawer beneath it, and I've got all my coffee mugs in the cabinet above the stove." She gave a wry smile. "I'm the only coffee drinker in this place, so having someone to drink with me is a real treat."

"Yeah, that Arnold Schwarzenegger wannabe said something to that affect." I laughed at Nora's words, but Teresa's smile was tight.

"Just a word of caution, you two. I would stay as far away from him as possible. And I'm very serious." Teresa paused with two coffee mugs in her hands (original CorningWare, if my eyes didn't deceive me), her expression grave. "He might be Martin's lapdog, but he's a mean son of a gun." She shook herself slightly, placing the cups on the granite countertop. "And he enjoys being mean."

"I take it you're Martin's wife." Nora was already taking the first sip of coffee, walking slowly, with the mug to her lips, as she headed toward the kitchen table. "I had no idea he was even interested in women."

Teresa made a sound that might have been a sob. I glanced at her quickly, but her face was hidden as she turned to remove the happily percolating pot from the stovetop. "Oh, he likes women, all right. Just not the one he's living with."

"Proof that the rotten apple doesn't fall far from the twisted tree, I'd say." Nora's voice was wry, but her eyes were kind as she looked at Teresa. "His dad was the same way." She gave a short bark of laughter. "And that's why he became my ex-hubby number three. He had to fork over quite a bit of moolah, though, so he wasn't too happy." She gave Teresa a wink. "Have you thought about that for yourself?"

To my surprise, Teresa burst into laughter. "You bet I have, but only because I'd be the one forking over the alimony. The money, as they say, is 'mine, all mine.'"

Chapter 9

"Don't tell me you didn't sign a prenup, girl." Nora sounded aghast, but Teresa only seemed amused at Nora's words.

Still smiling, Teresa carried the two full mugs over to the table, her robe flapping open to reveal a very skimpy bathing suit. "There's sugar on the table and creamer in the fridge, if you need it." Sliding into the chair across from Nora, she looked at her over the rim of her own cup. "Oh, there's a prenup, all right. But I'm holding out. If I can make it to our tenth anniversary, I'm home free and can ditch the *bas*—the weasel—ASAP."

"That makes absolutely no sense." I couldn't hold the words back, and Nora turned to stare at me, her eyebrows lifted as high as they'd go. Teresa, though, continued sipping coffee, her expression unconcerned. "Why in the world would you stay with someone so...so odious as Martin when there have to be a million men out there who'd treat you a lot better?"

Tears filled my eyes, and I hastily took a sip of coffee to cover my distress. Blame it on not sleeping in my own bed. And I was missing Herc. And Roger. Lala, her tiny face turned up toward me, looked as sympathetic as a dog could, and I wanted to bury my face in her fur and cry.

"It's none of your business." Nora didn't sound angry. "Maybe Teresa and Martin have some sort of plan."

Teresa nodded in agreement, her voice abruptly sad. "When I married Martin, against my better judgment, I might add, it was because I needed a husband in order to inherit my parents' money. So, Martin agreed that if I stayed with him for ten years and let him use some of my money to fund his ridiculous laundry business, he'd divorce me, no questions, no alimony, no nothing, when we hit that magical ten-year mark."

"Ten years? You couldn't get him to agree to something less? Seven? Or Five?" Nora, apparently forgetting she'd just told me to mind my own business, leaned forward in avid curiosity. "I'm not too sure I'd have been able to agree to something that smacks of servitude."

Teresa laughed, but there was no amusement in her voice. "Yeah, I thought about it. It made me remember those colonial stories about being bound to someone in order to earn freedom." She took a small sip of coffee, briefly shutting her eyes as though getting her emotions under control. "That's what I keep telling myself. I'm crossing the days off, believe you me."

"So, how much longer do you have to go with this agreement?" I was glad Nora had asked the question since I couldn't trust my voice at the moment. "Hopefully just a few more years."

Teresa smiled at her, a sad smile that didn't reach her beautiful eyes. "I've still got seven years left, and I hope I can last that long without killing him."

"Not if I get to you first, sweetie pie."

The three of us turned. Martin and Zeke were standing in the doorway of the kitchen, wearing twin smirks.

"Marty." Nora's voice was so heavy with sarcasm I was amazed the words had enough impetus to fly across the room toward the anticipated target. "I've been hearing all about how charming you are. Sounds like you took husband lessons from your dad."

Zeke's fists clenched, and his feet moved as if he intended to rush at Nora. Martin gave a nearly imperceptible shake of his head, though, and Zeke stayed put. I glanced at Nora, and the pulse in her neck was beating a little quicker; my own heart was racing. I'd faced down crazed parents and even a killer or two, but this man was in a league of his own.

Teresa stayed where she was, coolly observing her husband over the rim of her coffee mug as she took another sip. She set the cup down with a studied casualness. "Come to give me a hard time in front of witnesses, *dear*?"

The emphasis on that last word sent a wave of angry color into Martin's cheeks, but he clamped his mouth shut.

Zeke had no such compunction. "You need to learn some respect, Mrs. Pitt, and I'm just the person to teach it to you." He cracked his knuckles in a way I'd only ever seen in old-time gangster movies, and I wanted to laugh. His next words took the laughter right out of my mouth, though. "And you'd better watch what you're telling these two. We've got eyes and ears everywhere." He turned to look at Martin, his expression childlike, as though looking for approval. "Ain't that right, Boss?"

Martin stared at Zeke for a moment before waving one hand in the air, dismissing either him or the conversation. "Whatever. I'm outta here." He spun on one heel and strode out of the kitchen, leaving Zeke to scamper after him like the toady he was.

There was complete silence for a moment, broken only by Lala's quiet whine. I could feel her little heart beating as rapidly as mine through her smooth fur. Poor thing. She'd picked up the tenseness between her mistress and the two men, and I felt sorry that such a little animal had to experience it.

I stroked Lala's soft ears. "This poor thing is scared to death, Teresa. Someone needs to put a muzzle on that man's mouth." I cuddled the dog closer to me, her small body trembling.

"Which one? Martin or Zeke?" Teresa's voice was sardonic. "They're a two-headed monster, Gwen. Where one is, the other is sure to be somewhere close by."

"We didn't see Zeke yesterday," I volunteered before I could stop myself.

Beside me, Nora shifted uncomfortably while Teresa stared at the two of us, her face unreadable.

"I mean, we were only there for a few minutes, so maybe..." I was caught between Teresa's stare and Nora's scowl. Shrugging, I dropped my face to Lala's head and hugged the dog closer to my chest.

"Why were you at the cleaners?" Teresa asked in a controlled voice, but I could sense a coiled anxiety beneath her words. "Did he know you were dropping by?"

I raised my face to look at them.

"We weren't just 'dropping by.'" Nora's crooked fingers emphasized the two words and Teresa flushed. "Gwen and I drove all the way from Portland to talk to the rat." She gave a disgusted grunt. "His dad better really be dead, or I'm gonna make sure that happens. Trust me when I say that seeing my ex-stepson again wasn't on my bucket list."

"Ah. The will." Teresa lowered her gaze to her hands, both hands clutched tightly together on the table. "I'm hoping he'll inherit enough money to let me go." She looked at Nora. "Have you seen what he'll be getting?"

Nora shifted in her chair, hands palm up and shoulders lifted. "Not exactly."

I looked at her sharply, wondering where this was going. As far as I knew, she hadn't seen the will itself, only the letter declaring her executorship. And it wasn't like Nora to be so noncommittal. Normally her words were arrow straight and struck their target with accuracy.

"And what does 'not exactly' mean?" One thin eyebrow had risen on Teresa's forehead, a half-moon of skepticism. "You either have or you haven't."

"It means what I said. 'Not exactly.'" Nora looked at Teresa without batting an eyelash. Believe me, if she had, I'd have seen it. The mascara was so thick on her eyelashes that they had the appearance of tarantulas, poised above and below each eye as if waiting to grab any prey that might scuttle by.

Teresa held her gaze for another moment and then gave a half-shrug. "Okay. Whatever you say. But I'm not giving up hope that he gets the lot and can get the heck out of my life."

"And I'm not saying he's not." Nora took a sip of her coffee and grimaced. "Oh, good grief. Can I use your microwave, Teresa?"

"Sure." She motioned over her shoulder toward a stainless-steel microwave nestled above the equally shiny stove-and-oven combo. "Just press the number one, and it'll heat up quickly."

We sat in silence as the microwave whirred softly, heating the cold coffee back to a drinkable temperature. I was still turning Nora's comment over in my head (had she told me about actually reading the will and I'd forgotten?), and Teresa was staring at her hands as if trying to recall where they'd come from. Finally, the microwave gave a sharp ding, causing Lala to twitch in my lap. The poor thing was a bundle of nerves.

And I was a bundle of confusion. The longer we stayed in Seattle, the more convoluted this situation became. Give me good old Portland and an afternoon with Brent's wacky humor any day over this family drama.

We left a very quiet Teresa behind as we walked out of the house. Lala's sharp barks and Teresa's equally strident admonitions followed us, and I wondered for the thousandth time why some folks were allowed to have a pet.

Thinking of pets took me right to Herc, and I thought about his time away from me. Was he being taken care of as I would have done? Was Aggie, the little ham, hogging all of Brent's attention? I said as much to Nora as we stood waiting for our Uber ride to arrive.

"Are you kidding me?" Nora looked at me in amazement. "Herc can hold his own with that little mop of a dog. Trust me on this, Sis."

"I certainly hope so."

A silver Highlander slowed to a crawl, the driver lifting a hesitant hand in our direction.

"Looks like our taxi's here. Home?"

"If you mean the Airbnb, yep. I'm ready for a glass of something stronger than coffee."

The SUV came to a complete stop, and Nora opened the back door. "Thanks for getting here so quickly."

The driver, a thin man with an even thinner mustache and what had to be a toupee resting on his head, simply nodded in acknowledgment. He leaned over and did something on the touch screen attached to his console, still silent. Nora didn't seem to be bothered by his reticence, and I gave a mental shrug before following Nora into the back seat. Not everyone was a conversationalist. Some days I wished Brent was in that category, bless his loquacious little heart.

* * * *

"Are you sure you got our information?" Nora spoke up abruptly, startling me out of my Brent-centric thoughts. "I'm pretty sure we're going the wrong way, driver."

There was no reply, not even a gesture to let us know he'd heard Nora. Maybe the man was deaf. That couldn't be safe. Nora, however, leaned forward and grabbed the man's shoulder, giving it a good shake. The only indication he'd even felt her hand was a brief glance into the rearview mirror.

Nora and I exchanged a quick glance. Her lips had compressed into a line thin enough to thread through a needle, and my heart rate was beginning to climb. What was going on with this driver? My anxiety level was rising, right along with my heart rate, and if Nora's reddened cheeks were any indication, her temper was rising as well.

"Driver, pull over right now. I want to terminate this ride immediately." Her tone was as icy as river water in the dead of winter, a sure sign the listener had better comply quickly. "*Now*, driver."

This got a response. Without a glance in our direction, he said, "I've got my orders. I'll let you out when we get to where we're going."

I looked at Nora, baffled. What in the world had that meant?

My best friend had never been known to sit and let life happen to her. She wasn't sitting now, either. In one of the quickest moves I'd ever seen, she leaned over the seat and grabbed the steering wheel, forcing the SUV to the side of the road.

Closing my eyes, I said a quick "Now I lay me down to sleep," my go-to prayer, and held on for dear life.

With a screech of tires and a few cuss words I hadn't heard since leaving the high school campus, the driver managed to stop without crashing.

Nora had fallen back against the seat, one hand clutching her cell phone as she jabbed viciously at the keypad.

"Who're you calling?" I tugged at my seat belt, twisting my neck away from its scratchy webbing. It had done its job well and now had me in a strangle hold, cutting right across my windpipe. "Hopefully you're calling the local police." I glanced at the rearview mirror and met the man's gaze.

He was watching us with interest, almost as if we were a new species that had crawled into his SUV.

"And you, where did you get these so-called 'orders'? From a Cracker Jack box?"

He didn't answer—no surprise there—but his eyes crinkled in amusement.

"I'll certainly be letting Uber know not to employ you in the future, I can assure you."

Beside me, Nora was frowning as she stared at her phone. "Sis, check your phone and see if you've got a signal. This place is downright creepy." She glared over the seat. "And so are the people."

I slipped my cell phone from my bag and looked doubtfully at the readout. I had two bars in the upper-left-hand corner, surely enough for a connection, but there was also a small image beside them that I didn't recognize.

Before I could answer Nora, though, our driver cleared his throat. "Your phones ain't gonna work in here, ladies." He leaned over and pointed at the navigational screen, the one I had assumed held our route information. "This here's called a 'cell phone blocker.'" He smiled suddenly, showing the most impressive set of dentures I had ever seen. "And don't think about running, either." He nodded at the door's lock. "This baby's got childproof locks, and no one gets out until I say so."

Nora was building up a head of steam that could have powered a train's engine. "I don't give a flying rat what that's called, idiot. I can tell you one thing, though: *this*"—she motioned with irritation to the two of us—"is called 'kidnapping,' and that happens to be a class-one felony. Capiche?"

We were back to the silent treatment. Whether we liked it or not, Nora and I were headed for a meeting with someone who probably didn't have our best interests at heart.

And they most likely wouldn't have a cup of coffee waiting for us, either.

Finally, the scenery began to take on a familiar look. I spotted a corner store I remembered from our previous trip downtown, and I was trying to place it when Nora gave a snort of disgust.

"Oh, give me a flippin' break." Nora looked out the passenger window, a scowl on her face. "We're back at Marty's hole-in-the-wall laundromat."

Indeed, we were. To be exact, we were parked in the alley behind said hole-in-the-wall, but it was definitely the same place we'd visited the day before. This time, though, I was fairly certain we'd be going through the back entrance, not the front.

The driver, still not talking, switched off the engine and hit the car's horn with a syncopated beat. The back door popped open, and a man who might have been Zeke's twin stepped out, his not-so-friendly grin spread wide.

"Clever. Makes me think of 'Pop Goes the Weasel,' heavy on the weasel." Nora glared at the second man, her tone as dry as my mouth currently felt. I wanted a cup of coffee more than anything at the moment. Not literally, of course. First and foremost, I would have loved to be out of this vehicle and well on my way out of town. Coffee, though, came in a close second.

"Oh, that's hilarious, lady." Another flash of the dentures and he opened his door. "Meet Chuckles, which rhymes with knuckles, which is what you two are gonna get if you don't shut those traps of yours."

"Hey, wait a minute. I didn't say anything." I was talking to an empty seat. Nora aimed her frown at me, and I stared back, defensive. "Well, I didn't. It's been all you."

She threw her hands up in an exaggerated gesture. "Fabulous. First my ex-stepkid thinks he's a mafia godfather, and now my best friend wants to throw me under the bus." She dropped her hands and eyed the second man as he reached for her door handle. "And here comes the bus, if I'm not mistaken."

I preferred "Chuckles" to "Bus," to be honest. It had a friendly ring to it, almost chummy. Maybe he wouldn't be as unpleasant as our driver had suggested. Finding oneself under a heavy bus seemed uncivilized. Surely no one called "Chuckles" could be *that* bad.

I changed my mind, though, when Chummy Chuckles reached inside and roughly pulled us outside, one at a time. Being run over by a real bus was beginning to seem like the better option.

"Get your mitts off me, you big galoot!" Nora was furious.

I fully expected her to give Chuckles a kick with her stilettos. He must have had a similar idea. In one quick movement, he leaned over and scooped up Nora, tossing her over his shoulder as if she weighed next to nothing.

The fact she was about half my weight didn't help her cause. I almost laughed as I remembered something I'd overheard at Voodoo Doughnuts: "Eat more doughnuts. You'll be harder to kidnap."

"Gwen, call the cops!"

Before I could punch in 9-1-1, though, Silent Sam grabbed my wrist and wrestled the phone from my hand. He didn't, I noticed with chagrin, even attempt to carry me as Nora had been carried. Instead, I was all but dragged into the dry cleaner's back room, my protests punctuated by my imprisoner's heavy breathing.

So much for that sage advice about doughnuts.

"You'll have theft added to those kidnapping charges if you don't give that phone back, pal."

I sounded snappy, and I probably wasn't in a position to act that way, but I had about had it with Seattle and wills and exes. Next time Nora wanted to chase an errant stepchild, she could darn well count me out. Plus, I hadn't had that phone for very long, and I didn't want to fork out more money for a replacement.

I watched, open-mouthed, as Silent Sam tossed my phone toward Chuckles. Nora, still steaming from her inelegant mode of transportation and being unceremoniously dumped on the floor, reached up and snagged the phone as it sailed past her. She promptly tucked it into her personal carrying case, also known as her brassiere, and I grinned at the expressions on the two men's faces.

"*I* ain't going after that." Chuckles emphasized his words by holding up both hands. "Uh, flipping no way, no how. The boss didn't say anything about frisking ladies."

"Oh, for cryin' out loud. She's about as big as my little finger. What can she do to stop us?"

"I wouldn't ask that if I were you, boys" was all I got out before Nora went into action, springing to her feet, bending to rip off one shoe and driving the pointed heel into, shall we say, a very tender place on Sam's thin body. Without any padding to absorb the blow, he bent over double, his wheezing now completely gone. He wasn't breathing at all but was gasping as though he'd been body slammed by The Rock.

Nora, with a very satisfied look, tossed me the phone. "Call the cops, Sis. And tell 'em we've got a pair of kidnappers ready and waiting."

I glanced up from my phone and pointed at the back door. "Make that one." I looked at Sam and saw he was beginning to recover from Nora's attack. "You'd probably better give him a second dose of high heel before he gets away as well."

He moaned in response, waving one hand weakly in surrender. Nora smiled triumphantly and waved the shoe in return. He whimpered and shut his eyes, letting himself sink slowly to the floor.

"I think this one's ready for the pokey." She shot a stern look at Chuckles, pointing the shoe at him. "And don't even think of trying anything, my man, unless you want what he got."

Like most bullies, Chuckles had more bluster than muscle. With another wave of his hands, he backed off, a wary eye on the stiletto.

Chapter 10

Silent Sam, it turned out, was a petty criminal named Gerald Porter, also known as Jerry "Fingers" Porter to the local police department.

"I guess he's moving up in the crime world, or down, depending on your perspective." Nora was still high on adrenaline and had charmed the information out of the younger of the two officers who'd arrived. She'd had to relinquish the shoe as evidence. "No thanks, Sis." She'd looked at my Birkenstock-shod feet with distaste in response to my offer to run and buy her a pair of sandals. "By the way, he's done time for shoplifting, and they said kidnapping isn't usually his thing."

My own adrenaline surge was being replaced by shaky knees, dry mouth, and an insane desire to hop in the back seat of the cruiser and lock all the doors. On top of that, I was already calculating how much cortisol was now circulating around in my over-taxed hormonal system, happily depositing new fat cells alongside their relatives residing permanently in my belly and hips. Nora, of course, would remain as slim as always. It made me wonder why I'd stayed best friends with her all these years.

"Oh, look." The aforementioned best friend was pointing delightedly at someone carrying a cardboard tray. "Someone's brought us Dutch Bros. Hope there's a White Chocolate Zombie in there."

Of course she did. And that was another thing that wasn't fair. She could drink fancy coffee and devour pastries by the dozens without an ounce of it staying behind on her, well, on her *behind*. Just one look at a froth-topped, chocolate-sprinkled mocha and my fat cells sat up and took notice.

Of course, I'd read somewhere that chocolate was soothing to jangled nerves, and mine were practically vibrating with anxiety. And that Snickers

Mocha was calling my name. With a grateful smile, I took it from the hand that offered it…and almost dropped it all over the floor.

"Caleb? What in the world?"

Caleb smiled sheepishly at me as he handed around the to-go cups. "I needed a change, I guess." As if it had only then occurred to him that I was part of the ongoing hoopla, he paused. "What're *you* doing here, Miss Franklin?"

I have no earthly idea is what I wanted to say. What I said aloud, though, was, "Oh, my friend was visiting some family in the area, and I came along for the ride."

Caleb glanced over at Nora. She was sipping her dessert in a cup (my description of froufrou coffee drinks) and chatting animatedly with not only the two officers who'd shown up but also with a handful of the dry cleaner's employees, who'd come out to see what the ruckus was about. Was anyone still minding the shop?

"She's the one who was with you at The Friendly Bean, right?" He looked back at me with a sharp expression. "So, have you two been friends for long?"

I could hear the inflection as he said "friends," and my cheeks grew warm. Taking a hasty sip of my drink, I stalled while I considered what to say. I could simply give him an ambiguous smile and say nothing, but that might not be the best route.

Instead, I stared sternly at him from over the rim of my coffee cup. "Not that it should matter to you, Caleb, but Mrs. Goldstein and I have been best friends since we met at school."

His eyebrows began to rise.

"In kindergarten, to be precise. So, yes, I guess you might say we've known each other for a long time." Before he could ask how long that had been, I got in my own query. "Have you contacted Hannah? Made a phone call, sent a text, anything?"

Now it was Caleb's turn to seem uncomfortable. He began breaking down the empty coffee carrier as if he alone could save the planet with his recycling efforts, and his cheeks had developed two bright pink patches. I must've hit a conversational nerve.

"No, and I'm not gonna either." The words had none of the friendliness that had been there only moments before. As he turned to walk away, he tossed one more thing over his shoulder, his voice tight with anger. "And you can tell her to stay out of my business."

And with that, he stomped away, heading back the way he'd come. I stared after him, not sure of what to make of his abrupt change of attitude.

"Well, that's one way to win friends and influence enemies. What'd you say to get *his* tighty whities in a wad?" Nora's amused tone in my ear made me start.

I blamed it on my still-rattled nerves. So far, the chocolate drink hadn't done much to soothe either them or my mind. I tried to keep my voice light, though, as I gave her a half-smile.

"Oh, I mentioned something about contacting his girlfriend in Portland, and he blew up." I shrugged, sipping my cooled coffee. "Maybe he came here to forget her or something equally sappy." I held out the Dutch Bros cup, wrinkling my nose. "Want this? I don't think I can drink anymore."

"I don't want your secondhand coffee, thank you very much." She took it from my hand and added it to the pile tottering above the edge of an old trash can. "Besides, mine was a little on the too-sweet side. I tossed it as well."

"Any idea of how we'll get back to our Airbnb?" I twisted my neck to watch the officers, both leaning against the cruiser's hood as they completed paperwork. "And how soon we can leave?"

"Leave? Who said anything about leaving?" Nora waved a hand in my face. "I want to talk to whoever is working in there and see if I can figure out who's behind these shenanigans." She hooked a thumb in the direction of the office. "And I want to get it done before Marty shows his ugly mug around here, which will probably be soon." The thumb now jabbed in the direction of the police. "I overheard them say that they called him to come join the party."

I groaned. "Nora, I'm worn out." It was my turn to hold up a hand. "Listen to me, please. I have been kidnapped. I want a cup of good coffee. I need to rest before we drive home. If you want to stay and play detective, fine. I, however, am calling a cab."

Nora stared at me, her eyes narrowed and her mouth a tight line. I'd made her mad, but I was beyond caring. I'd care later, of course, but at the moment, I was too upset to worry. And Fern's coffee maker was screaming my name.

"Fine." Nora threw up both hands, clearly annoyed. "You win. I'll ask someone to give us a ride, though, because frankly, I have no desire to get into another Uber."

"I've felt that way since experiencing that first ride with Brent." I smiled tentatively at her, waiting to see how she'd respond.

Nora wasn't one to stay angry for any length of time, unless it had something to do with Marcus.

"You can say that again." She smiled a wide smile that showed enough teeth to make a shark jealous. "I don't know about you, but I'm thinking a ride home with those boys in blue might be just the thing we need."

I watched as she sashayed over to the cruiser and said something that made the officers laugh. When they nodded in unison, I sighed. She'd done it once more. Nora would never lose that magic touch with those of the opposite sex, although I sometimes wished she'd tone it down a bit.

Still, a ride was a ride, and a free ride with security was even better. I could have done without the lights and sirens when we pulled in front of Fern's home, though, but that's what happened when Nora took control.

When we finally put our belongings into my car and pulled back onto the highway, I was so happy I almost cried.

* * * *

When I pulled my car into my home's detached garage later that evening, I was tempted to stay seated. I was weary from the drive, true, but it was the mental strain of the past few days that had me ready to curl up and sleep right where I was. Sighing, I laid my head back against the headrest and closed my eyes. I'd just rest a moment and then get myself inside and into a hot bath.

I should have known better.

"Hey, Miss F. Are you asleep?" Brent's volume control operated on three settings, in my experience: loud, louder, and mumble. Right now it was roughly on the louder end of things, and it was being broadcasted directly into my left ear as he leaned into my open car window.

I jerked upright, nearly giving myself whiplash, and glared at him. "Brent, I'm not deaf. And don't sneak up on me like that. You might give me a heart attack."

He only grinned. "Me and Aggie brought Herc home for you. See?"

I swiveled my gaze from Brent to the ground. There sat my precious tuxedo-furred dog, Herc, and his fluffy white companion, tongues out and tails thumping on the ground. They were not, I noticed sleepily, running around or barking.

"Brent, back away so I can get out of the car, please. And if you could carry my suitcase inside for me, I'd greatly appreciate it." Opening my door and ignoring its protest, I got out and stretched both arms over my head before dropping down to pet both dogs. "What's wrong with these two?"

"Huh?" Brent's forehead wrinkled as he looked from the dogs to me. "There's nothing wrong with them, Miss F." He reached through the open back window and dragged my Goodwill special suitcase out with a thump. Still, the dogs were silent, parked in one spot and watching us with bright eyes. "I got 'em trained, that's all."

Sometimes Brent's confusing syntax sent my mind into a spin as I tried to translate. This comment was no different. "Are you saying *you* trained them or that you had them trained?" I looked back at the two dogs and wondered what had happened in the short amount of time I'd been away.

He juggled my case to one shoulder, a young Paul Bunyan in jeans and a T-shirt. "Rachel did it, Miss F. She's really good with animals. And with me," he added with pride. "She keeps telling me she's almost got me trained too." He pointed to the two dogs. "If you want them to follow you, just slap your leg."

"You can tell her 'thanks' and 'good luck' for me. I'm sure she'll know what I mean." I patted my leg hesitantly, waiting to see what Herc would do. To my amazement, both he and Aggie stood, tails still wagging, as they waited for their next command. I looked at Brent. "Now what?"

"Just start walking. Herc'll follow you. Well, so will Aggie, but I'll get her as soon as I put your case in the house." He suited action to words, giving his own leg a smack. Both dogs trotted after him, without the usual chaotic barking and running in circles. Rachel had performed a minor miracle, in my estimation. If she could also get a handle on her beau and his "Brentness," she'd be ready for sainthood.

I followed the trio around the front of the house to the door. I'd left my porch light on the entire time I'd been away and was relieved to see it still casting its yellow glow over the porch.

"You should make me a house key, Miss F." Brent set the case down and picked up Aggie. She nuzzled his face and gave a small bark, but that was all. "That way I won't have to crawl in the doggy door anymore. Besides, I got really embarrassed when your neighbor called the cops."

"What?" I froze, the key turned halfway in the lock. "Which neighbor?" I quickly ran through the various people living around me and wondered to whom I'd need to apologize.

"Just kidding, Miss F." He seemed delighted with his joke. "But I could still use a key."

I opened the door, and he walked in ahead of me, still talking.

"You might fall down and break a hip, or whatever old people do." He feigned falling and Aggie scrabbled on his chest with her paws. "You know, like 'I've fallen, and I can't get up!'" He grinned as he straightened up.

I did not grin back.

"Brent Mayfair." I spoke sternly. "Number one, I am *not* giving you a key. And secondly, I am *not* old." I was only in my mid-fifties, for Pete's sake. It'd been an early retirement because I'd begun teaching directly out of college and had earned my full state pension.

He shrugged. "Fine by me, Miss F. But don't expect me to come running when you fall down and bust something."

"Cross my heart and hope to..." I let the words trail away to nothingness. Saying "hope to die" in this type of conversation might not be wise. Instead, I lifted one hand and pointed to the door. "And now, I'd appreciate it if you'd take your shadow and leave, Brent. I've had a long drive, and I'm tired."

He gave another careless lift of one shoulder. "Sure thing, but it's nighttime, and I don't have a shadow right now." He shook his head and looked at me almost sorrowfully. "It's a good thing you didn't teach science. You'd probably get things all mixed up."

Thankfully, he was gone before I could say something in reply. I might have said something I'd either regret or, even worse, have to explain.

Herc was sitting quietly at my feet, his gazed fixed on my face, as if transmitting a message. Of course, he only had two messages in his repertoire, namely "feed me" and "pet me." He'd had another, "outside," but, with the advent of the doggy door, that had disappeared.

"Okay, boy, I'll feed you. Give me a chance to unload this case in my room first." Talking to Herc was comforting, almost therapeutic, and even Nora's teasing couldn't deter this habit. "I'll bet you've already eaten, though."

He didn't respond but followed me through the short hallway and into my bedroom. It was almost spooky, having a noiseless dog. It reminded me too much of Silent Sam for me to like it. Maybe a treat could get him animated.

I'd just opened the cabinet where I kept Herc's food and treats when a sharp knock on the front door made me start. I was still on edge and debated ignoring whoever it was. When Herc trotted over and began sniffing along the bottom of the door, tail wagging, I took that as a sign it was safe to see who was there.

Roger and his two lovely golden retrievers, Max and Doc, stood there, the first handing me a bunch of cheerful daisies and the other two exchanging typical canine greetings with Herc.

It made me thankful I was a human and not a dog. I'd take a bouquet of flowers any day over a bouquet of canine—well, you get the picture. Besides, daisies seemed to smile while a dog's hind quarters definitely did not.

I smiled at Roger, reaching for his arm and drawing him inside. "How'd you know I was home?"

The three dogs headed for the kitchen and the back door. Roger and I chose the couch and sat down, the flowers still in my hands.

"Turning psychic?"

His cheeks flushed slightly as he shook his head. "No, nothing that exciting. I was passing by and saw your lights on." He gave me a smile that reminded me of a little boy who'd gotten caught doing something nice. "So, I ran and got those for you and got back here as quickly as I could. I wanted to catch you before you went to bed."

It was my turn for my fact to warm. Even the word "bed" sent a shiver up one side of my spine and down the other. To cover it, I stood. "Let me get a vase for these beauties and then we can catch up." I glanced back at him, eyebrows slightly lifted in question. "Coffee?"

"Sounds good. I can make it, if that's all right." His eyes smiled into mine, and I almost tripped over my own feet.

How in the world had Nora managed to handle so many exes? I was having a difficult time with one beau.

"I'm pretty handy in the kitchen."

Oh, thank the stars above and all that was holy. A man who knew his way around a kitchen. Although I was pretty sure my thoughts had appeared over my head in one of those cartoon bubbles, I tried to keep it casual.

"Sure. The Keurig's right there." I helpfully pointed to the coffee machine obviously squatting next to my stove. "And the pods are in the cabinet above it."

I fumbled my way through several places a vase might be hiding before deciding to put the flowers in an old Tupperware pitcher I'd picked up for a song at a yard sale. When I placed it in the center of the kitchen table, it looked almost elegant. It certainly added some color to my rather dark kitchen.

We'd barely sat down again with our coffee when my cell phone began to do a jig across the table. I snatched it up as it headed for a tumble, frowning slightly when I saw the name on the tiny screen.

"Excuse me, Roger. It's Nora." What in the world could be so important? Had we left something behind at Fern's? She was intruding on my time, and I'd make sure to tell her the next time I saw her. Punching the icon with more force than was strictly necessary, I barked into the phone. "What now?"

When I heard what she had to say, I almost dropped my phone.

Martin Pitt had been abducted.

"Good grief. Did Teresa tell you when it happened?" I glanced at Roger, who was busily tapping away on his cell phone. "Do we need to get back up there?"

"It was earlier this afternoon, and she said we don't need to come back yet." Nora took a gulp of something, reminding me of my cooling coffee. "Here's hoping that whoever took the numbskull realizes they took damaged goods."

Reaching for my mug, I took a quick sip. "He's not the brightest bulb in the chandelier, that's for certain, so maybe they'll return him quickly."

Nora only grunted. "I'm fairly sure Teresa will be fine however it turns out."

"Agreed. She seems like a strong woman." I set my coffee down, brushing against Roger's legs as I reached for the coffee table.

His smile gave me a kick the coffee hadn't managed to do, and I returned his smile with one of my own.

"Well, keep me informed. And if we need to go back, we can."

The three dogs came back inside, the flap of the doggy door nearly catching Herc's tail.

"That's what I told her." Now Nora was doing something that required a lot of crinkling and rustling. "Have you tried the new Reese's Peanut Butter Pumpkins? They're stuffed with Reese's Pieces, Sis. You gotta get some, I'm telling you."

I never knew how much candy Nora had stashed at any given time, but it was guaranteed to rival the local convenience store's display. The woman had a sweet tooth the size of an elephant, and she thrived on hitting the half-price sales following any holiday. She ate Halloween candy in March and Valentine's Day goodies in September.

"I'll try some the next time I see you." I gave Roger another smile and made a "talking" gesture with my fingers. "I need to cut this short, but don't forget to text or call when you hear back from Teresa."

I'd almost tapped the icon for disconnecting when Nora said very loudly and clearly, "Got your boyfriend there, do ya?"

I managed to cut off the wild laughter in mid-cackle, and my cheeks began growing warm.

"She's something else." Roger was now grinning from ear to ear. "I'd say she was pretty perceptive, though."

I snorted, reaching over to give Herc's ears a rub. "I've got another word for what she is, but it's not very polite." I stayed bent over my dog for an extra moment, giving my face time to cool off. I could see Roger from the corner of my eye, though, and he still looked amused.

"What? I'm not your boyfriend?" Roger tapped his chin, pretending to consider some idea. "Could we at least be friends? Walk the dogs together, have coffee now and then?"

I glanced up quickly, nearly giving my neck a kink. Surely the man was teasing me. Wasn't he?

"I–I—aren't you—aren't we—" I, who for so many years used my words daily in my teaching career, couldn't put together one cohesive sentence. I didn't need to speak right then anyway. I was too busy returning Roger's kiss as the three dogs pressed around us.

It was the most enlightening evening I had experienced in a long time.

Chapter 11

The sun seemed extra bright the next morning for some odd reason, and I was smiling at the coffee maker as if I could see a certain face imposed on it. Roger and the retrievers had left at what, for me, was an ungodly hour—after *midnight*, for Pete's sake—but I felt as though I'd had a full ten hours' sleep.

I'd just taken the first sip of a wonderful Ethiopian blend when a voice from behind me caused me to jump.

"I see someone's looking awfully jolly this morning." The laugh that followed these words made me close my eyes and shake my head. "Well, spill it. What was the good doctor doing here so late last night?"

I ignored her question. "Nora, if I tell you it's illegal to pick locks, will that make you stop?"

Another volley of laughter shot from behind me, making me cringe. "Nope." She headed for the Keurig. "D'ya have more of that Island Coconut I had last time I was here?" She sniffed the air as if she could smell the coconut-flavored brew. "That stuff was the bomb."

I rolled my eyes at her word choice, but I waved at the cabinet above the coffee maker. "You know where it is, and since you've already made yourself at home, just keep at it."

"Will do." She turned and gave me an exaggerated wink, exposing the bright teal eye shadow that covered her eyelid. "And don't go anywhere until you give me the complete scoop."

"There's nothing to scoop." I made myself sip my coffee slowly and placidly, watching her over the rim of my mug. I'd chosen one that had TEARS OF MY STUDENTS printed on the side. I'd liked using this one during tests. "Besides, I was almost asleep when he left."

I wanted to jump all over those words as soon as they left my mouth and drag them back.

"I knew it!" Nora's voice managed to find an octave and decibel combo I'd not heard before.

Herc, who was lying under the kitchen table, covered his muzzle with his paws and whined.

"Now I'm definitely not leaving without the deets."

"The *what*?" I stared at her, trying to interpret the meaning of "deets."

"The details, you old fogey, the details." Nora moved her neck as I'd seen my students do in the past when they were on their way to being sassy. "You've gotta get with it." Here she gave me another wink. "Kinda like you and the doc."

I'd heard enough. "Let's get one thing straight, O Hipster of the Geriatric High-Rise." I set my mug down carefully so I wouldn't be tempted to throw it. It was one of my favorites, after all. "Nothing, and I repeat, *nothing* happened. At least not in the way you mean it. We might have kissed, and he may have read poetry to me, but that's it." I shrugged, enjoying her expression. "That's why I was almost asleep when he left. James Whitcomb Riley always relaxes me."

"James Whit-who?" Now she was stuttering, and I almost felt sorry for her. Almost. She deserved a little dose of her own medicine. "Where was Roger when this James was reading to you?" She sniffed disparagingly. "And no wonder you were falling asleep. Poetry's as boring as it gets."

I had to laugh. Her anticipated salacious "scoop" had all but vanished, and I actually wanted to tell her about my evening.

"James Whitcomb Riley was a poet from Indiana. And since Roger and I both like to read his writing—poems such as 'Knee Deep in June' and 'Little Orphan Annie'—I let him read aloud to me while I rested on the couch." I took another drink of coffee. "It was a rather long day, after all."

"Sheesh." Nora shook her head in amazement. "Can you even begin to imagine Marcus reading poetry to me, much less something like that?"

I laughed again. "Maybe. Have you ever asked him to?"

"As if." She snorted the words and then chuckled, tilting her head as she smiled at me. "Do you need me to tell you what that means as well?"

"'As if.'" I gave her the air quote motion. "I'm pretty sure I've heard Brent use that a time or two."

"True. Speaking of the Boy Wonder, has he called or texted yet this morning?" She reached inside her neon-pink top and produced her cell phone, studying the screen before looking up. "Nothing on my phone yet."

I shook my head. "No. I think the first job today is later than usual, so maybe that's why."

"Or maybe he was reading poetry to Rachel last night." Nora gave me a sly expression, one eyebrow lifted. "Sound plausible to you?"

"Oh, you." I stood and waggled my coffee mug at her. "Want another cup?"

We spent the next half hour going over the day's schedule, enjoying coffee, and chatting about our Seattle experience.

"I don't know when I'll be able to trust an Uber driver again." I shuddered, and Nora nodded in agreement. "Either I drive or someone we know and trust drives."

"Agreed." Nora took the last sip of her coffee and placed the mug on the table. "I'm not too sure who I'd be able to trust. Not Brent."

"Definitely not. Rachel would be fine, though, and even Marcus." I rose and took both empty mugs to the sink. "Or we might consider calling Detective Day and get his suggestions."

"Rachel's dad? What'll he be able to tell us?" Nora leaned over and gave Herc's soft fur a pat. "I mean, he'll know the drunks and whatnot, but what else could he tell us?"

I lifted one shoulder and let it drop. "It was a thought, that's all."

Nora's phone made a sound like crickets chirping, and she snatched it up. "Speaking of, here's the Brentmeister now."

Brentmeister? She was suddenly speaking like someone a third her age, making me feel suspicious. Maybe she had a new man in her life, someone much younger. Or she'd been sampling old Mr. Wyrick's special brownies, the ones his wife made to ease his glaucoma symptoms. Knowing Nora, I wouldn't put it past her. Giving my head a slight shake, I rinsed out the mugs before setting them to drain on the sink's edge.

"Yo, I know where the dog park is, buttercup."

I swung my head around and stared at Nora as she spoke into the phone.

"You just make sure *your* hiney is there on time. Understand, rubber band?" She listened for another moment before adding, "After 'while, crocodile."

Oh, good grief. I thought I'd left this all behind in the high school hallways.

"Care to share?" I came back to the table and sat down. "From what I could hear on this end, Brent has something at the Portland Pooch Park today, right?"

She nodded, standing. "Yep. He's got a dog-walking job at noon with a new client."

"At the park?"

"Sort of. The owner wants to watch him interact with the dog first before he turns Brent loose with his precious pooch." She wrinkled her nose. "He's some kind of celebrity."

"Who is? The owner?"

Nora chuckled. "The dog, goofy. He won last year's 'Portland Pup of the Year.'"

I threw up both hands before letting them drop to the table. "That's a contest at the local mall, not the Westminster Kennel Club Dog Show."

Pet owners never ceased to amaze me. Some of them could get downright batty when it came to their furred and feathered companions, almost surpassing that modern breed known as the "helicopter parent." I gazed at my own dog, admiring his handsome fur tuxedo and striking eyes. Now *that* was a fabulous animal, and with the recent training Rachel had done with him and Aggie, Herc would be a natural for the honor.

I almost snorted out loud as I considered the new client and his dog. Celebrity, indeed.

"Did you hear me?" Nora's tone was heading toward sharp, a sure sign of irritation. "Yoo hoo. Earth to Gwen."

I glanced away from Herc and across at Nora, trying to refocus my thoughts. She was staring at me with a knowing expression, and I felt my cheeks warm.

"Yes, I heard you." I sounded guilty, even to myself. "And personally, I think Herc is a much better candidate."

"What've you been drinking? Been adding a little something to your morning coffee?" Nora's thinly plucked eyebrows rose. "I asked if you were ready to go back to my place."

"Oh. Sorry." I reached over and grabbed her hand briefly, giving it a gentle squeeze. "I was thinking about the Portland Pup contest. I might enter Herc this year."

"Sure you weren't dreaming about a particular retired dentist?" Her smile was teasing, and I gave her my best raspberry in reply, startling Herc from under the table.

He ducked out the flap in the back door, giving me a wounded look before disappearing into the backyard.

Everyone was a critic.

"Let me grab a shower first." I headed for the short hallway, running my mind over my limited wardrobe. Since comfort was my first and foremost fashion requirement, it would be some age-softened denim capris with a souvenir T-shirt from Multnomah Falls, my favorite beauty spot in a state full of them. Paired with my faithful Birkenstock sandals, I'd be ready to face the day and maybe my first-ever celebrity pet sighting.

From the living room, Nora yelled, "Get a move on it, Sis. We've got things to do, people to see, yada."

I cranked the old shower handle marked "hot" as far as it would go, returning her comment with one of my own. "And as a certain William Shakespeare once said, 'They stumble who run fast.' I intend to take my time." I stepped into the old shower, sticking my head out for one last remark. "That's from *Romeo and Juliet*, in case you want to look it up."

"Yeah, yeah. Just hurry."

I could hear the smile in her voice, though. Whether she admitted it or not, she was proud of my literary training, almost as if she herself had pushed me to do it.

When I was clean and dressed, we headed, on foot, for Nora's luxury apartment building. Neither one of us was too crazy about calling for a ride, especially with the memory of the last driver hanging like a specter above our heads. I wasn't sure Nora could walk from my house to her place in those ridiculous heels, but she didn't seem to notice the extra four inches under her feet. I'd never minded it, though, and thought of it as my own exercise program, free as the air I breathed.

Free was always good, especially as I tended to count pennies.

It was quiet in the lobby of Nora's building. The concierge, a youngish woman with thick auburn braids worn coronet style and a generous dash of freckles across an upturned nose, was on the phone as we passed by. She lifted her gaze briefly from the paper she was jotting notes on, her smile more perfunctory than warm. Nora, bless her heart, tended to divide those who knew her into two camps: lifelong fans and cautious observers.

The concierge was clearly in the latter category. I tried to make up for my best friend, though, and gave the young woman my widest smile as we walked past the desk. She only stared at me, with a startled expression, and almost dropped her phone. Maybe I'd used the Big Bad Wolf version instead, the kind I'd usually trotted out during parent-teacher meetings.

"What'd you do? Did you see that gal's face?" Nora looked at me curiously as she jabbed at the button to call the elevator with one manicured thumb. "You must've given her a weird look or something."

"I only—oh, never mind." I stepped in the elevator with a toss of my head, a la Brent Mayfair, and hit the fifth-floor button. "Speaking of whom, when do we need to be at the Portland Pooch Park?"

Nora consulted her cell phone, for once being carried in her hand and not her brassiere. "In about twenty minutes." She glanced at the moving numbers, jolting forward slightly as the elevator stopped at her floor. "I've got some Girl Scout cookies in the freezer we can take with us. Can you grab those while I make some hot tea?" She gave her flat stomach a gentle rub. "I've gotta start cutting down on the caffeine, and there's no time like the present."

"You know that tea has almost the same amount of caffeine in it as coffee does, right? And what about your sugar intake? Shouldn't you focus on that first?"

Nora inserted a shiny brass key into the door's lock and flung the door open, nodding for me to enter first.

"Well, smarty-pants, the tea is peppermint, therefore no caffeine, and the cookies are frozen." She headed for the kitchen, leaving me in the living room, baffled at her explanation.

"What in the world does 'frozen' have to do with watching your sugar intake, if you wouldn't mind telling me." I followed her into the kitchen, admiring the shiny stainless-steel appliances as I always did. If only…but I was happy with my house and its outdated design. It sometimes made me feel as though I'd fallen into a time warp around 1950, but it was mine.

"They're frozen, goofy, because it takes longer to eat them. See?" She demonstrated by reaching into the freezer and pulling out a familiar green box. I almost groaned: Thin Mints, my cookie Achilles heel. Ripping open one of the inner cellophane sleeves, she snapped a frozen chocolate cookie from the stack and popped it into her mouth.

It disappeared in a fairly short amount of time, despite being in its frozen state. Clearly her plan hadn't worked. Shrugging, she tugged out the second stack and offered it to me. I gave in without a whimper.

Drinking herbal tea was the first step. It really wouldn't do to rush something as serious as this, and we'd both work on the sugar issues later. Besides, I'd just discovered my new favorite combo: peppermint tea and peppermint cookies. Lifting my half-eaten chocolate cookie in a toast, I managed to restrain myself while we waited for the water to boil.

* * * *

The Portland Pooch Park was directly across the street from Nora's building and was actually the impetus behind us starting 2 Sisters Pet Valet. We'd counted on the built-in clientele from the park as well as the many pet owners who resided in the same building as Nora.

With teacup in one hand and cookies in the other, I settled myself on one of the benches that ringed the perimeter of the park. Nora sat beside me, swinging one slim leg over the arm of the bench. She looked relaxed as she sipped her tea and looked around the park. Based on the admiring glances she was getting from a few doggy dads, she must've looked alluring as well.

I looked at the cookies and sighed. Maybe if they came with Velcro strips that directly attached to my hips and thighs, I might not eat as many. They didn't, though, and I was in the middle of chewing a minty cookie when Nora suddenly sat up and pointed across the grass.

"Oh, my goodness! Is that who I think it is?"

Cookies forgotten, I squinted slightly as I looked where Nora pointed. "Are you talking about that man in the red shirt or jacket?"

Nora nodded vigorously, standing up and brushing her hands off on her legs. "Yep. And if that isn't Mayor Dinwitty, I'll start wearing flats."

I did my best to jog after Nora. She could move faster in heels than I could in sandals.

Running in Birkenstocks, though, required very flexible toes. I had to curl them as I ran in order to keep the shoes on my feet, and this made my pace much slower than Nora's...or at least that was what I told myself. The cookies I'd just consumed and all their sugary predecessors had nothing to do with my puffing and huffing, right?

"Well, well, well." Nora had come to an abrupt halt in front of a startled Mayor Dinwitty as he stood with a small hairless animal cradled to his chest. "I had no idea you were an animal lover, mayor."

I gaped at the dog, amazed at what I was seeing. The closer I got to the mayor, the more I saw of the animal's odd appearance. Its body wasn't only free of fur, it was also very thin, almost delicate. The ears, though—I couldn't help it.

Without thinking, I blurted out, "What did you do to those ears?"

"I was just getting ready to say the same thing." Nora leaned in closer to gaze at the strange-looking dog. "Did you have them groomed that way on purpose? If not, you need to get your money back, pal."

Mayor Dinwitty's mouth thinned out, and he half-turned his body in a protective movement, sheltering his odd dog from our curious stares. "It's a Chinese crested, I'll have you know. This is how their ears look, and these dogs are very, very exclusive." He looked at the small dog and crooned, "Aren't you, Dinky?"

Nora let out a hoot of laughter. "'Dinky'? You've named that 'exclusive' thing 'Dinky'?" Nora stared from me to the mayor, her eyes wide in amazement. "Whose bright idea was that?"

In nature, animals have telltale signs that indicate danger to those around them: a ruff of fur might flare, large teeth might become bared, and the animal may growl. The mayor was no different. His teeth stayed covered, and I saw nothing that resembled a ruff, but his cheeks and the tips of his ears reddened in anger, and he all but snarled as he spoke.

"That's none of your business, and if you'll excuse me, I see someone I'm supposed to meet." The mayor began walking away from us, his head held high and his gaze fixed on the other side of the park.

Nora and I turned in unison, watching the mayor as he headed toward Brent. *Brent*?

And then it hit me.

"Oh, no! I think the new client is Mayor Dinwitty." I covered my eyes with the hand not clutching the cookie sleeve, half-laughing and half-crying. "And we completely made fun of his dog."

Nora began to giggle, leaning over to clutch my arm. "Yep, Sis. We dogged his dog."

Shakespeare she was not, but it was the funniest thing I'd heard all day.

"His *celebrity* dog," I chortled, ignoring the interested stares of those standing near us. "That was the Portland Pup of the Year, and we didn't appreciate it."

"Well, I'd say we'll probably be kissing this job goodbye." Nora wiped her eyes with the back of one finger, careful not to touch her mascaraed lashes. "I don't know about you, but I'm okay with that." She shook her head and pulled me along with her toward the bench. "Kinda reminds me of my idiot ex-stepson, you know? All show and no substance."

The mention of Martin sobered me quickly. We still had that issue hovering over us, and if Teresa called, we'd need to go back to Seattle.

The Pitt family was beginning to feel like a giant albatross.

Chapter 12

"Man, that Mayor Dinwitty is really dumb, Miss F." Brent strolled over to where Nora and I were sitting, a puzzled expression on his face. "You know what he told me?" He didn't give me a chance to respond. "He said you and Mrs. G. were from Palestine. I told him you were from Portland, the same as him and me." He shook his head as if amazed at the ignorance of someone in such a high position.

My eyebrows shot up in confusion, and I forgot to correct him for calling the man "dumb," although I'd used that same term often when referring to the mayor. I was used to the malapropisms of teens in general, and Brent Mayfair in particular, but this one had me stumped. What had made the mayor say we were from Palestine?

Then my internal translator kicked in, and I had to chuckle. "I think he said we were 'philistines,' Brent not 'Palestines.' It's not complimentary, but it's not awful. It's a word some use to mean 'uncivilized.'"

Nora snorted. "I'd say the only philistine in this scenario is Mayor Dimwit, not us. And that's not for repeating, young man." She shook her finger at Brent, one hand on her hip. "If I hear that word anywhere else, I'll know you've been blabbing."

Brent's eyes grew rounder, and he made a crossing motion over his chest. "Cross my heart and hope to die, stick a needle in my eye, Mrs. G." He dropped his hand and his voice, leaning closer. "So far only you and Miss F. have been blabbing. You're the only two I've ever heard say that."

As per most extended conversations with this kid, my emotional equilibrium was beginning to spin out of control. I held up one hand, eyes closed. "Aaand we'll leave this topic right here, won't we?" When I didn't get an immediate answer, I opened my eyes and stared firmly at Brent. "Did you hear me, Brent Mayfair?"

He nodded vigorously, with a self-righteous expression. "I heard you, Miss F. But you just said the topic was closed, so I couldn't say anything else."

Between Chinese crested dogs, angry mayors, and philistines, I was done for the day. What I needed was caffeine, and I needed it right then.

I turned to look at Nora. "You can come with me or not, but I'm marching down to The Friendly Bean right now. I can hear an Americano calling me from here."

"Oh, believe you me, Sis, I'm with you."

"Me too, Miss Franklin. Besides, I gotta make sure no one else thinks you're not from Portland. They might not let you have any coffee."

Sometimes you just had to choose the hill on which to die. Sighing inwardly, I motioned for Brent to follow us. Besides, the kid might be useful if Hannah happened to be at work.

We'd had a quite a few days of decent weather, according to Portland standards, and the walk to the coffee shop was pleasant. Brent kept us entertained with Aggie tales and told us how Rachel had trained Herc and Aggie in only a few days. As usual, Nora drew a few catcalls. I wanted to throw up a three-fingered salute and yell, "Read between the lines!" to a particularly obnoxious driver.

I restrained myself. I didn't want Brent adding it to his own repertoire.

As luck would have it, Hannah was indeed at work behind the counter. She looked perky, joking with the customers in line ahead of us. Watching her, I tried to decide if this was due to moving on from Caleb or reconnecting with him. I was pulling for the latter since it might lead to more information on what was going on at the dry cleaners.

I gave her a cheerful smile when we reached the counter. "It's nice to see you again, Hannah. How have you been?"

That was ambiguous enough to give her an out if she wanted it. Or it might prompt her to share information. To my dismay, however, she clammed up tighter than a drum.

"I'm fine. What can I get you?" Her glance flickered over the three of us before dropping to the counter.

Aha. So something *was* up, and there was something she was determined not to reveal. Had Caleb gotten to her and warned her not to talk? If so, what was it she wasn't supposed to say? Needless to say, her reticence became a bright red cape, flapping wildly in front of the bull that was my curiosity.

"I'll take a hot Americano with room for cream. Have you heard from Caleb lately?"

Without answering, she punched the order into the register and looked at Brent. "And what do you want?" The tone was vaguely impolite, and the other barista shot a surprised look in her direction.

Brent, of course, noticed nothing and beamed at her. "Hey, Hannah. I didn't know you worked here."

Hannah only shrugged in response, her fingers poised over the register. "You want coffee or something?"

"Yeah, I'll take an extra-large café mocha with double chocolate and lots of whipped cream." Brent paused and turned to look at me. "Is that okay, Miss F.?"

"I'm getting it, kid." Nora gave him a poke in the side with one fake fingernail, making him jump. "Get what you want." When a delighted smile spread across his face, she added, "Within reason, of course." She turned to look at me, with a wry grin. "I think I just opened a can of worms."

"Or at least a counter of pastries," I replied with amusement. "Better keep well back. There'll be crumbs flying like snow around here."

By the time we finished our order with the sullen Hannah and grabbed a newly vacant table, I'd come up with another strategy to get her to talk.

I left Nora and Brent squabbling over the baker's dozen of pastries and walked back to the counter, beckoning over the woman I knew to be the shift manager.

"Can I help you?" She smiled at me, an open smile arranged in carefully professional lines. "Is there anything wrong with your order?"

"Oh, no." I fluttered one hand as if waving away the idea. "No, our order was perfect, as usual. We love this place."

She smiled again but remained silent.

I took in a breath and blurted out the words before I could talk myself out of them. "Can we borrow Hannah for ten minutes?" When she looked hesitant, I added quickly, "I promise it's nothing bad, and we'll talk in here, right over there." I turned and pointed to the table, where Nora and Brent were now laughing, each holding up a chocolate-filled croissant as if toasting one another.

Or about to begin a duel.

"Well, I don't know." She glanced over at the register, where a smiling Hannah was entering a new order. "I mean, we *are* kinda busy at the moment."

I nodded. "Yes, I know you are. But when it slows down, can you send her over? Please?" That last word had a tinge of begging in it. I prayed it hadn't sounded that way to her, but I was beginning to feel slightly anxious. What if Hannah knew something that could help us and her manager refused to let her talk with us?

"Weeelllll." She let the word drag from her lips as she tapped her chin with one finger. "I guess she can. But only if she agrees, okay?" Her gaze looked sternly at me. "I don't want any of my staff being harassed."

"Of course not. And thank you."

Before she could change her mind, I turned and hurried back to the table, slipping awkwardly into my chair. The sweat that had sprung up on my forehead felt cool against my skin, and I was aware I was breathing more heavily than usual. I felt as though I'd just run a mile (not that I ever had, but I imagined that this was what it felt like), not walked a mere twenty feet.

Nora and Brent stared at me and then at each other, twin expressions of interest on their faces. I held up one hand before taking a gulp from my cooled Americano. I'd forgotten the cream, of course.

"Everything all right?" Nora's recently Botoxed brows tried to draw together in concern. She managed to twitch them slightly, but I appreciated the gesture all the same.

"Nothing's wrong, per se. I asked that Hannah join us for a few minutes, that's all."

"She's cute." Brent blushed. "I mean, she's not as cute as Rachel or Aggie."

"And I'm sure Rachel will be delighted to hear that," I said drily. "There's nothing quite like being compared to a dog."

Beside me, Nora snorted. "Oh, I've heard that many times, trust me. Only a different word was used, if you get my drift."

I did. Brent, thankfully, didn't. When he opened his mouth to ask, I shushed him with a quick gesture. "That's not important right now. What we need to do is think of a few questions we can ask Hannah before she bolts."

"And are we expecting her to 'bolt'?" Nora's tone gave the word implied quotation marks. She took a sip of her latte, looking thoughtfully at me over the edge of the mug.

I nodded. "You saw how she acted when we were ordering. She barely looked at us. It was as if she wanted us to move away from the counter as quickly as possible."

Brent nodded vigorously, a small avalanche of crumbs falling from the front of his shirt. "Yeah, I saw that, Miss F. She didn't even smile at me. I mean, she acted like she was mad or something."

"Indeed she did, Brent." I gave him an approving smile.

His comment was right on target.

"And that's what I want to find out. Why is she mad? Did we do something?"

"She wasn't all that comfortable talking with us last time," Nora pointed out. "And if Caleb What's-his-name has called her recently, she's really going to clam up."

"We can only hope she doesn't." I looked at Brent, my lips pursed. "Brent, how well do you know her?"

He glanced up briefly from the large cinnamon roll he'd begun eating, crumbs clinging to the edge of his mouth. I automatically handed him a paper napkin.

"Um, maybe not as good as Rachel, but I remember her from school."

I did a quick calculation in my head. "She was a freshman when you were a senior, right?"

He nodded as he forked in a large bite, chewing rapidly. Brent ate as though the food in front of him would disappear or be removed at any moment. He spoke around the mouthful and sent a mini snowstorm of icing across the table. "Yeah, and she could do three flips in a row."

Nora and I both stared at him, trying to couple his commentary with my original question.

I finally gave in. "Flips?"

"Yeah, you know." He made a circling motion with his fork, nearly putting out Nora's eye. "Like cheerleaders do." He took another bite. "And her boyfriend was there too."

"Ah." It made sense now. "Hannah was a cheerleader when you played football, and Caleb was on the team with you."

He looked up at me, his forehead wrinkled in consternation as he took another bite. "That's what I said, Miss F."

Of course he had, in his own way. I shook my head slightly at Nora. What I needed was more information on Hannah, not on Brent's lack of conversational skills.

"Okay. This is what I'd like you to do when she comes over to talk." When I had his attention, I quickly outlined my plan.

He would get her talking about their common school activities and ask her about Caleb. I would insert a comment about seeing Caleb at the dry cleaners. Nora would do the final honors and tell her about our Seattle experience.

"Does everyone understand their part?" I looked at both of my tablemates but was really talking to Brent. "Okay, get ready. She's headed our way now."

"My manager said you want to talk to me?" Hannah stood beside our table, arms folded across her apron and her lips compressed in an unfriendly manner. She clearly didn't want to be there, and I smiled at her, trying to put her at ease.

"Thanks for coming over, Hannah." I motioned at the empty chair between Brent and me. "Can you sit down for a few minutes? It'll be quick. I promise."

"I guess." She spoke curtly, but she sat on the edge of the chair. "What?"

I gave Brent's leg a nudge under the table, hoping he'd take the hint.

"Hey, remember that time you tried to teach me how to do a back flip?" He grinned disarmingly at Hannah, a piece of icing hanging from one eyebrow like a miniature icicle. The boy certainly ate with abandon, I'd give him that. "And I got knocked out?"

Hannah began giggling, and I relaxed. This might work after all.

"Yeah, I remember." She leaned forward, uncrossing her arms and planting her elbows on the table. "And Coach thought I'd killed you." She slid a shy glance in my direction. "Did you ever hear about that, Miss Franklin?"

I shook my head. "I can't say I did, Hannah. Of course, I didn't get out of my classroom much," I added wryly. I smiled encouragingly at her. "So, what happened after that?"

"Well, Caleb got to take his place for the next game." She clamped her mouth shut as soon as the words were out of her mouth. The very mention of Caleb's name was as good as a dash of cold water. She made a move to stand, but I put out one hand and caught her arm.

"Oh, please stay for another minute. We wouldn't bother you, but it's very important we ask you something. Is that okay?"

She hesitated, and her muscles jumped under my hand. I reluctantly let go, hoping she wouldn't leave.

"I guess." She was back to speaking in a curt, unfriendly tone.

"We saw Caleb recently, Hannah. Has he called you?" I watched her face carefully for any reaction to my comment. "Did he tell you we talked to him when the police were called?"

That got her attention. I gave Nora a tiny nod. It was her show now.

"Listen, Hannah." Nora leaned closer, lowering her voice. "Miss Franklin and I were kidnapped when we were in Seattle. And it has something to do with the place where Caleb works. And my ex-stepson."

Hannah's expression sharpened, and she slumped back, her gaze fixed on Nora. "You were kidnapped? And you think Caleb has something to do with that?" She sounded defensive, and her arms had resumed their crossed position over her chest. "He'd never do anything like kidnapping someone. That's just—just stupid."

I frowned at Nora. "Listen, Hannah, we're not saying he had anything to do with it. In fact, he brought us some coffee while we were making the report afterward." I gave her shoulder a little shake. "He's a good kid. You know it, and I know it. What we need to know is why he's working for Martin Pitt."

Her eyebrows bunched together. "I don't know, Miss Franklin. I really don't. I don't even know who this Martin Pitt is."

"I can tell you that. He's my rat of a stepson. Ex, that is." Nora's mouth screwed up as if she'd tasted something unpleasant. "Only now he's been kidnapped as well. We're hoping Caleb might know what's going on."

"And that he'll tell you," I chimed in, nodding at the cell phone sticking out of her apron pocket. "Do you think you could call him?"

Hannah gave a tiny smile. "I don't use my cell for making calls. I text if I want to talk to someone."

Of course. Like the rest of the younger population. Maybe we were seeing the beginning of the first silent generation.

"Do you think you might text him, then? Maybe you could ask him about Martin and what's happening about that situation."

To my relief, she nodded. "I will. Just not right now." She glanced over her shoulder at the counter. "I need to get back to work. I promise I'll ask him tonight, though." She stood and looked around the table. "So, how can I get hold of you?"

Nora reached into her top and pulled out her cell. I wanted to burst into laughter at Hannah's reaction at seeing this. Nora was completely oblivious. I had a feeling the rest of the crew at The Friendly Bean would be hearing all about this soon. "Give me your number, and I'll text you so you can have mine. That okay?"

"Sure." The exchange made, Hannah began to walk away. Suddenly, she turned around, a serious expression on her face. "Listen. I don't know what Caleb's really doing, or even if *he* knows what's up. But I can tell you one thing for sure." She lowered her voice, bending toward the table. "I overheard my sister talking to Caleb's sister, and they were both crying. I think he's involved in something really, really bad."

The three of us watched her walk back to the front of the coffee shop, and my heart dropped. I hated hearing something like this about a former student, even if it was Caleb Greene, and now I was more determined than ever to get back to Seattle.

"Sis, did it ever occur to you that we've gotten ourselves in a whole lotta trouble?" Nora tucked her cell phone away as Hannah disappeared behind the counter. "I don't recall having this much action, exes aside, before you took early retirement."

"Speak for yourself, pal. It wasn't *my* ex-husband and stepchildren who created the current chaos, if I remember correctly." I almost gave a toss of my head but stopped when I saw Brent's curious gaze fixed on me.

"You know what I mean." Nora drank the rest of her coffee and set the mug down with a decided thump. "Besides, I blame it on pure nosiness. On my part," she added hastily when I narrowed my eyes.

"Miss F.'s pretty nosy too."

I'd been waiting for Brent's contribution. I shifted my glare toward him, but he gave me a cheeky grin.

"You remember, you always used to ask us about our weekend and if we did our homework."

"Oh, good grief, kid." Nora stared at him, her expression incredulous. "That's called being a caring teacher. Ever heard of it?"

Brent shrugged. "Yeah, whatever. But she was the only one who bugged me like that, though."

I was tempted to give him lunch detention. "I rest my case, Brent. I cared then. I still care. I care so much that I'm telling you to hit the road." I made a shooing motion at him with both hands. "Go home. Call Rachel. Just leave Mrs. Goldstein and me alone so we can get our plans together." I glanced at Nora, who nodded at me. "We're going back to Seattle."

Brent shrugged at my words. "Okay, Miss F. But me an' Rachel could help you guys. You should take us with you."

"Not on your life." I shook my head decisively. "It could be dangerous. Besides, you two need to stay and take care of the pet business and Herc."

Nora glanced from me to Brent and back again, tapping her chin with one finger. "You know, Sis, he might have a point. We could always use the extra eyes and ears, and a driver."

I saw Brent processing this comment and hurried to speak before he could ask another silly question. "That might be true, but do you really want to have the added responsibility? I'm pretty sure the parents of those two wouldn't be too happy if something worse than a kidnapping occurred."

"Kidnapping? Cool, Miss F.!" Trust Brent to latch on to the one thing I didn't want him to catch. "I know how to get out of a trunk, and Rachel knows how to use car keys to poke someone's eyes."

I rolled mine. I really didn't want to know exactly how he'd gotten his information on escaping from a trunk.

"Brent, being kidnapped isn't a YouTube video, all right? It's scary. Really scary. Mrs. Goldstein and I are extremely lucky we got out of the situation in one piece." I looked at Nora. "And, you know, we'd have to house and feed them as well."

She lifted an eyebrow. "It couldn't be any worse than dealing with them here. And we already feed this kid like he's our own. Besides, if Rachel goes with us, it'd be three against one." She smiled triumphantly. "I call those pretty good odds."

"Fine." I lifted my hands and let them fall to the table. "We take them with us. Brent, I know you're over eighteen, but I want you to ask your mom if it's all right. That's called being respectful."

"I'm always respectful to my mom." He looked affronted. "My mom would twist my ear if I gave her any sass."

Nora and I nodded approvingly in unison. "And rightly so, kid." She leaned over and gave Brent's shoulders a quick hug. "You've gotta stay polite in life if you want to get anywhere." She gave me a teasing grin as she rose. "And in this case, 'anywhere' happens to be Seattle, and if we're going, we need to find a place to stay."

"Oh, that's easy, Mrs. G. We can stay with my Uncle Charlie." Brent stood as well, looking extremely pleased. "He's got a really neat house, super old and creaky."

"Hmm. And is this uncle old and creaky as well?" Nora's head tilted in question.

"Nora Goldstein." I spoke firmly. "Is there any chance we can focus on the issue at hand? This isn't a dating game."

"Oh, you wouldn't like him anyway, Mrs. G." Brent's eyes widened as he looked earnestly from me to Nora. "He's got hair comin' outta his nose and ears and none on his head. You'd have to take him to a groomer first."

Nora and I both laughed. A couple at the next table, both busy on their phones, stared at us as if we were doing something odd. I wanted to tell them, "It's called conversing, folks."

"I'm pretty sure you mean 'barber' and not 'groomer.'" I finished my coffee and stood as well.

"Nope, I meant groomer, Miss F. He looks like one of those upside-down animals. You know, they hang in trees and stuff."

"They hang in trees? What in the world are you talking about, kid?" Nora's hands were on her hips now, her head tipped back as she stared at Brent.

"Possums. He means possums. Right?" It was my turn to crane my neck to look up.

He nodded vigorously. "Yeah, that's what I mean." He gestured at his face. "They've got all this weird hair on their faces, just like Uncle Charlie." His eyes grew even wider. "And my mom says he's kinda crazy too."

Great. As if Brent wasn't already one sandwich short of a picnic, now we might stay with an equally nutty relative. Still, free was free, and I gave

Nora a tiny shrug of acquiescence. "It can't be any worse that dealing with Marcus, in my opinion." I also made a mental note to contact Roger about caring for Aggie and Herc yet again. I felt a tad guilty about leaving my dog but knew he'd be well taken care of at Roger's.

"At least Marcus doesn't have nose hair." She closed her eyes and gave a shudder. "Okay, kid. Give your hairy uncle a shout. Emerald City, here we come, ready or not."

Chapter 13

Before I knew it, I was behind the steering wheel, chauffeuring my passengers to Seattle. If we were headed to the Emerald City, where were Dorothy and her trio of misfit pals?

I moved the rearview mirror slightly and snuck a peek at my back-seat passengers. Brent, his blond hair sticking up as though he'd combed it with a rake, was the perfect Scarecrow. Next to him, Rachel, with her charcoal gray sweatshirt and metallic-toned eye makeup, could be a Tin Man stand-in.

And sandwiched between Rachel and the passenger door sat our own Cowardly Lion, Marcus, in all his plaid glory. How he'd ended up on this road trip was still a mystery.

That left Dorothy and the Wicked Witch. Wishing I'd worn my red Birkenstocks, I glanced over at my seatmate. The bright neon green of Nora's top and her dangling peridot earrings made me smile. The gang was all here, minus Toto One and Two. They were staying with Roger and the golden retrievers, safe from flying monkeys and other misadventures that might await us.

"Hey, Miss F." Brent leaned forward and tapped my shoulder, drawing me back to reality. "Can we stop and get something to eat? I'm starving."

"You had two cheeseburgers and fries barely an hour ago." Rachel's voice was gently reproving. "You need to give that stomach of yours a break."

"My mom says I've got a hollow leg." He kicked the back of my seat as he demonstrated. "My stomach feels pretty hollow too."

Nora looked back at him, shaking her head. "I'm thinking it's your head that's hollow, kid. No one could possibly need to eat as much as you do."

"I could use some coffee." Marcus, who'd been silent for the most part, spoke up. "That stuff I got at that last gas station had to have been the bottom of the pot."

"Didn't you pour it yourself?" I glanced at the mirror and met Marcus's gaze. "Common sense would say not to get it if it's that bad."

"You'd think that, wouldn't you?"

His words were as dry as the desert, and beside me, Nora shifted in her seat. Apparently, she'd struck again by offering to get his coffee, and if I was Marcus, I'd probably get my own coffee (and everything else) from here on out. A Shakespearean quote about a woman's scorn and fury popped into my head, and I smiled inwardly. When my best friend got on a roll, she stayed on it until she was satisfied and felt she'd made her point.

And that point was aimed directly for Marcus.

"I vote for a break." Rachel leaned forward and spoke in my ear. "Maybe we could stop at a fast-food place? That way Brent can get his food refill, and we can get freshly brewed coffee."

"That's fine with me." I pointed to a large sign that advertised several places to eat. "The next place is only seven miles, if that works."

"Works for me. I just need to visit the facilities." Nora reached behind her neck and gave it a brisk rub. "And if we run into a masseuse, I definitely need someone to get these kinks out of my neck and back. All this car travel isn't good."

My gaze slid to Marcus's face as Nora spoke. If her comment had been a hint, or her version of an olive branch, he didn't seem interested. Good for him. Maybe he had more gumption than I'd given him credit for.

Pulling the car off the freeway, I stopped at the light at the end of the ramp. "Which place should we choose?" I leaned forward slightly, looking in both directions. "I see McDonald's, Taco Bell, KFC, and something called Pete's Diner."

"Oh, let's try the diner," Rachel exclaimed. "Brent, I'll bet they'll have an all-day breakfast menu."

"Nora? Marcus?" I glanced at them and then back at the light. "Hurry, folks. It's getting ready to change."

"Pete's is okay with me." Nora reached down and adjusted the strap of one high heel. She gave a slight toss of her head. "And, Marcus, you can watch the staff pour it so you won't be able to blame me if it's bad."

Pete's Diner sat behind a convenience store, whose windows were blanketed in posters of scantily dressed girls selling beer. The dark blue garbage container that sat between the two businesses was overflowing, and a layer of flies hovered above it like a shape-shifting black mist. A few cars were parked in front of the diner alongside a large truck, its bed filled with construction equipment and its doors streaked in what looked like tobacco juice. I wasn't sure about this place to begin with, and visions of botulism were beginning to tap-dance through my mind. In fact, it was beginning to elevate chain fast-food joints to the level of fine dining.

"Boy, this place looks like it's right out of *Deliverance*, Miss F." Brent opened his door and stepped out. "You know, that movie where those guys end up almost gettin' killed by the crazy locals?"

I glared at him but was unable to find the words to disagree. I didn't. If a place could be said to have vibes, this diner was putting out some fairly unsavory ones.

"Maybe I need a tough man to keep me safe." Nora sashayed over to Marcus and slipped an arm through his. "Know anyone like that?"

"Me, Mrs. G." Brent stopped walking and struck a pose, both arms flexed. "I'm the strongest one here, just ask Rachel." He looked at Marcus, a sheepish grin on his face. "No offense, Mr. Avery."

"None taken, kid." Marcus looked at Nora, and his expression softened. "Will I do, sugar? Even if I'm not the toughest?" He waggled his eyebrows at her, and she looked adoringly at him, her eyes as soft as the clouds overhead.

"You betcha, honeybunch." Nora stretched up and gave his cheek a loud kiss, causing Brent to make gagging noises and Rachel to giggle.

I just shook my head and headed for the entrance of Pete's Diner. I was ready to take my chances with whatever lay on the other side of the door. Surely it couldn't be any worse than watching the rerun of *Wild Kingdom* being played out in front of me.

It was quiet inside Pete's, and the décor reminded me of any number of small cafés I'd visited before. The few customers I could see scattered around the diner seemed intent on their phones, not too different than folks I'd observed in Portland. My anxiety level dropped significantly as a ponytailed young woman approached us, her polyester uniform pants creating a swishing noise as she walked.

"Five? Right this way." She headed for a circular booth at the back of the room that sat higher than the rest of the booths on a dais-like platform. "Mind the step up." She nodded toward the floor and slid a handful of laminated menus onto the table. "Can I get you all something to drink first?"

"Coffee," said Marcus and Nora in unison, causing Rachel to grin. I had to smile at the obvious makeup session happening in real time. As long as it didn't progress to a make-*out* session, I could handle them.

"I'll have coffee as well." I glanced at Rachel and Brent, my eyebrows lifted in question. "And you two?"

"Do you have Pepsi or Coke products?" Rachel glanced at the waitress.

"We've got Coke, Diet Coke, Sprite, root beer, Mr. Pibb. And iced tea." The plastic tag pinned to her top said SUSIE, a name I hadn't seen, or heard, in years. "Or I can mix 'em together and make you a Kamikaze."

That sounded absolutely repulsive, but Brent's face lit up. Rachel, however, kept a firm grip on things. "I'll take an iced tea, thanks, no lemon." She turned to Brent. "Do you want Mr. Pibb or Sprite?"

Brent hesitated, and I could see why Rachel had kept his selections to only two. "Mr. Pibb. And I'll take her lemon."

"You've got it. Give me a sec." Susie beamed around at us and swished away toward the kitchen.

"You put lemon in Mr. Pibb?" Nora wrinkled her nose, scooting closer to Marcus. "That's sure different."

Brent shrugged. "I like it. Kinda gives it a kick, you know?" He gave Nora a quick smile. "Maybe you should try it."

"Oh, don't you worry, chum." Nora all but oozed over Marcus's arm as she got even closer than I thought possible. "I've got my own 'kick' right here."

She gave Marcus another kiss, this time right on the lips, which sent both Brent and Rachel into another fit of giggles.

Ugh. The make-out interlude was starting to gain steam.

"He said 'kick,' not 'kiss.'" I frowned across at Nora and Marcus, where they sat looking more like a two-headed creature than a pair of adults. Maybe I should've asked for iced water as well. It might come in handy if I needed it to put a damper on their ardor. "Now, I have a question." Perhaps a change of subject would help cool things down. "Are we going straight to Brent's uncle's house or to Teresa's?"

Nora shrugged. "Whatever you think, Sis. I'm okay with either." She turned to look at Marcus, her eyelashes fluttering fast enough to start a breeze. "Unless you've got a preference, sweet cheeks."

"'Sweet cheeks'?" Brent looked at Nora with something akin to admiration. "That's really kinda cute, Mrs. G."

"Cute?" It was my turn to parrot. "It's not cute at all, Brent. And I'm sure Rachel wouldn't like to be called that."

"Oh, I call her other things, Miss F." He turned his gaze on me, eyes widening earnestly. "You wanna hear some?"

"No!" Rachel and I both burst out, she with a red face and me with a churning stomach. This was getting out of hand quickly.

"Okay, folks. Here ya go." Saved by the waitress, thank goodness.

As she handed around our drinks, I took a moment to breathe in deeply, trying to get my emotional equilibrium back. I needed all my marbles if this trip was going to be successful, and losing my cool over Brent's and Nora's shenanigans wasn't helping.

I took a small sip of coffee, wincing at the heat. I'd need to wait a moment to drink it. In the meantime, I needed something sweet to go with it. I pointed at the menu. "Do you have anything like a Danish or bear claw or something?"

Susie nodded. "Yeah, we've got both of those, plus we have really awesome cinnamon rolls. You want one of those? They come with or without raisins."

"Definitely with raisins." I gave a satisfied nod. "And I think there might be a few other orders as well." As if our heads had been attached to the same neck, we all turned to look at Brent.

"What?" He looked around at us with an expression of pure innocence. "Don't blame me because I'm hungry all the time. I'm a growing boy. Right, Rachel?"

"Just order already, okay? We don't have all day, kid." Nora gave the menu lying in front of Brent a jab. "Get something that'll stick to those ribs of yours."

"She means to eat something with lots of protein," I said hastily. "Order a steak or a double cheeseburger."

"We've got a Protein Lover's Platter." Susie leaned over and used her pen to point. "See? It's got bacon, sausage, and chorizo, along with a three-egg omelet. You can ask for extra cheese, too."

"Oh, yeah." Brent all but rubbed his stomach as he looked at the laminated menu. "And can I have some of those pancakes?" His gaze had wandered to the next page, where pictures of pancakes, toast, and muffins were featured. "No syrup. I shouldn't eat too much sugar."

"Drop the word 'sugar,'" Nora muttered. "Kid, your mother's grocery bill must be astronomical."

Rachel laughed, slipping an arm around Brent's waist. "No, we're giving her a break, Mrs. Goldstein. He's at my house more than his own lately."

"No wonder her dad was snippy with us at the lawyer's office." Nora turned up one corner of her mouth in a half-mast smile. "He probably blames us for the kid eating him out of house and home."

I chuckled. "Or maybe he was irritated with us trying to play detective."

"Who's playing?" Nora reared back in mock offense and looked at me, both penciled brows hovering near her hairline. "Certainly not *moi*. I'm serious about this, you know, in it to win it and all that jazz." She blew an air kiss in Marcus's direction. "Isn't that right, sugar pants?"

That was what worried me. When Nora was fixated on accomplishing a goal, there was no stopping her. Not even a kidnapping gone wrong had deterred her plans. I sighed inwardly, keeping my worries to myself. Maybe everything would turn out just fine.

And maybe pigs would fly. Of course, watching how quickly the heaping plate set in front of Brent had emptied, I could almost believe in winged porkers. It was almost too bad the two-winged monkeys who'd attempted to stop us hadn't succeeded.

"At least this place isn't as bad as we thought. No food poisoning so far, right?" The comment popped out before I could put the brakes on it.

Susie, walking past with a tray full of dirty dishes, stopped abruptly.

I stared at her, and the warmth of embarrassment spread over my face. "I'm sorry, Susie. That was rude of me."

She returned my stare, and then, with shake of her head that sent her ponytail whipping around her shoulders, she pushed past us and into the kitchen. I felt as small as the crumbs left on my plate.

"Someone sure looks mad." Brent gave Rachel a sly nudge with his elbow. "Think we should blow this pop stand before she comes out here with Bubba and a shotgun?"

"Don't be silly, kid. Things like that don't happen in real life." Nora began scooting across the bench quickly, as though she didn't believe her own words. She jabbed Marcus. "Move, you."

"I'm moving, I'm moving." Marcus used the table's edge to lever himself up, causing a resounding groan from the rivets that held the tabletop to the center leg. I watched anxiously, worried the table was going to slide onto the floor. It certainly wouldn't endear us to Pete or whoever owned the diner.

"Hang on a minute." I reached over and grabbed the edge of Marcus's flashy jacket, halting him in his tracks. "Nora, what's with you? Nothing is going to happen to us. Look around." I motioned to the room. "There are too many people here. No one in their right mind would commit a crime in plain sight of so many witnesses."

"What in the world are you squawking about, woman?" Nora slipped from the booth and stood, both hands on her hips. "I just need to use the little princess room, all right?"

"Oh." I felt silly. And scared.

Susie was headed our way with a very large, very angry man in tow.

Chapter 14

"Who's got a problem with my food?"

The man stood, his beefy arms crossed high above a protruding belly, tree-trunk legs splayed. Whoever he was, he was clearly annoyed.

"There's no problem, sir," I began hesitantly when no one in my party spoke. "I made an ill-advised joke, and I'm sorry."

I looked at my traveling companions, willing someone to speak up. Instead, the four of them had become as silent as the grave, which was exactly where I was certain I was heading. This man appeared as angry as an antagonized bull and just as lethal.

"I might have overreacted, Dad." Susie peeked out from behind him, with an apologetic expression. "It's just that after, well, you know…" She raised her hands and let them drop.

Dad? Maybe this was a *Deliverance* scenario after all. I snuck a peek toward the front door. Would I be able to run fast enough to beat the rest of the group? Everyone knew it was the one who lagged behind that got caught.

"Actually, we *don't* know what you're talking about." Nora spoke up, her mouth set in a careful smile, but her eyes snapping angry sparks. "Perhaps someone else has complained over the—the *food* here? Would you care to enlighten us, sir?"

The word "sir" was spoken as if it was an afterthought, and I was fairly certain it was. Nora wasn't given to using words such as "sir" or "ma'am," and when she did use them, it generally indicated the opposite meaning.

I really hoped this mountain of a man didn't catch that. Susie, however, was another matter. She aimed a sharp glance at Nora. Nora's attention, however, was still on Susie's dad. Marcus had begun a nervous shuffling beside her, his hands moving nervously over his receding hairline. Rachel and Brent were bent over his cell phone, giggling at the small screen. Probably watching a video about silly cat tricks or dancing bears.

"Yeah, I'll enlighten you all right." Susie's dad's voice took on an aggressive tone, and the muscles in his arms began twitching. "No one disses my diner or my cooking. You got that?"

"Ha!" Nora gave a short laugh as she looked around the room. "You call this dump a diner? I'm thinking you need a dictionary, pal."

"Now, Nora," Marcus began nervously, giving Nora's shoulder a hesitant pat. "Let's not make the nice man upset." He made an odd bow, dipping his head in the direction of the very angry man. "If we can have the bill for our drinks, we'll be on our way."

"I'm not paying for squat, not after this treatment." Nora shrugged out of Marcus's grasp and crossed her arms, mirroring Susie's dad's stance and his expression. "In fact, I'm thinking Mr. Dump here owes us an apology."

A tense silence fell over our little group as Nora and Susie's dad glared at one another. If the situation wasn't verging on serious, I might have been amused. It could have been played out on any playground in this state—or in this country, for that matter.

"What's with the mad faces, kids?"

As if on command, every neck swiveled around. Standing a few feet away was a mirage from another decade, gray wool fedora tipped low over his forehead and the snappiest suit I'd seen since watching Bing Crosby in *White Christmas*.

"Oh, give it a rest, Bud." Susie gave her head a toss as the suit-wearing Bud pointed a forefinger at her and winked. "No one cares if you're in *Guys and Dolls*, all right?"

Yanking off the fedora with more force than was necessary, he made a face at the waitress. "You could at least introduce me to your friends, cuz."

"We're not her friends, *cuz*," Nora snapped. "We're ex-customers who are quite dissatisfied." She turned back to Susie's dad. "Ever hear of Yelp, pal?"

"Aw, c'mon, lady." Bud was clearly finding it difficult to switch from his script to everyday language. "What'd Uncle Lou do this time? Salt your dessert?" He bent over, slapping his knees, guffawing loudly.

I wanted to sink through the cracked linoleum floor as several pairs of eyes turned in our direction. It would be just my luck to find out later someone had recorded this little escapade for the entertainment of the masses.

YouTube had a lot to answer for, in my opinion.

"Nothing's wrong." I'd had enough of this charade. "In fact, we were just leaving. Susie, we'll take the bill, please."

"Okay," she mumbled, her head down and bright spots of red on her cheeks. "I probably overreacted."

Lou craned his beefy neck and looked at his daughter. "Yeah, I'll say you did, kid." He gave her a little push. "Get in the kitchen and give your mom a hand." He glared at me as if I'd started a fight he'd had to break up and motioned toward the front door. "And you take your friends here and get out of my business."

Oh, Nora. She never could leave well enough alone. With a feisty sashay, she moved around me and aimed one lethal fingernail straight at Lou.

"You haven't heard the last of this, buster. My boyfriend here's a detective, and he'll dig up any and all dirt you're hiding in this—this *business*."

Marcus, a startled expression on his face, weakly waved off the suggestion, but neither combatant paid him any mind. If I didn't get Nora and the rest of us out of here soon, I wasn't sure if I'd be able to keep Lou from taking a swing.

"Nora, let's just go, all right? We've got enough problems with Martin Pitt, and we don't need to collect more." I grabbed her arm and pulled her toward me. If it took all my strength, I was going to march this gal out the door and to the car.

"Wait a sec." Lou's eyebrows lifted, and he motioned for me to stop. "Did you say Martin Pitt? You got an issue with him too? What's he done to you?"

Susie and Bud moved closer together, their expressions an identical mix of concern and eagerness that struck me as odd. Did these two knew something about Martin that we didn't?

"What's he done to *me*?" Nora returned Lou's question with one of her own. "Besides being my ex-stepson and a piece of work, he's now gotten himself kidnapped. His wife's asked us for help, and that's why we're here." She scowled at Lou, her hands back on her hips. "And trust me when I say that coming to this neck of the woods is *not* on my bucket list."

"And having you here in my establishment ain't on my bucket list either." Lou's scowl had returned, and I gave a deep sigh. Same song, second verse. Or maybe it was the third. Either way, I was finished with this song and dance.

"Look," I moved to stand between them and stared fixedly at Lou, "if you know something that might help us find Martin, please let us know. If not, we're out of here."

Lou looked at me as if seeing me for the first time. "Whaddya mean, help you find him? I say let him stay missing. I'm tired of those two thugs of his always showing up here, threatening to close me down if I don't do what they say."

"Two thugs? You mean Chuckles and Zeke?" I could see those two making life miserable for others but not playing the part of Mafia-type enforcers.

"Yep." Lou gave a grunt. "A pair of idiots. Always asking for free food."

Nora and I exchanged glances. Free food? Not money?

"Sounds to me like a pair of freeloaders and bullies." Nora looked around at Susie. "Did they bother you?"

The girl dropped her gaze to the floor before looking back at me. "Yes."

We waited for her to elaborate. When she didn't, I leaned forward and placed a gentle hand on her arm. "Susie, it's all right. We've met that type before." I directed the last statement to Nora, who nodded in agreement. "Trust me. All it'll take is someone to stand up to them and they'll run."

Nora flexed one arm, and Brent laughed.

I gave him the hairy eyeball and looked back at Susie. "In fact, we'd be happy to have a heart-to-heart with them."

"*You*? You gotta death wish, lady?" Bud's brows were lifted as high as they could go. "They'll eat you alive."

"We've already met them both." My tone was Saharan desert dry. "They aren't the brightest bulbs in the chandelier."

Bud and Susie exchanged a furtive look. What was going on here? The dynamics were as unstable as a three-legged dog.

I decided to dig a little deeper. "Did either of you know Zeke or Chuckles before they began giving Lou a hard time?"

Susie's hand fluttered to her chest, and her eyes widened in confused innocence. I'd seen that act too many times before, however, to be fooled by this one now. I'd let her dig her own hole, though.

"Um, I—uh, we might have met them once or twice. Maybe at a concert or something. Isn't that right?" Susie gave her cousin a poke in the side with an elbow, knocking him off balance. Classic deflection tactic. I'd seen that move before as well. "They were some sort of security."

Bud appeared as confused as Susie, but his confusion seemed genuine. He was going to play the part of the stooge in this little scenario. Before Bud could respond, Lou dropped one heavy hand on his daughter's shoulder and spun her around to face him.

"What's all this about, young lady?" Lou's voice rose, and Susie winced. Whether it was from the grip on her shoulder or her dad's anger was difficult to tell. "You'd better tell me the truth, and don't leave one detail out. You understand me?"

"Ye-yes, Dad." She sounded scared now, but I was certain it was because she'd been caught. Being dragged into a parent's kangaroo court, especially in front of others, had to be a frightening experience.

I almost felt sorry for her. Motioning with my head toward the door, I gave Nora a meaningful glance. She nodded, but I could see reluctance there. She wanted to see the entire scene play out. It wasn't our business, though, and I reminded her about that once we were settled back in the car. "Chalk it up to youthful indiscretion." I started the car. "Susie made a silly choice about her friends, and it sounds like it backfired on her."

"We could've stayed long enough to ask about Martin," Nora objected. "Don't you think so, sweetie pie?"

The endearment, thankfully, was directed at Marcus and not me. I watched in the rearview mirror as he gave a noncommittal shrug. Smart move.

"I say let's get to Uncle Charlie's and settle in before we do any sleuthing." I aimed my comment at my passengers in general and got a chorus of agreement in return. "How much longer, Brent?"

"Um, maybe an hour. Depends on how fast you drive, Miss F." He leaned forward, giving me a whiff of Protein Platter. "Want me to drive? I can get us there in thirty, forty minutes."

"No!" Nora, Rachel, and I spoke in unison, and Rachel punctuated it with shove at Brent's arm.

"It's not like I'll get us killed." Brent's expression in my rearview mirror was that of a petulant child being told he couldn't have another cookie. "I know how to drive. I used to drive for Uber."

Nora and I looked at each other, and I shivered at the memory of our first ride with him. I liked to say we saved the rest of Portland from certain chaos when we hired him to work for us as a dog walker.

"I'll drive, thanks." I put my foot down a little harder on the accelerator. "I want to get there in one piece."

Uncle Charlie's house wasn't that far from Fern's, which surprised me. I pointed this out to Nora, noting the coincidence.

"It makes me think Seattle isn't such a big place after all." I lifted my overnight bag out of the trunk and slammed the lid shut. "I guess it's the Starbucks and Amazon affect that made me think it was a big city."

"Bigger than a bread box?" Nora let her case swing against the back of my knee, nearly sending me flat on my face.

"Watch that thing." I reached down to rub the offended spot. "And yes, definitely bigger than a bread box. It's just a hair bigger than Portland and not as large as Las Vegas."

"And I know which town I prefer." Nora gave an exaggerated hip wiggle and a wink. "Vegas doesn't know what it's missing."

I started to roll my eyes but was stopped by the appearance of an older man on the front porch of the small house. Brent was right, the man was as hirsute as a possum.

Firmly fixing my gaze on his, I did my best to ignore the hair poking out from his nose and ears. Surely he'd heard of grooming. Nora, standing behind me, made a sound like a gurgle.

"It's nice to meet you." I offered my free hand, speaking loudly enough to cover Nora's amusement. "I really appreciate you letting us stay the night."

Uncle Charlie lifted one hand and cupped his furry ear. "What? I don't hear too good anymore."

"I said," I projected as loudly as I could without yelling, "thank you for letting us stay here."

He dropped his hand and gave me a wounded look. "No need to shout, young lady. I can hear you."

Oh, *this* was going to be fun. When I saw the sleeping arrangements, there was no doubt in my mind.

The five of us distributed our things in the various rooms offered by Brent's uncle as places to sleep. Nora, Rachel, and I took the back bedroom, which overlooked a small strip of yard, an old-fashioned clothesline strung from the back of the house to a tree.

I leaned down and pressed on the mattress of the double bed that stood under the one window, my hand sinking nearly up to the wrist.

"This is really soft. It's a backache in the making." I looked around at Nora and Rachel. "I'll be happy to sleep on the floor."

"Well, you can scooch on over, Sis. I'll be right there beside you." Nora aimed a sassy grin at Rachel, nodding at the bed. "Looks like you get the entire thing to yourself, girlie."

"Can't we just say we forgot we needed to be somewhere else and go get a hotel room?" Rachel clasped her hands together as if in prayer. "I'll even pay for it. Please?"

It was tempting.

"I think we'd hurt both Uncle Charlie's and Brent's feelings." I gave her an impulsive hug. "I've got an idea. We can drag the top mattress onto the floor and use the box springs as a bed." I smiled at Nora. "Remember when we went to science camp in fifth grade?"

"Oh, those awful beds." Nora grimaced at the memory. "We lined up all the mattresses on the floor and had one big slumber party in the girls' dorm." She gave me a wide smile, her eyes twinkling with mischief. "And the boys did the same."

"How do you know that?" Rachel's expression was the perfect mix of curiosity and "I don't want to know."

I knew exactly how she felt. It was like driving past a car accident and not being able to look away. But we were in fifth grade, for goodness' sake, and into playing jokes and not into boys.

"Only because she snuck out with a couple other girls in order to TP the porch that ran around the boys' cabin." I chuckled, remembering the hoopla when Nora tripped over one of the sleeping counselors when they snuck back inside. It made her the most admired girl in fifth grade...and the only one grounded for the rest of the school year.

"Oh, that's cool, Mrs. Goldstein." Rachel sounded as impressed as the rest of our friends had been that year. "I never got to do anything like that." She made a wry face. "You know, having a police officer for a dad can be a wet blanket."

"I'd say that was probably a good thing for you, Rachel." Turning back to Nora, I spoke briskly. "Let's get this show on the road. We need to decide what our next step is going to be." I glanced at the hardwood floor and grimaced. This wouldn't make a comfy foundation for a mattress. "I'd guess a good night's sleep won't be part of it."

Chapter 15

Dinner that night was—*interesting*. I could find no other word to describe the repast set before the five of us, and the glow of pride on Uncle Charlie's face told me this was a Special Meal, capitals implied.

"I can't say I've ever eaten anything quite like this." I used my fork to prod the tough cut of meat on my plate, only just managing not to wrinkle my nose at the aroma. Maybe it was something gamey, perhaps venison or moose.

"Isn't this awesome, Miss F.?" Brent enthusiastically sawed at a large piece of meat and popped a bite into his mouth, chewing with clear enjoyment. "Nobody does squirrel like my Uncle Charlie."

Squirrel? Did people actually *eat* squirrel? Or was this Brent's idea of a joke?

I glanced across the table at Nora and Rachel. Nora's nose was wrinkled in disgust, and Rachel's face had lost all color. So help me, it was as white as Aggie's fur after it had been washed.

Pushing her plate away, Rachel grabbed her glass of water and took large gulps, her eyes wide over the rim. Poor thing. She looked like she was going to be sick. I certainly felt that way myself.

Only Brent, Marcus, and Charlie continued to eat, apparently with complete satisfaction. If I knew Nora, she'd make him sanitize his mouth before she'd ever let him kiss her again. The thought caused me to smile.

"What's so funny?" Brent stared at me in curiosity, his fork suspended over his nearly empty plate.

"What?" I looked at him, momentarily startled out of my thoughts. "Oh, it's nothing." I forced myself to take a bite of squirrel, if that was really what it was, and then laid my fork across the plate. "That was amazing." I smiled brightly at Uncle Charlie, hoping I didn't appear as manic as The Joker.

He glanced at my still-full plate and grunted, pointing at it. Panic rose in my chest. I feared I'd offended our host. Maybe we'd need to find somewhere else to stay the night. It might not be a bad idea at that.

"You gonna finish that?"

"This?" I looked at the food as if I'd never seen it before.

"Yeah, that. If you're not gonna eat it, pass it this way."

I gladly slid my plate across the table, noting Nora's amused expression from my peripheral.

"You want mine?" Nora indicated her plate with one manicured finger. "I'm so full now I'm not sure I can sleep." She gave her stomach a little pat, miming satisfaction.

"And mine." Rachel's voice was shaky, but I was glad to see her color was returning.

"You ladies sure? I don't make this stuff very often."

Brent acknowledged his uncle with a lifted fork. "Yeah, Miss F. This is a family delicacy."

"We're sure." I spoke firmly, and Rachel's stiff shoulders relaxed. Poor kid. She was too nice for her own good at times.

I stood, gesturing for Nora and Rachel to follow me. "Let's leave these gentlemen to finish their dinner without us. We need to discuss our plans for tomorrow."

It was an excuse as transparent as the picture window in the dining room, but I didn't care. If I didn't get away from the pungent smell of fried squirrel, I was going to be sick.

"Let's go outside," Nora murmured in my ear. "This place is getting weirder by the minute."

"Agreed."

I led the way to the front door and opened it, taking in a big gulp of fresh air. I wasn't sure if staying here had been such a great idea after all. Would Brent and Uncle Charlie be offended if I rented a motel room for the night? Maybe I could claim a relapse of some obscure illness.

"He seems like a nice person." Rachel's voice seemed steadier now. "I just didn't think Brent was serious when he told me his uncle was a bit different." She shrugged, with a wry expression. "I mean, you know Brent. He's a little different himself."

"Ha. That's putting it mildly, girl." Nora slid her arm around Rachel's shoulders and gave her a brief hug. "Sure you want to get involved with a family like this?"

Rachel smiled slightly, and I could see she'd shaken off her sickness from dinner. Oh, the resilience of youth. My own stomach was still roiling, and the thought of putting anything in it only increased my nausea.

"She's old enough to make up her mind." I turned to Rachel. "Of course, Mrs. Goldstein might know what she's talking about when it comes to relationships." I didn't mention the litany of divorces or exes, but my meaning was clear.

"Oh, don't worry about me, Miss Franklin. We don't plan on getting married anytime soon." Rachel's eyes twinkled, and her smile grew wider. "In fact, we're talking about getting our own place and staying status quo for the foreseeable future."

"Yeah? What do your folks think about that?" Nora sounded genuinely curious, but a tiny frown formed between her eyebrows. She clearly didn't care for Rachel and Brent's plan.

"Believe it or not, my mom is okay with it. And she said not to worry about my dad, that he'd come around. Eventually."

And I've inherited Windsor Castle. I was certain Detective Day would have quite a few things to say about that little arrangement, but it wasn't my business.

The door opened behind us, and we turned. Brent was standing there with a pleased grin, holding an enamel bowl. "Hey, you guys want some blueberries?" He walked over to us, holding the bowl carefully as though it was a precious offering. "He picked these yesterday right out there." He motioned with his chin to the thick woods that grew up to the edge of Uncle Charlie's property. "When he was out squirrel hunting."

That did it for me. I loved fruit, especially when it was fresh, but the thought of squirrels being near the berries—maybe even eating them—sent my tummy into another round of nausea. Shaking my head, I waved off the bowl as it was held out.

"I'll take some." Rachel stepped forward and took a handful of the round berries, popping them into her mouth with apparent enjoyment. "Wow, these are really sweet. You two need to try them."

"Not for me," I said weakly. "Bad issues with the plumbing, I'm afraid." I gave my offended stomach a gentle pat.

"Oh, there's nothing wrong with the plumbing, Miss F. The toilet works just fine. I used it before—"

I cut off Brent's comment with a stern shake of my head, looking at Nora for help. She instantly pushed the bowl away.

"You two stay here and enjoy the berries. Miss Franklin and I are going to take a little walk before turning in." She slipped a hand under one of my arms, steering me toward the woods. "We'll be back in a few."

The graveled driveway crunched under our shoes as we moved away from the house. I fancied I could still smell fried squirrel trailing behind us, and my insides did a flip. The farther away we got, the better I felt. It was most likely the product of an over-active imagination combined with a delicate stomach, but, at that moment, I swore off eating anything fried for the rest of my life.

"Wanna go into town and grab a salad or something?" Nora tugged at my arm, stopping our progress. "You've got to eat something, Sis. For that matter, so do I." She chuckled, and we continued our stroll. "In all my days, I never thought I'd be served anything like that."

"Don't say it." I forced the image of our dinner from my mind. I needed something else to think about, a sort of mental palate cleanser. "Let's talk about Martin and Teresa instead. We still need to decide how to deal with his disappearance."

Nora grunted. "Sounds to me like he's a chip off the old block. His dad used to do the same thing. Some days he'd be home, some days he wouldn't. I got tired of playing single mommy to those two brats of his and told him so, right before I served him with divorce papers." She grimaced at the memory. "You should've seen his face. But I managed to get a few dollars out of the deal, so I guess it wasn't all bad."

"A few dollars" was a misnomer. Nora had become a millionaire because of her divorces. Alimony and marriage seemed to go hand in hand in her world, and I was thankful she'd stopped looking for the next ex-husband. Cross my fingers, toes, and eyes.

Of course, there was Marcus, but as far as I knew, he didn't have a spare cent to his name. That was probably his saving grace, if I was honest.

"Should we go to the nearest police station before we visit Teresa?" I forced my mind back on track, trying to come up with the next step. "It seems odd she hasn't reported this already."

"I don't know. Maybe." Nora stepped carefully around a tree stump. "Seems to me Teresa's a funny gal when it comes to her privacy." She gave a small shrug. "At least that's what I picked up from the time we spent with her."

"But her husband is missing. I'm not sure this falls into the category of a privacy issue."

"I'm not saying I don't agree with you. I just want to make sure she'll be okay if we report it. I mean, who knows? She might be safer with him gone."

I'd forgotten about that. Teresa, poor thing, had endured mistreatment at Martin's hands. She probably *was* better off with him out of her life.

"Hey, Miss F., Mrs. G." Brent's voice followed us into the woods, sounding excited about something. "You need to see this."

"If it's another animal carcass, I'm gonna lose my cookies." Nora looked at me, one eyebrow quirked. "You ready to go back?" She fished into her top and brought out her cell phone. "We need to shed some light on the subject, so to speak. We should've remembered flashlights."

"It's not that dark yet. But yes, I'm ready to head back. I think I'm going to see about making some hot tea anyway. That usually helps when I feel like this." The crackle of footsteps on fallen leaves met my ears. "Nora, hold that light up. It sounds like a bear is headed this way."

Brent was jogging toward us, his face alight with excitement.

"It seems Brent's wound up over something."

"Look what I got." He held up cupped hands, proudly looking at something moving there. "Uncle Charlie says I can keep it."

"What is it?" I leaned forward, curious to see what he'd found.

A tiny bird was lying there, its small wings tucked under its body, bright eyes peering at us. It made a cheeping sound, and I jumped back.

"Brent, it needs to go back to its mother. It's too young to leave the nest."

"Don't you know nothing, Miss F.? Mama birds don't take back babies that've been handled by people." He brought his hands closer to his face, crooning softly. "I'm gonna be your mama, little bird."

"Not in my car, you're not." I spoke firmly but kindly. "Leave it here for your uncle to care for, and when you come visit, you'll have a pet."

"Oh, c'mon," Brent pleaded, his gaze fixed on the tiny creature. "He won't hurt a fly."

Rachel came forward and placed one hand gently on his arm. "Miss Franklin's right. This poor little thing will be better off staying where he's more comfortable." She smiled at him, her expression soft. "I know you love animals, but can you imagine keeping a bird inside an apartment? That would be cruel."

I watched Brent, clearly struggling between keeping the tiny bird and letting it go. Finally, he sighed and held his hands closer to his face. For a moment, I thought he was going to kiss it, but he just whispered something before placing it on Rachel's waiting palm.

"Aggie might get jealous if you bring home another pet, kid." Nora, her voice soft, reached out and squeezed his arm. "And we need to focus on our task at hand. And speaking of which"—she looked back at the house—"go get that no-good Marcus and tell him to get his fanny out here. We need to talk about tomorrow."

"I'll get him for you." Rachel moved away from us with the bird. "I need to get this little guy settled for the night first."

Nora and I watched as she walked back to the house, her hands cupped gently around the little bird. Brent stayed where he was, the expression on his face as bereft as if I'd told him he couldn't have dessert. He really was a big teddy bear, a softy where all animals were concerned. We were really lucky to have him with us at 2 Sisters Pet Valet Services.

With a sigh, Nora rubbed her eyes and yawned. "It's been a really weird day, you two. I might turn in early." Her smile was mischievous, and she gave my arm a light tap. "You ready for a night on the floor?"

"On the floor?" Brent's eyebrows shot up as far as they'd go. "Uncle Charlie has beds, Mrs. G. You don't need to sleep on the floor."

Nora started to speak, but I cut her off, not wanting to go into any great explanation. Sometimes less was the better choice where Brent was concerned, bless his heart.

"It's a girl thing, Brent." I brushed at the mosquito that buzzed near my ear. "And I think we'd all better go back in or we'll get eaten alive out here."

"Here comes the bigshot himself." Nora nodded toward the door as Marcus appeared, Rachel just behind him, chattering happily. "Let's convene in the living room, maybe with some coffee."

"That'll wake you up," I pointed out. "How about herbal tea, if I can find any?"

"You're turning into Fern, you know that?" Nora teetered slightly in her heels as she stepped on a small rock. "Brent, give me your arm. I'm gonna break my neck out here."

"You should wear shoes like me and Rachel, Mrs. G." Brent obligingly held out an arm for Nora to grasp. "Those shoes you wear'll make your toes ugly. I saw a video on YouTube that showed some really bad feet."

"That's a bunch of hooey." Nora stumbled again and muttered something under her breath. "Besides, I've been wearing high heels for as long as I can remember, and my feet are just fine."

"You betcha, sweetcakes." Marcus met us before we reached the door, planting a loud kiss on Nora's upturned face. "You've got some fine feet and fine everything else."

Per usual, Rachel and Brent giggled, Nora preened, and I rolled my eyes. At this moment, when things were feeling par for the course, it was difficult to recall the reason we'd landed in this slice of Washington.

Once we were all settled on the various lumpy chairs and couch that filled the small living room, I took drink orders and headed for the kitchen. Uncle Charlie had taken himself off to his bedroom, and I could hear the tinny sound of canned laughter filtering downstairs.

I busied myself heating water for tea and collecting cups, spoons, sugar, and milk. I felt the need for some alone time so I could get my mind fixed on the task at hand. I was still confused about why Teresa had called us first and not the police.

A missing person, even if it was a husband whose actions might not be aboveboard, was cause for concern. In fact, I wasn't sure what she expected us to do.

Chapter 16

"I think the best thing to do is for Gwen and me to go talk directly with Teresa." Nora placed her teacup on the antique packing crate enjoying new life as a coffee table. "Marcus, you and these two," she waved at Rachel and Brent, "can swing by the cleaners to see if anyone's heard from Martin. We'll drop you off before we head out to Teresa's place."

"And what if no one has, Mrs. Goldstein?" Rachel looked over the rim of the teacup, her brows drawn together, her eyes troubled. "Do we go to the police?"

"I think we should call them first before we do anything else." I cradled the warm mug between my hands. "I've never heard of someone going missing without the family notifying the police." I shook my head. "It doesn't feel right."

"I saw a TV show once that was about this man who killed his wife and told everyone she'd gone to Mexico with some friends." Brent glanced at Rachel. "Remember? That one where they find her buried in the garden? It's that show we like, something about snapping."

I knew exactly which show he meant, and in a strange way, Brent's comment made sense to me.

"My point exactly." I motioned with my empty mug. "Who's to say that someone with a grudge didn't kill Martin and dispose of his body? There's a big ocean out there."

"Do you have any idea who might want Martin dead?" Marcus shifted against the sofa's cushions, moving closer to Nora. "I thought he had a couple of bodyguards. Seems they'd know something if there was an issue bad enough for someone to want him erased."

"Zeke and Chuckles." Nora spit the names out with disgust. "I've never met more incompetent idiots than those two."

Something triggered in my mind. Hadn't I recently heard those names? Then it hit me. I snapped my fingers. "I know—the diner's owner and his daughter."

"That's right." Marcus swung his head around to me, his eyes wide. "Those two were bothering them for free food."

The five of us sat there silently, letting this new train of thought chug its way through our collective minds. The connection was tenuous, but it meant something. It couldn't have been a coincidence that Martin's hired thugs had harassed Pete and his daughter. Maybe Martin's racket, if that was what it was, involved taking what they wanted from small businesses. It could be anything, including money. Someone could have finally said, "Enough."

Finally, Nora sighed and wiggled out from under Marcus's arm. "I don't know about you folks, but I need to get my beauty sleep. You ready?"

This last comment was aimed at me, and I nodded absently. Hopefully, my unconscious mind would make some connections as I slept. Leaving Nora and Rachel to say good night to their respective beaus, I headed to the bedroom to prepare for sleep.

The mattress wasn't as uncomfortable as I thought it would be, and Nora only snored for a little while before turning onto her side. Rolled into a musty down comforter between Rachel and Nora, I quickly fell into a dreamless sleep.

* * * *

I didn't wake up with any great revelation, though. In fact, all I had to show for the night was a stiff back. So much for my unconscious brain working out the problem. After showering under the tepid water and donning a pair of cropped jeans and a loose shirt, I made my way to the kitchen in search of caffeine. Memories of last night's dinner were still hovering in my mind, and stomach, and I'd already decided to skip any breakfast that might be offered. Maybe a piece of fruit, if I could find one, or some dry toast would help my innards gain their equilibrium.

"Hey, Miss F. You want some coffee?" Brent leaned against the counter, his hair still tousled from sleep, holding a coffee mug. He motioned toward the coffee maker, a pleased expression on his sheet-creased face. "I made it myself."

I eyed the dark brew suspiciously, wondering just how much coffee he'd used. It looked strong enough to lift weights. Brent was looking expectantly at me, though, and I couldn't hurt the boy's feelings. I could always pop a few antacids to counteract any unwelcome effects.

"Of course," I smiled at him. "I always need a shot of caffeine to get my day started."

"You need a shot? Like a needle?" His eyes twinkled as he pointed to his cup, embossed with a picture of Seattle's Space Needle. "I got the only one there was. Maybe you could drink out of a fish."

He pointed to the sink, and I saw that the mugs from the night before were still sitting where we'd left them. I spied the mug he meant, its sides covered with various types of fish found in Puget Sound. Since these seemed to comprise Uncle Charlie's entire mug collection, I gave it a brief swish under the tap and poured myself a cup of coffee. Hopefully the coffee would be strong enough to kill any lingering germs.

I took a tentative sip and was pleasantly surprised.

"This is really good." I sat at the kitchen table. Its surface was scarred with various stains and scratches, with no evidence of any coasters. "Do you know what the blend is?" I took another drink, inhaling the rich aroma.

He cocked his head, one eyebrow lifted in question.

"I'm talking about the coffee. Did you notice what kind it is?"

"I'm not too sure." He jerked his chin toward the coffee maker. "I just used the coffee that was already in there."

In there? I hesitated, the mug halfway to my lips. "You mean the filter basket?"

"Yep." He looked pleased with himself. "I figured it was still okay. I didn't see no mold or anything."

I was saved from answering by Rachel. Breezing in to the kitchen with a cheery smile for me and a kiss for Brent, she looked ready to tackle the day, even without caffeine.

Nora, looking as rough as I'd ever seen her, trailed behind her, sans the ever-present high heels, with a hairdo that looked like raccoons had nested there. Marcus followed close behind, bags big enough to pack clothes in underneath both eyes. It seemed I was the only one who'd managed a decent night's sleep.

"Coffee," Nora croaked, slipping into a chair, "I need coffee." She folded her arms on the table and dropped her head. "I feel like a Mack truck rolled over me."

"I second that." Marcus sat down heavily, groaning as various joints popped in protest.

"Comin' right up." Brent plucked a mug from the sink and held it up for inspection. Giving it a quick once-over, he filled it and sat in front of Nora. "You oughta be careful how much of this stuff you drink, Mrs. G. My mom says it'll stunt your growth if you drink too much."

Rachel giggled. "*My* mom says it'll put hair on your chest." She gave Brent a playful poke in the arm. "Maybe you should drink some."

"I got hair," he protested. "Look."

Rachel squealed, launching herself at Brent as he started to lift his T-shirt.

"Okay, you two. Get it together." Nora peered up from her arms, her eyes bleary as she drew the coffee closer.

"Ah. This smells good." Marcus accepted a mug as well, sniffing the surface before taking a tentative taste. "Smells like that Ethiopian stuff you buy, Nora."

I decided to not mention the used grounds. Instead, I sipped my own coffee and waited for Nora and Marcus to join the land of the living. I needed Nora functioning on all cylinders in order to set our plans in motion.

Rachel, still exhibiting more energy than I usually felt in a week, chatted brightly with Brent as she started a sink of sudsy water. "You should've let me wash those mugs first," she playfully scolded him. "Anyone want some toast or something?"

Nora, her head now at half-mast, lifted one hand before letting it fall again. "Me."

"I'll take some." Marcus stretched his neck, letting his head loll from side to side. "I need to sit in a hot tub."

"I'll help, Rachel." Toast sounded good, and it would tide me over until getting a more substantial meal.

I opened the old Amana fridge, bending down in order to find butter. Instantly a strong scent rolled out at me, filling my nose and the back of my throat. I quickly slammed the door, one hand covering my mouth.

"Dear lord in heaven," Nora groaned. "What crawled in there and died?"

"What in the heck was that?" Rachel, her hands covered in soap suds, stared from me to the fridge. "Please don't tell me Uncle Charlie kept the leftovers from last night."

"Well, sure he did. You can't throw out perfectly good food." Brent reached for the Amana's tarnished silver handle. "You wanna heat some up?"

"Young man, don't you *dare* open that door." I stood there, my hands on my hips, glaring. Pointing to his chair, I used a voice I hadn't needed since the time a student let a mouse loose in my classroom. "Get away from that fridge. *Now*."

With a startled expression, as though I'd just executed a complex dance step on the ceiling, Brent fell back into his chair and spoke in an injured tone. "You don't need to get so mad, Miss F. I just thought you'd like something besides toast. You didn't eat your dinner last night."

Uncle Charlie shuffled in, tufts of wiry gray hair sticking up all over his head and his mouth opened in a wide yawn. "Did I hear someone say 'dinner'?"

We left Uncle Charlie's house as quickly as we could get ready, without the toast. Brent was still protesting that squirrel was "better than chicken."

"If you want, I can make us some when we get back to Portland, Miss F."

"Thanks but no thanks." I pulled my car onto the road. "I'll stick to meat that's been packaged and sold in a store." After the squirrel, though, I wasn't certain I could ever eat any type of meat again.

"I could use a breakfast burrito or something. Could we stop at a McDonald's?" From the back seat, I could hear Rachel tapping on her cell phone. "It says here that if you turn right on the next street, there'll be one about half a mile up the road."

I followed her directions and found the fast-food restaurant without any problem. How I'd ever managed without GPS I couldn't imagine, and I said so as we entered the brightly lit lobby.

"I'm pretty sure we used things called maps," Nora said wryly, and I had to chuckle.

"You're right. It seems a lifetime ago, though." I patted the pocket of my cropped pants. "My phone is practically an extra limb."

Nora gave me a sly grin. "Mine's extra padding, if you get my drift."

I wanted to roll my eyes, but I refrained. I definitely got her drift.

Once the five of us had placed our orders and found a clean booth in which to sit, I decided to broach the topic of that day's plans.

"I think we need to drop them off at the cleaners as soon as we eat." I nodded across the table at Marcus, Brent, and Rachel. "Maybe they can take an Uber and meet us at Teresa and Martin's house once they speak with the employees."

"Not on your life." Brent's face was serious, and he leaned forward. "I know how crazy those drivers are."

Nora and I exchanged amused glances. My first encounter with Brent post high school had been when he'd driven us from The Friendly Bean to Nora's apartment. We'd arrived in one piece by sheer luck and the grace of God.

"We could meet them at the Chinese restaurant." Nora popped the last piece of an Egg McMuffin into her mouth. "It's the one that's kitty-corner from the dry cleaners."

"Yeah, that's a great idea," Brent agreed enthusiastically. "I love egg foo young. And fried rice."

"Do you ever stop thinking about your next meal?" Nora shook a finger at him, but her tone was teasing. "Marcus, Rachel, is that all right with you two?"

Marcus lifted one shoulder in answer, still chewing a mouthful of pancakes. Rachel, having neatly folded and disposed of her breakfast burrito wrapper, nodded.

"That sounds fine with me too, Mrs. G." She gave Brent a playful punch on his arm. "And I'll keep a close eye on this one and make sure he doesn't clear out the buffet."

"It's a buffet?" Brent's eyes lit up as brightly as child's at Christmas. "That's awesome. Maybe I can take some for the road."

"Not in my car you're not," I said firmly. A dropped and forgotten French fry was bad enough, leaving behind an odor much like dirty feet. The scent of leftover egg foo young and chicken chow mein would be almost impossible to eradicate from the upholstery. "Besides, I'm fairly certain most buffets don't allow take-home boxes unless you're paying for another person."

I left Brent to puzzle over that revelation as I concentrated on navigating the narrow road. Seattle seemed to have packed a lot of trees and houses into a small space, and the streets were congested at this time of day. I couldn't have stayed at Uncle Charlie's any longer, though, and one could only sit in a fast-food joint for so long.

"I think I'll go inside with you when we get there." Nora turned to smile at Marcus. "I want to check on something first before we head out to Teresa's."

I glanced at her. "What's on your mind?"

"Oh, just something." She turned around and resettled the shoulder harness over her padded chest. "If I find it, I'll show you."

"I can help you look." Brent leaned forward, sending a gust of breakfast breath over my shoulder. "Is it bigger than a bread basket?"

"I think that's a game, kid." Marcus shifted in his seat. "But I'm curious as well. Is it bigger than a bread box?"

"Oh, good grief, you two." Despite the words, Nora sounded more amused than irritated. "I'm looking for a picture of Martin's father, all right?"

"Don't you have one, Mrs. Goldstein?" Rachel asked. "Not that it's any of my business."

"It's fine." Nora didn't seem bothered by all our questions, which surprised me. She tended to get "tetchy," as my granny would say, when any of her past marriages were mentioned. "I need it for identification purposes."

Her words sank as deftly as a stone in water as the meaning hit me. "Have they found a body?"

"No, silly. Besides, a picture probably wouldn't be much help after all this time." Nora's voice held a trace of sadness. "He's been missing for quite a while now."

"That's right, Mrs. G. I saw a show about a missing person, and when they finally found the body, it was—"

I cut off Brent's enthusiastic comment. "We get the point." I looked at Nora briefly and turned back to watch the road. "Who last saw him, and where? Have you ever found that out?"

"No. Those two ex-stepkids of mine tend to hold their cards close to the vest."

I noticed she didn't use their names and glanced in the rearview mirror in time to see Marcus flush. Merry Pitt was still a topic best left untouched.

"What made them report their dad as missing?" Rachel asked, and I nodded as I navigated a left turn and pulled up in front of the dry cleaners.

I'd been wondering the same thing. If they'd been estranged from their father, I wouldn't have thought that contacting him was high on their list of priorities.

Nora threw up her hands and let them drop to her lap. "Don't ask me. That whole family is as nutty as fruitcake. Who knows why they do anything?"

"I think it might be better if you go in by yourself." Marcus placed a hand on Nora's shoulder, and she covered it with hers. "Or, if you'd like, I can go in with you to make sure you're okay." He gave her a lopsided smile. "I don't want them to feel like they're being raided."

"You're a sweetie." She undid her seat belt and let it slide back into the holder. "It won't take me but a few minutes. I'll be all right." Opening the door, she leaned back in and flashed a mischievous smile. "But if I'm not out in twenty minutes, send in the hounds."

Chapter 17

I wasn't crazy with this arrangement, knowing Chuckles might be lurking somewhere. She could flirt her way into anything, though, plus she was wearing a pair of powerful weapons on her feet. I turned around so I could see both the front door to the cleaners and my back-seat passengers and settled in to wait.

"What type of questions are we going to be asking, Mr. Avery?" Rachel shifted in her seat so she was facing Marcus. "I've tried to think of some myself, but I'm stumped."

"Well, we first need to find out when Martin was last seen at the business. I'll ask about any type of security cameras and hope that they have some." He opened his door. "That's better. Need to get some air circulating." He patted his bulky middle, smiling wryly. "I have my own heat supply."

I shivered as a cool breeze filled the car and pulled my sleeves down as far as they'd go. I wasn't often chilly, so this was a welcome change from the menopausal heater I normally carried with me.

"I wonder what Teresa's told the employees." I looked back at Marcus, and he shrugged.

"Judging from what Nora's told me and what her stepdaughter said about Teresa, most likely nothing." Marcus's cheeks were pink, but whether it was from mentioning Merry or his own internal heat source, I couldn't say. "Here comes Nora." His voice sounded relieved as he stepped from the car and hurried to meet her.

"Teresa most likely didn't want to start a panic." Rachel nudged Brent. "Let's get out. Mr. Avery's already headed inside."

"We'll meet you three at the restaurant as soon as we can." I gave her an encouraging smile as they got out. "Maybe you should text me when you're finished so we have an idea of when we should wrap things up, okay?"

"Sounds good." Rachel leaned down and peered through the driver's-side window. "You two be careful out there."

Nora looked up from fastening her seat belt. "We'll be fine, but thanks anyway." She flexed one thin arm, winking at the concerned girl. "Miss Franklin's got me as a bodyguard."

I made a face at Rachel, who laughed and waved as I pulled away from the curb. She was such a great person and perfect for Brent. And for 2 Sisters Pet Valet Services.

Thinking of Rachel brought my thoughts to her father. "Do you think it would do any good to talk with Detective Day?"

Nora snorted. "Whatever for? The man's a walking nuisance."

"He's also an officer of the law." I steered the car onto the road that led to Teresa and Martin's home. "He might have some insight into the search for your ex's body."

"I doubt that." Nora lifted her arms above her head and gave a little twist and groan. "I swear my back will never recover from that sorry excuse for a bed. Next time Brent offers to find a place for us to stay, remind me to say no."

"I'd say we're too old to be sleeping on any floor. That mattress just about killed my back. Besides, science camp and sleeping under the stars was a long time ago."

"Everything was a long time ago." Nora sighed and settled back in the passenger seat. "And having to look for Martin isn't exactly the way I thought I'd be spending my precious time. It was bad enough when he was a kid and always getting into trouble."

"They say your children are always your babies, no matter how old they might get." I smiled to myself, waiting for her reaction. I wasn't disappointed.

"I'd like to remind you, Sis, that he wasn't my child. Never was, never will be. And right now, he's just a huge pain in the bum."

"Well, let's pretend we care when we're speaking with Teresa, all right?" I slowed down and made the final turn onto the road that ran past the house. "She might not be happy in her marriage, but she's still worried, and I don't want to make it worse."

"You're right. As usual." She reached over and squeezed my shoulder. "It's a good thing I have you to keep me balanced."

I smiled at her and patted her hand, If was nice to have my best friend next to me, even if it was on a search for one of her nutty stepkids.

To my surprise, the gates that were normally closed stood open. I drove through them cautiously, praying it wasn't a faulty mechanical issue that would cause them to close on the tail end of my car. It might be an oldie, but my vehicle was still a goody. *And* fully paid for.

"This doesn't look good." Nora craned her neck to look around the grounds. "No cars, gate wide open, and dog running lose." She pointed, and I spotted the small dog normally tucked under Teresa's arm huddling under a large hydrangea bush, strangely silent as it watched us with bright eyes.

I drew up to one side of the driveway, leaving enough room in case someone else needed to pull in and park. Cutting the motor, I sat and listened to the silence. I could hear nothing but the sound of the breeze as it rustled the leaves of the trees and bushes and the click of the cooling engine. The entire scene was as eerie as a scene from a Stephen King novel, not the genteel imaginations of Agatha Christie's books.

Opening my door, I stepped out and waited for Nora to join me. "I think we need to check on that poor thing first." I leaned over and snapped my fingers at the dog and then stood up abruptly, my eyes wide. "Nora, the poor thing's muzzled. Help me get it off."

With a little coaxing, I was able to reach the dog and held it closely as Nora worked to unbuckle the sides of the tight contraption. Crooning softly, I stroked its soft ears as the muzzle came off.

"I hope she's all right." I looked at Nora with concern, my fingers massaging the dog's small face where the straps had been the tightest.

"Who? The dog or Teresa?"

"Both, although I was talking about this poor little thing." I leaned closer to examine a mark on the side of the dog's face. "Whoever put that muzzle on meant business."

"Probably that idiot Zeke," Nora muttered darkly. "Sounds like his speed."

"Let's get inside so it can at least have some water." I led the way to the front door and waited for Nora to ring the doorbell. I didn't expect anyone to answer the door, especially since I hadn't noticed any cars. I wasn't going to leave this sweet little pup behind if no one was home, though.

Nora reached out and ruffled the dog's soft ears. "You know you can't take it home with you, Sis."

She knew me so well. That was what fifty years of friendship turned into: a relationship closer than some marriages. Yes, we'd had a few years where our meetings had been few and far between. She'd been busy getting married and divorced, and I'd just begun my teaching career. When we finally made the connection once more, though, it was so easy to pick right back up where we'd left off.

And now she could almost read my mind.

"I know." I held the dog a bit closer. "But I can't leave it here without food or water."

"Let's cross that bridge when we get to it, shall we?" Nora lifted her hand and pressed the doorbell again, adding a sharp rap with her knuckles for good measure. "I think I hear someone." She listened, a small frown crossing her face. "I don't think that's Teresa. At least it doesn't sound like her. Too heavy."

I cocked my head to one side and listened intently. Footsteps were moving toward the door, apparently not in any hurry to see who was standing on the porch. Weirder and weirder. Shades of Stephen King flashed through my mind again, and I shivered, taking a step back.

It was Nora's ex-family, after all. She should be the one in front.

When Chuckles yanked open the door, a scowl already on his face, I was glad I'd moved back. Nora, however, didn't budge an inch. In fact, she stepped even closer, almost nose to nose, or nose to chest, with the muscle-bound bodyguard.

She didn't give him a chance to speak either. In an icy tone, she asked, "What in the Sam Hill are you doing here? And where's Teresa?"

"And good morning to you, too, sunshine." Chuckles's bulky arms, held close to his chest, flexed visibly, and I cringed. I wasn't certain Nora would be able to reach her heels again to use as a weapon on the behemoth man. "She's sleeping. What's it to you?"

"Sleeping? At this time of the day?" With a shove, Nora pushed past him and into the foyer. "And pray tell, who muzzled this poor dog?" She motioned toward me and the pup. "It's a good thing we got here to rescue the poor thing."

Chuckles snorted. "Don't look at me. *She's* the one who shut that yappy thing up so we could get some rest around here."

Nora and I exchanged startled glances. That didn't seem like the Teresa we met.

"What's going on?" I hadn't heard Teresa walk up behind Chuckles, a snowy-white bathrobe tied tightly around an enviable small waist. "And what are you doing with my dog?"

I mutely handed the trembling animal to his owner and was relieved to see her cuddle the pooch. That wasn't the action of someone who'd muzzle a defenseless animal all night long.

"We found that poor little thing outside. Any idea how this muzzle came to be on it?" Nora, one eyebrow lifted, dangled the offending object from one finger.

"Muzzle? On my darling baby?" Teresa sounded as mystified as she looked, and she lifted the dog to her face for a kiss on its snout. "I have no earthly idea." A light suddenly dawned in her eyes, and she turned to glare at Chuckles. "Do you have something to say about this?"

I felt so sorry for her. Not only had she had to endure an unhappy marriage to Martin, now she was saddled with his henchman. If I was her, I'd call someone and have the man removed pronto. I still didn't understand why he was allowed to be out in public after nearly kidnapping Nora and me.

"Look, we didn't come here to referee an argument," Nora stated firmly. "We came to talk about Martin and ask why you haven't called in the police yet." She scowled at Chuckles before looking back at Teresa. "And we'd prefer to do it without the goon squad standing around."

Chuckles's face darkened at her words, but he said nothing. I had to hand it to him. If I'd been called a goon by someone half my size, I might be tempted to remove the irritation. Permanently.

I gave an inward gasp at that last thought. Maybe that was what he meant to do with Teresa. Maybe Martin's kidnapping was actually a ruse, something to keep Teresa's attention occupied while a plan was laid to get rid of her, just as Martin's dad had disappeared. With her gone, Martin would be the one to inherit the entire estate, finances included.

I gave Nora's elbow a discreet tug. "Could I speak with you a moment? In private?" I jerked my chin toward the door. With a smile for Teresa and nothing for Chuckles, I added, "It'll only take a moment."

"No problem." Teresa shrugged, then leaned over and placed the fluffy pup on the floor. "I'll make some coffee for us while I'm waiting, And Chuckles," she threw over her shoulder, "you need to feed the dog."

She didn't see the dark scowl that filled his face as she walked away, but I did. Something was definitely going on here that wasn't right. Nudging Nora, I steered her out the front door, closing it behind us.

"We've got to get Teresa out of here." I kept my voice low in case someone was listening. "I have a feeling she's being held here against her will. And you saw her face when you told her about the dog."

"Hold on, Sis." Nora held up one hand. "Are you saying you think Teresa's a prisoner in her own house?"

"Yes, that's exactly what I think." I began ticking the points off on my fingers. "First, the dog's muzzled. Clearly that's something she would never do, and I think it was to keep it from barking at Chuckles. Point two. What in the world is he doing here? Doesn't he have his own place in town? And three, I think he's here because he's planning on making her disappear as well. Besides," I whispered, "I've started getting this gut feeling that Martin somehow instigated his own disappearance."

Nora's expression said it all. She was amused, astonished, and worried. Reaching out one hand, she felt my forehead. "You sure you're okay? Maybe that squirrel gave you some sort of mad cow disease or something."

I pulled away from her with a snort of irritation. "Mad cow disease isn't found in squirrels, at least not to my knowledge. And I'm fine. I'm beginning to think Martin is behind all of this." Nora started to speak, but I waved her off. "Listen. His dad's missing and declared dead, and he'll probably get money from that once you've gone through the legalities. Teresa has to remain married to him for the next seven years before she can escape with her inheritance, but if she conveniently 'disappears' as well, Martin might get that fortune too. All I can say is his sister needs to watch her back." I aimed a finger at Nora to make my point. "And you can't tell me Teresa would actually want Chuckles to stay here. I think that's all part of Martin's plan."

Nora stared at me for a moment. "You know, you're making sense in an odd way." She pulled me away from the door and down the front steps, lowering her voice. "Let's say you're right. How do we approach this now? I was all set to talk about Martin and how we should be contacting the police."

"And that's another thing. Calling you might have been the only way Teresa was able to get the word out. I'll bet that numbskull in there is listening in on all her calls."

"Or maybe he's got her cell phone." Nora shook her head. "I keep saying a planet without men would be a step in the right direction."

"Even Marcus?" I teased. "I can't imagine you going more than a day or two without having a man on the string, pal."

"Whatever." She poked her tongue out at me. "Let's get back in there and see if we can figure out what's really going on. You've got my brain in a spin right now."

The door was yanked open with a force strong enough to fling it back against the wall, revealing a glowering Chuckles. "Teresa says the coffee's ready."

"How kind," Nora drawled, the sardonic tone as thick as molasses and deceptively sweet. "In the meantime, *dear*, could you tell us why you're here? Shouldn't you be looking for your employer? Or staying at your own place and not mooching off a defenseless woman?"

"It's none of our business, you old bag." He started toward us and then halted as if reconsidering. Maybe he'd rather we come inside so no one would see us being pummeled by those big hands.

"Oh, I think it *is* my business," Nora shot back, all pretense of sweetness gone. "I'm the executor of Martin's father's will, and depending on how long I want to make a legal fuss, I can hold up any money or property he might be entitled to receive." She moved closer to Chuckles and poked him in the chest with the tip of one long nail. "And that, smarty-pants, means your salary. Capiche?"

"Let's have that coffee now, shall we?" I needed to diffuse this blossoming argument before it came to blows, especially since I knew who'd be on the receiving end. "Teresa's waiting for us, Nora."

The combatants both stared at me as if I'd magically appeared, and I smiled weakly at them. If this encounter escalated, there would be no way for me to stop it. Grabbing my best friend by her arm, I steered both of us around Chuckles and toward the kitchen.

"Don't antagonize him," I hissed in her ear as we moved away from the front door. "He might have some information that could help."

"Not if he's in on the plan as well, as you seem to think." Nora jerked her arm from my grasp and gingerly rubbed it. "You've got quite a grip there, Sis."

"And it's a good thing, too. If you'd kept getting in that man's face, there might not be much left of you." I sniffed appreciatively as we entered the bright kitchen. "That smells wonderful, Teresa. Thanks for making it for us."

Teresa was sitting at the kitchen table, a cafetière and several coffee mugs before her. With a wan smile, she indicated we should join her. As I sat down, I examined her face closely. What I saw was a woman whose sleep wasn't restful and who appeared to have more on her mind than brewing the perfect pot of coffee.

"I'm glad you stopped by." Teresa busied herself pouring the coffee. "There's sugar in the bowl and creamer in the fridge, if you want any."

She kept her gaze down as she ran one finger around the rim of her coffee mug. She either had something to share with us or nothing at all to say. I fervently hoped it was the former. I had questions waiting to be asked, and I was sure she had the answers.

"I want creamer. No, don't get up." Nora motioned Teresa to remain seated. "I can get it."

I sipped the fragrant brew and thought about the various tables I'd been at lately, drinking coffee and talking about Nora's current situation. I wondered how Herc was getting along with Max and Doc and smiled to myself. He was most likely in hog heaven—or dog heaven, in this case. I'd have to find a way to thank Roger for taking on the task.

I must have blushed at the thought. Nora glanced at me as she sat back down, cocking her head in curiosity. "What's on your mind?" When I didn't answer, she grinned knowingly. "Ah, it's gotta be a certain retired dentist."

"I was thinking about Herc," I said haughtily. "I miss him."

"Yeah, and my last name's Astor." She chuckled and turned to Teresa, who was looking at me with a quizzical expression. "Gwen's got a beau, and he's watching her dog Herc right now. I'm guessing that one thought led to another. Right?" She leaned over and nudged my arm.

I ignored her. Instead, I set the mug down and faced Teresa. As long as I had her attention, I might as well take advantage of it.

"We think you might be in some kind of trouble." I leaned forward slightly, lowering my voice. "Is there anything we can do to help?"

She stared at me, eyes widening at my words. "I–I don't know what you're talking about. It's not me who's in trouble. It's my missing husband." Her eyes abruptly filled with tears, and she lowered her head.

Nora and I exchanged looks, and I shrugged.

"I think what Gwen is trying to say is we're concerned about why your husband's personal bodyguard is still hanging around." Nora took a sip of coffee. "I know Zeke is normally the one with him, but this Chuckles character is bad news as well."

"I can't get rid of him." Teresa looked up, her face full of desperation. "I don't know what to do, to be honest. I keep thinking he'll help me find Martin, but…" She lifted both shoulders and let them drop. "You saw what he did to my poor baby." She leaned closer. "He said he'll do the same to me if I go to the police."

I shot Nora a triumphant look. This neatly dovetailed into my theory that Martin's bodyguards knew something. I maintained that "something" was that he wasn't missing, just conveniently out of the picture so Teresa could become the true victim.

"Teresa," I began firmly, "I think you need to come with us when we leave. You could be in danger. In fact, I don't think your husband is missing at all. I'm fairly certain he's orchestrating your demise."

To my surprise, Teresa began to laugh, a hysterical sound that filled the space between us. The small dog sitting on her lap began to bark sharply, and she gently shushed it.

"I think I need to tell you that I've convinced Chuckles to be a sort of 'double agent.' I figured I needed someone on the inside, so to speak, to keep me informed about Martin's cheating ways." She shook her head. "It's like he's determined to run through as much of my money as humanly possible, and I can't let that happen."

"So, let's get this straight." Nora had apparently recovered more quickly than I had, and now I saw both her incredulity and her anger. "Everything you just told us about Chuckles threatening you is a lie? What kind of game are you playing?"

"It's not a game." Teresa's voice was as eerily calm as if we were discussing the weather. "It's called survival. You have no idea how awful it is living with your son—"

"My ex-stepson," Nora interrupted coldly.

"Fine. Your 'ex-stepson.'" She gave the word air quotes. "His dad was just as bad. I'm glad they're both gone, to be honest. Now I just have to wait to get Martin declared dead, and I'm home free."

"But what about your dog?" I couldn't get my focus off the small pooch. "Why did he need to muzzle it?"

"You know Chuckles." Teresa's expression was resigned, and her mouth drooped into a pout as if emphasizing just how victimized she felt. "I only got it to bug Martin. Since he's not around anymore, well…"

I shot Nora a quick glance. She lifted one eyebrow slightly in response. Just how did Teresa think we "knew" Chuckles? And why did she seem so blasé about the current predicament? Maybe she was taking something to help her cope and it was making her compliant.

And maybe she wasn't as concerned about her husband's disappearance as I'd thought. I was losing my ability to read people, something I'd always prided myself on. It had certainly helped me in the classroom and when dealing with parents.

"Is there something else you're not telling us?" Nora seemed to have caught on as well. Good for her.

"About what?" Teresa gave a short laugh. "You mean do I have any more surprises up my sleeve?" She mimed peeking inside the lose robe and gave Nora a mocking smile. "Nope. Nothing else to hide. I'm just a woman who's glad her ball and chain of a husband isn't around to pester her. For all I care, he can stay missing."

"Wait a minute. You called us, remember?" Now Nora was working up a temper.

I couldn't blame her. In fact, I was angry myself. No one liked being manipulated, especially when it required making a long car trip and being served a squirrel dinner.

"I think we've done all we can here." I took another sip of coffee and stood. "Let's get over to the meeting place and then head for home. I'm rather anxious to shake the dust of Seattle off my feet."

"I completely agree, Sis. And I say the sooner, the better."

At the kitchen door, I turned around. "By the way, Teresa, don't be shocked if you get a visit from the local SPCA."

I'd never been one for using the proverbial parting shot, mostly because I usually thought of what to say long after I was gone. And I didn't wait for a response. My gut was telling me to run before one of them decided to stop us.

Back in the car, belted in, doors locked, and motor running, I finally calmed down enough to remind Nora to text Marcus.

"Let him know this entire trip was a waste. We should be at the restaurant in less than twenty minutes."

"Already on it." Nora's nails were busy tapping out a message on her cell. "I'd better include Rachel and Brent in the text as well or that kid'll bug the heck out of Marcus until he finds out what's going on."

"That kid" was Brent. Reticence wasn't one of his strong suits. I put the car in gear, and off we went, leaving behind a very selfish woman who'd managed to fool me but good. I sincerely hoped Martin would turn up today, safe and sound, and ready to stick out the remainder of his marriage agreement with her. She deserved nothing less.

Chapter 18

"I love eating at a buffet." Brent worked his way down the line of food. "I don't know why my mom doesn't take us to one more often."

"I'd say it's because they've been tossed out of every buffet in the Portland area," Nora murmured in my ear as we filled our plates with the various aromatic dishes. "If I owned one and saw that boy coming back for fifths and sixths, I'd ban him for life."

"At least he appreciates his food." I used a pair of metal tongs to snag a spring roll. "I just hope he doesn't get car sick."

"If he doesn't, I might." Nora glanced over at Brent's overflowing plate and made a face. "How one person can eat all of that is beyond me."

The red Naugahyde of the booth made a series of hissing noises as the five of us settled into our seats. A half-moon design grouped us around a laminated table, the years of service apparent in its marred surface. It was clean, though, and the food smelled absolutely delicious. Of course, anything smelled good after last night's debacle of a meal.

Finally, I sighed and pushed away my plate. If I ate any more, I'd need to find a corner in which to nap. Nora had done something like that, letting her head fall over on Marcus's shoulder. I gave her a sympathetic look. If Roger had been there, I might have done the same.

"I keep thinking," Nora said drowsily, "that Martin is probably under our noses. I can't imagine anyone taking him anywhere far away, unless he orchestrated it himself. Or that weird wife of his did it."

"He could be on a beach someone, soaking up some rays and having cocktails delivered by a bikini-wearing waitress." I reached for my glass of iced water and drank. There was something in Chinese food that always made me incredibly thirsty. "Or he really could be in trouble, if not lying dead somewhere."

Nora lifted her head and blinked blearily. "And you'd never know it by looking at the bimbo wife of his, would you." She snorted in disgust. "What a piece of work."

"Do you think she's got that thing that kidnap victims get when they begin to identify with their captors?" Rachel snapped her fingers. "Stockholm Syndrome. I think that's what it is."

That made me pause. I hadn't considered that. I looked at Nora, a feeling of unease rising.

"Bah." She shot down the suggestion. "If anything, I'd say she has a case of the 'me me me' syndrome."

"I don't know about syndromes, but there's definitely something weird going on here." Marcus looked around the table, his expression serious. "Not one person gave us anything even vaguely helpful, and all the videotapes were conveniently wiped clean."

"And one of them told us that the police had already asked them the same things so they didn't have anything new to add." Rachel took a sip from her iced-water glass, her eyes thoughtful. "I think that one kid does have information, though. He was clearly nervous when we showed up."

"Are you talking about Caleb? Sort of thin and a mop of hair he's constantly pushing out of his eyes?" I asked.

"Yes, that's the one." Rachel nodded, pushing her water glass away. "I think if we can get him by himself, we'll get useful info out of him. I'll bet he knows Martin is involved in criminal activity"

I agreed, but I couldn't help it: I was beginning to feel goose bumps.

Despite the heavy conversation at the restaurant, the drive back to Portland was fairly pleasant if you didn't count the various burps and belches coming from the back seat. Marcus and Brent had eaten their fill and then some, and the food was insisting on a return visit. Nora had fallen asleep almost as soon as we'd left the restaurant's parking lot, and my passengers in the back seat soon followed suit.

I was trying to make a solid connection between Martin's disappearance, his dry-cleaning business, the wacky marriage agreement with Teresa, and Nora's position as the executor for her ex-husband's will. The more I looked at the big picture, the more I understood that this entire fiasco began with that letter from Ione's law office.

I sighed, put my foot down on the accelerator, and steered for home. It was all too convoluted for me to find a common thread. Maybe if I ran my thoughts past Nora, she'd be able to help me find that connection. In the meantime, I'd enjoy the view as I drove.

The steep hillsides were thickly covered in trees. From the smoky blue of balsams to the deeper greens of Douglas firs, the landscape was a lovely contrast to the clear blue skies overhead. We had more days with fog and rain than not during the year, but the mid-summer months could be picture-perfect. I cracked my window and inhaled the scent of pine.

"Do you have to sniff so loudly?" Nora stirred in the front seat, groaning as she moved her neck from side to side. "That's so annoying."

"And good afternoon to you too, sleeping beauty." I glanced quickly at the rearview mirror. The other three were still out for the count. "As soon as your brain catches up, I have something I want to run past you."

"Hilarious." She sat up straight and rubbed her stomach. "I can't believe I'm hungry again already."

"Chinese food can do that to you." I was beginning to feel the stirrings of hunger pangs as well, but I wasn't going to admit it. "Listen, about the will. Do you see any connection between it and Martin's disappearance?"

"Between the will and Martin? Besides his inheritance?" She turned in my direction, and I heard the question in her voice. "That's all that jumps out at me."

"That's one thing, certainly." I rolled up my window to cut the noise from the road. "I wonder who'll get his share if he remains gone or is eventually found dead."

"His sister, of course." She hesitated a moment. "This is beginning to sound like my ex-husband all over again."

"You mean the 'missing, declared dead' aspect?"

"Yes. Exactly. And I wonder just how much Merry is involved in his life." Nora let the name hang there a moment. "Makes me wonder how close she and Teresa are."

I looked at her and then back at the road. "Do you think they could be in on this together? I mean with Martin?"

Nora shrugged. "Why not? Sometimes money means more than people, even if it is your husband."

"Or your brother," I said grimly. "For that matter, I wonder what they know about your ex-husband's disappearance."

"Wait." Nora swiveled completely around to face me, her voice incredulous. "Are you thinking Merry might be the one behind both disappearances?"

It was my turn to shrug. "She's the only one with direct connections to both men, right? And she possibly stands to gain from both." I tapped my fingers on the steering wheel, thinking. "Do you remember what she inherits from her dad?"

"Sure. Half of everything, and her brother's share if he..." Nora's voiced halted in midsentence. "No. No way. I can't picture that mealy-mouthed girl turning into a cold-blooded killer." She drew her brows together in thought. "On the other hand, there's another woman with a connection to both Martin and the Bottomless Pitt." When I didn't bite, she added almost impatiently, "Martin's wife. She's right in the thick of things, if you ask me."

"You said money means more to some folks than relationships do." I turned on my right blinker and exited the freeway. "And if he had a lot of money, Merry might not want to share with her brother. The same probably goes for Teresa."

"Yikes." Nora turned around and stared out the windshield. "So, when he was declared dead and the will began moving through the system, it basically sealed Martin's fate." She slowly shook her head. "I just can't see Teresa being involved for the money, though. She's got plenty of her own."

"I don't know that for a fact, but it does make sense." I turned left at the end of the exit ramp, nearly rear-ending a slow-moving car. "It's the pedal on the right," I muttered as I pulled out and passed the car. Glancing to my right, I caught a glimpse of an old woman, both hands firmly clamped on the steering wheel, her nose barely above the dash. "There should be an age restriction on driving."

"Or a height restriction." Brent was awake. "Hey, Miss F., remember when I was talking about that TV show you need to watch?" He didn't give me a chance to respond but babbled on. "Well, I thought of another one, and it's called *Buried in the Obvious Spot*, and it's all about people who get killed by their loved ones and then buried right behind their house and—"

"Hold up there, motormouth." Nora twisted around to face Brent. "Do you ever take a breath?"

"Well, duh, Mrs. G." I watched in the mirror while he stuck out his chest in a parody of inhaling. "I'm breathing all the time, except when I'm asleep."

"Oh, dear lord." Nora let her head fall back against the neck rest. "Brent, do you really think you stop breathing when you sleep? Really?"

"How do I know? I'm not awake when I'm sleeping." He sounded so proud of his logic that all I could do was laugh. Serious or not, he had the ability to make me chuckle.

"Getting back to the show." I interrupted this exchange before it went any further. "Do you watch a lot of true-crime programs?"

Brent nodded vigorously. "Sure do. Me and Rachel like watching how they find a body and solve the murder. Kinda like you and Mrs. G., only you don't really solve anything, you just find the bodies. Well, at least you did one time," he amended. "Does that still count?"

Nora and I exchanged amused looks.

"Absolutely it does," Nora assured him. "And was there any particular reason why you brought up this program about burying someone behind a house?"

"Yep." He answered without hesitation. "Me and Rachel—well, and Aggie too—were talking about that missing guy in Seattle, and we think he's buried by his house."

"Brent, how in the world do you know that? Did you see a grave?" Nora's voice was light, but I had an abrupt chill as goose bumps again broke out along my arms. Premonition or temperature dip? I glanced up at the sky, and it was still as blue and cloudless as it had been minutes before. My suspicions about Chuckles and Zeke, however, just shot up from a five to a ten.

"Maybe." Brent leaned forward, his voice excited, and I angled the rearview mirror in order to see his face. "All you need is a bunch of yard work going on. That's a great cover for planting a body six feet down. You just gotta stick a tree or something on top, and you're home free." He settled back again, his expression as proud as if he'd discovered buried treasure.

A quick look at Nora showed me she was as concerned as I was. In that weird connected way that best friends sometimes had, we exchanged a glance that spoke volumes. This was definitely a topic to be explored later, and definitely more fully.

I gave her a brief nod before turning my attention back to the road.

After dropping off Marcus at his office and Brent and Rachel at her house, I turned to Nora and raised an eyebrow in question. "My place or yours?"

"Better be mine. If we go to yours, that dentist is gonna turn up, you can mark my words." She gave me a sassy wink and then laughed. "I'm not saying that's a bad thing, but we need to talk about this newest theory."

"And from Brent, of all people." I decided to let the dentist comment slide. "Do you think it's feasible?"

Nora pursed her lips. "Maybe. It makes as much sense as anything so far. And quite honestly, it could explain Teresa's change of attitude."

"You think she did it?" I couldn't help the astonishment in my voice. "Surely not."

"No, no, that's not what I mean. I think she's found out what those two clowns did to him, and she's playing along so she doesn't join him in a dirt nap."

"Do you think we could get Teresa on her own, at least enough for a quick talk? We need to see if that's really what's going on." I neatly pulled my car up to the curb beside Nora's luxury apartment building and shut off the engine. "Guess we're going back to Seattle."

"I'd better call Fern and see if she's got room for us." Nora gave me a wry smile. "It might make more sense to rent a room from her on a monthly basis, as often as we seem to be there."

Once we were in her apartment, I sank down on one of her overstuffed sofas and kicked off my sandals. Wiggling my toes, I sighed and leaned back against the cushions, briefly closing my eyes. "I sure could use a coffee."

"I can take a hint." Nora's stilettos landed next to my Birkenstocks as she headed for the kitchen. "I might have some leftover apple strudel, if you're interested."

"Silly question. Can you heat it up, please?"

"Come in here and do it yourself, woman. I'm busy making your coffee."

I grumbled my way into the kitchen, muttering something about not being the one who lived there, but I knew my way around her kitchen almost as well as I did my own. I found the strudel, cut a large slice for each of us, and microwaved them until I could see the filling beginning to bubble. Carefully plating them without burning my fingers, I set them on the kitchen table and waited for the coffee.

"This sure beats the coffee we had at Uncle Charlie's." I slid a full mug closer. "Brent didn't bother emptying the old coffee grounds before brewing the next pot."

"Sounds like the entire family has issues when it comes to all things culinary." Nora shuddered. "I thought I was going to pass out when I realized what we'd been given for dinner."

I held up a hand and let it drop weakly. "Let's not go there, all right? My stomach is just beginning to settle."

"We can check that off our bucket list, I guess." Nora chuckled and reached for a fork before cutting a bite of apple strudel.

I couldn't find the humor at that moment, however, and my stomach was beginning to make that odd gurgling noise that indicated bad times ahead. Pushing my plate away, I focused instead on the coffee. At least I knew what was in my cup, a freshly ground blend Nora bought at The Friendly Bean.

Or was it? I abruptly set it down and stared at the steaming liquid. Exactly what was this made of?

I had to bring these thoughts to a screeching halt or I'd be condemned to growing my own food, buying a cow, and picking my own coffee beans, not to mention preparing homemade dog food for Herc.

"Hey, you okay there, Sis? You're looking kinda green." Nora's face was filled with concern a she leaned toward me. "Maybe you're coming down with the flu."

I jumped off the train of thought chugging through my brain and smiled, albeit faintly. "I'm fine. I just don't want to think about...about certain food anymore."

"You've got it." Nora pushed my plate back in front of me. "Take of bite of this. That'll cleanse your palate."

It did. Just to make sure, though, I had another piece.

Before I left for home, we'd made a plan to return to Seattle. "We need to say it's for rest and relaxation purposes." I took the final bite of strudel. "We'd better not mention Seattle, though. We could tell everyone we're headed to that new resort near Mount Hood, the one that features hot stone massages."

"Why lie?" Nora carried our plates to the sink. "Let's really go there first and then make a detour up to Washington."

"Not on my retirement I can't. And this last check from our pet valet business went straight to my rainy-day fund."

"Oh, we'll call it 'business expenses for corporate bonding' and put it on the books." Nora casually brushed aside my monetary concerns as she walked me to the front door. "We need it, after all we've been through lately."

* * * *

Needless to say, the resort was amazing. No, it was more than amazing. It was fantabulous, a word I learned from Brent. There really were hot stone massages—my first—and the food was beyond perfect. I decided vegan could be a viable way to eat and mentioned this to Nora as I sipped an almond milk smoothie.

"You'd have to give up Voodoo Doughnuts." She waved a forked at me, a piece of grilled zucchini trembling on the tines. "They have animal products in them." She took a large mouthful of veggies and chewed thoughtfully. "And even if they do make a vegan doughnut, it won't taste the same."

"You're probably right." I set my smoothie down and frowned at it as if the fault lay with the creamy drink. "Why do animals taste so good?"

The overly tanned, overly thin woman at the next table turned and glared at me. At least I thought she glared. Her forehead moved slightly, and her eyes narrowed. I added "overly Botoxed" to her description as I smiled brightly at her before looking back at Nora.

"Let's take this stuff to go. We need to get to Puget Sound before Fern turns in for the evening."

* * * *

Fern was as welcoming as before and seemed delighted to see us.

"I've just made a pot of chamomile lavender tea." She ushered us inside and closed the door behind us. "Why don't you take your luggage to your room and then join me in the kitchen."

"Sounds good." I smiled at her gratefully and headed for the stairs. Winding down from the drive with a cup of herbal tea was exactly what I needed.

Fern's kitchen was as warm and inviting as ever. Pulling out one of her eclectically designed chairs, I sank down gratefully and watched Fern pour the steaming golden liquid into a hand-thrown pottery mug.

"You would love the place Nora and I visited earlier today." I took the mug from her with a smile. "It's completely natural, using no animal products whatever in their treatments and food. And I have to say the smoothie I had was really tasty."

"You say that like you're surprised," Fern chuckled. "I've subscribed to that lifestyle for nearly thirty years now." She glanced around at her kitchen, a satisfied expression on her face. "I've never regretted the decision either. I feel amazing, and I'm contributing to a cleaner environment as well."

I nodded and sipped the herbal tea. I'd miss bacon-wrapped chicken breasts and the occasional burger too much, but more power to Fern and those who shared her convictions.

When my fellow carnivore strolled into the room, trailing the scent of an expensive face wash, my thoughts turned from food choices to family issues. We were here to do more digging about Martin, and some of that might be literal.

"That smells good, Fern. Is there enough for me?" Nora plopped into the chair next to me and sighed loudly.

"Absolutely." Fern smiled and handed her a full mug. "Enjoy."

I waited until Nora had swallowed a mouthful of tea before I spoke. "We need to decide if we want to go out there this evening or early tomorrow morning."

"Yeah, about that." Nora set the mug down carefully, her gaze fixed on it as if expecting it to dance across the table. "I've been thinking we should ask permission to dig around in the backyard."

I stared at her, flabbergasted. "Ask *permission*? Nora, if they did it, they're not going to let Teresa give us the okay." I was careful not to mention the names of the two bodyguards in front of Fern. The less she knew, the better it would be. "I thought we were in agreement."

We needed to be able to poke around the house's property. I was certain that if there had been any funny business, aka a body buried there, we'd be able to see disturbed ground. And now Nora was getting cold feet.

Chapter 19

"We're not going to get all the answers we need until we pay another visit to Teresa," I pointed out. "So far, all we have are a handful of suspicions, nothing the police will take as gospel truth."

"Maybe. Maybe not." Nora narrowed her eyes as she stared at the ceiling, and I could almost hear the wheels turning and the puzzle pieces locking into place. Finally, she looked at me and gave a brusque nod. "Okay. You've got a deal. Let's get back over to that wannabe mansion and do some serious digging. In fact," she stood, "there's no time like the present."

"Finish your tea first. We both could use a little grounding right now." I took a final drink of the chamomile lavender tea and smiled at Fern. "That was delicious. And it tasted just like lavender smells, if that makes sense."

"It sure does." Fern stood and grabbed the apron on the back of her chair. "I'm making a batch of my famous zucchini muffins. And I'm in for the rest of the evening, so don't worry about being locked out." She walked with us to the front door, the apron enveloping her from neck to knees. "Listen to your gut reactions, gals, and get out of there if something doesn't feel right. Let someone else be the hero, okay?"

"You bet. I plan on being around for a long time." I gave her a reassuring smile. "We'll go there, take a look around the yard, and be back before you know it." I looked at the sky. "Besides, it'll be completely dark soon."

Nora waggled her manicured fingers at Fern as we stepped off the front porch and walked to the car. "Maybe we ought to do some type of exercise as well." She patted her perfectly flat stomach and gave an exaggerated grimace. "I swear all this food is going straight to my belly."

"And where else should it go, goofball? Your leg?" I shot Fern my "see what I have to put with?" look, and she gave me a commiserating smile. Why did thin people always complain about the amount of food they consumed? "Let's focus on this one task so we can get back here and feed that stomach of yours."

"Someone got up on the bossy side of the bed today." Nora's words were punctuated with a quick squeeze around my nearly nonexistent waistline. "Don't worry, Fern. We'll be back before that first batch of muffins has time to cool."

With another wave and a smile, Fern shut the door behind us. I slid a sidelong glance at Nora and was surprised to see worry lines forming around her mouth and eyes. Was she nervous about approaching Teresa at her house? I fastened my seat belt, giving it an extra tug.

"We've already done this, so it's not anything new." I put the car in DRIVE and pulled onto the quiet street. "The only person we really need to worry about is Zeke."

"I'm not thinking about that, silly." Nora shifted in her seat and then fished out her cell phone from her shirt front and peered at the small screen. "I'm waiting for a text from Marcus."

"Another lover's tiff?"

"No. He's looking into something for me. For us, really." Before I could ask what in the world she was talking about, she slid the phone back into her top. "I asked him to look into Teresa's background."

"Teresa?" I risked a glance across at her before turning back to the road. "Why? She's as much a victim as your ex-husband, at least in my opinion."

"And I'm not saying she isn't, Sis. It's just that—oh, I don't know. I keep thinking Zeke is holding something over her head, something that might help us discover what really happened to Martin's dad."

"Holding something over her head?" I was well and truly puzzled. "Like what? I can't think of anything."

"That's why I asked Marcus to do some digging. If there's anything to find, he will."

"Ah. I see." I couldn't think of anything else to say, and I needed to focus on my driving.

As often as I'd been in the Seattle area lately, I was still uneasy with the layout of the town and its suburbs. And as crazy as it was to drive in Portland, at least I knew my way around.

The driveway was deserted when we pulled up to the gate at Martin and Teresa's house. I hesitated a moment, glancing at Nora for direction. "Should we try the buzzer?" I motioned toward the drive and the side garage, whose open doors showed empty bays where Teresa and Martin's cars normally parked. "Maybe we should've called before driving out here."

Nora's chest began buzzing, and she reached inside her top again. "Maybe this is Marcus. Hang on while I check this."

"I swear I'm going to get you one of those nerdy phone belt clips."

Watching her fish around inside her shirt while in public was a tad embarrassing.

"And where would I put something like that, if I might ask?" Without waiting for an answer, she abruptly pumped the air with one fist. "Aha! Just what I thought."

"About what? Teresa?"

She nodded with a look of triumph. "I just knew something was up with those two."

This was beginning to feel as though I was talking to a brick wall.

"Nora, for goodness sake." I slammed my hands on the steering wheel and winced at the sting. "Who are you talking about?"

"Zeke and Teresa, that's who." Sliding the phone back into her carrying case, aka her Wonderbra, she smiled widely and pointed to the gate buzzer. "Hit that thing already. If either one is home, they've got a lot of explaining to do."

I wanted to point out that Teresa might be out searching for Martin and that Zeke could be with her. If Roger was missing, I know I wouldn't be able to sit around the house and wait for someone else to find him. Whether she loved him or not, I couldn't understand Teresa's blasé attitude toward a missing husband. With a tiny shrug, I pressed the call button with one finger, not expecting to hear anyone on the other end of the speaker.

"What now?" Zeke's unmistakable voice crackled through the speaker, causing me to jump in my seat. "We don't want to talk to you two old ladies any more. And isn't it kinda late in the day for you two to be out?"

"Tough lug nuts, oatmeal brains." Nora leaned across me and yelled into the speaker. "Open these gate right now or I'm calling the police."

A bark of laughter burst from the speaker. "This is private property. What can the SPD do?"

"You're right about the private property part, numbskull. It happens to belong to me. Now open the gate before I—"

With a protesting groan, it began to swing open. I nosed my car between the two sides of the wrought-iron gate and moved up the graveled drive, parking in front of the empty garage. Behind us, the gate slowly creaked back into place. If this was a bad idea, it was a bit too late to worry.

I cut off the engine, and we sat in silence for a moment, the clicking of the still-warm motor the only sound. Not even the yapping of Teresa's dog could be heard, and Zeke was nowhere to be seen. I spotted a few bags of mulch stacked at the side of the house and several potted trees waiting to be planted. Brent's words came back as loudly as if he'd been speaking in my ear. An uncomfortable feeling started working its way across my scalp and down my spine.

"Shouldn't someone have come out to meet us?" I shifted in my seat to face Nora. She was peering at the windows, her forehead wrinkled with concern. "What are you thinking?"

"The same thing as you. Something's not right here." Nora slipped the cell phone out once more, a finger poised over the screen. "Should I call the police?"

"I have no clue." I unclipped my seat belt. "But sitting here won't get us an answer." I opened the car door and motioned toward the house. "Keep that phone handy, just in case."

In case of *what* I wasn't sure. And I didn't know if I really wanted to find out, to be honest. We were here, though, so it would be a wasted trip if we didn't at least take a peek in the backyard. First, however, I wanted to double-check and make sure we weren't walking into a trap.

"Well, let's do this." I got out of the car and waited until Nora joined me. I hooked an arm through hers and all but pulled her along with me to the front door. This bothered me more than the odd non-greeting, especially since Nora never shirked from confrontations.

"I don't know about you, Sis, but I'd rather be eating a zucchini muffin right about now." Taking in a deep breath, Nora reached out and punched the doorbell. "If Lurch's brother hurries up and opens this door, we can hotfoot it right back out of here."

The door was abruptly wrenched open, and to my surprise, Teresa stood there, fluffy pooch cradled in her arms. Her expression was as sour as unsweetened lemonade and twice as bitter. Something had her upset, and I had a gut feeling it might have been us.

"Zeke said you two were here again. What do you want this time?" Her eyes, once so friendly and confiding, were now two laser beams of dislike bouncing between Nora and me.

I wisely said nothing but gave Nora a jab with my elbow. She was already wound up, however, and didn't need any help from me to get started.

"Oh, just call this a friendly visit from your landlord, sweetie." Pushing past a now-scowling Teresa, Nora walked into the entryway and beckoned for me to follow.

I gave an apologetic shrug and walked inside. We'd get this over and done with as quickly as I could push Nora and then never come back again. I hoped.

"Wait. Hold up, you two." Teresa's voice was as harsh as the sunlight streaming through the skylight in the entryway. "Whaddya mean, 'landlord'?"

Nora swung around, the crystals on her bright pink Jimmy Choo stilettos winking in the sunlight. "I don't stutter. I mean exactly what I said." She made a grand gesture, indicating the house around her. "I own this. Every last foot. It's in the will."

I'd read about a person's expression becoming dark but had always thought it was simply a figure of speech. Teresa's carefully made-up face became infused with a rage so palpable it took on a life of its own. I backed away from her as quickly as I could—and straight into the steroid-plumped arms of Zeke.

This visit wasn't going the way I'd foreseen. And when Chuckles—he of the stiletto to the groin, courtesy of Nora—appeared as well, I knew the two of us were toast.

Grabbing Nora by the arms, Chuckles reached down and roughly removed Nora's heels. "Better safe than sorry, right?"

I watched in horror as he none-too-gently pitched the two shoes through an open doorway just off the foyer. Nora, however, didn't take kindly to this and gave Chuckles a backward donkey kick with all the force she could muster. I groaned inwardly. Making the situation worse wasn't a smart move.

Chuckles, it seemed, was prepared for something like that and easily stepped to one side. Wrenching Nora's arms behind her, he nodded at me. "Zeke, watch that one. You never know with these old ladies."

"I am not an old lady," I said hotly. "And you, you watch your mouth. What would your mother say? Or your grandmother?"

"Nothing, since they're both dead. Get her shoes too, Zeke." Chuckles, a scowl on his broad face, turned to Teresa. "Whaddya want us to do with these two?"

Teresa's gaze slowly ran over Nora and me, one carefully shaped eyebrow quirked in derision. "I want to say I don't care because I really don't, but I suppose we've got to do something with these two until I get my hands on that money." She turned to Zeke. "How's the other prisoner?"

Nora and I exchanged a worried glance. *Other* prisoner? Did she mean *Martin*?

"Guess I should get over there and check on him." Zeke leaned down and yanked my Birkenstocks from my feet and tossed them in the same direction Nora's shoes had gone. "Can you handle these two?"

Chuckles nodded. "Sure thing. Pass her over."

With a rough shove, I was pushed into Nora. Before I could recover, though, Chuckles pinioned both of my wrists in one hand. The man was as strong as an ox.

A silence fell as Zeke left, slamming the front door behind him. Teresa, who'd watched him leave, with a smirk, leaned over and set the dog on the floor. With a toss of her head, she said, "Let's see what we can get out of these two before we offer them a permanent place to stay." She motioned to Nora, the sneer broadening into a wicked smile. "Oh, I almost forgot. Check them for cell phones, would you?"

Without a word, Chuckles ran a rough hand over me, making me feel as grubby as the bottom of my sandals. Finding nothing, he dropped my hands and did the same to Nora. When he reached her chest, a wide grin split his face. With a flourish, he reached inside her top and extracted the cell phone.

"Here ya go." He tossed it toward Teresa, who caught it with a deft hand.

"So sorry, but I can't let you keep this." Dropping the phone on the floor, she stamped as hard as she could. Sharp pieces of plastic and glass shot across the floor, scattering like buckshot.

"You're not going to get away with anything." Nora's voice was as cold as I'd ever heard it before, and an icy shiver snaked its way down my back.

Teresa wouldn't hesitate to shut Nora up, and I had a feeling she'd planned to do exactly that.

This woman wasn't the person I'd been convinced she was. In fact, she'd been playing possum all this time, making me feel sorry for her. She'd gone from victim to bully so quickly my head was spinning.

Chapter 20

There was a brief moment of complete silence before Teresa threw back her head and roared with laughter. Nora and I exchanged confused looks, unsure of what had just happened.

"Did I miss the joke?" I murmured.

Nora made a tiny movement with one shoulder. "If you did, I did too."

Teresa, her face flushed with amusement, stepped closer to the pair of us, one finger crooked as though inviting us into her bedroom.

Will you walk into my parlor? said the spider to the fly.

Or flies, in this case. Nora lifted one bare foot, as if stepping forward, but I quickly grabbed her wrist.

"Stay right here." I spoke calmly, surprising even myself. My heart had begun a rumba against my ribs, and Nora's equally rapid pulse beat beneath my fingers. "Teresa, I don't know what you're thinking, but neither one of us is going with you. In fact," I added with a boldness I wasn't feeling, "we're leaving. Now."

Teresa gave a deep sigh, as if I'd said something disappointing. With a gesture to something behind us, she turned to leave.

Chuckles marched us across the room, his grip making my wrists burn. What was this thug doing here anyway? Wasn't he on Martin's payroll too? What in the world was going on here? First Zeke, now Chuckles. Who else was cozying up to Teresa?

"Move it." He gave me a not-too-gentle push in the small of my back. "You too, granny."

Beside me, Nora gave a disgusted snort. "I am *not* a granny, you idiot with birdseed for brains." She twitched her hips and straightened her shoulders, glaring back at him. "Not to mention you must be as blind as a bat."

Chuckles grunted, shoving Nora ahead of him and causing her to stumble. Maybe she wasn't comfortable walking without her heels. I peeked at my own bare feet. It really wasn't much different than walking around in Birkenstock sandals.

Teresa sat in a faux sixties armchair, legs crossed, looking as relaxed as if this were a planned visit. Nora and I were shoved onto the rather stiff leather couch that faced her. Chuckles sat in the matching armchair near Teresa, leaning forward, hands dangling between his knees. He gave me the impression of someone sitting on a coiled spring, ready to leap into action at a second's notice.

"So, gals," Teresa's voice held a note of amusement that mirrored the expression on her face. "What brings you back to this neck of the woods? Figuratively, of course." She glanced out of the large picture window that stretched along one side of the room. The view was magnificent, her extensive gardens spreading toward the green lawn that encircled the entire house. "Come to see me? Or to see something else?" Her voice hardened with this last comment.

I shifted closer to Nora, the movement seeming to not escape the fixed stare of the man who was clearly now Teresa's sidekick. He made a small movement of his own, as if to rise, but one quick gesture from Teresa stilled him.

The woman could have been a master dog trainer.

"We've come to uncover the reason behind the death of my ex-husband." Nora's voice was chilly. I couldn't read her face, but her eyes were as cold as the Columbia River in winter. "I won't say 'disappearance,' because it's clear to the both of us he's dead."

Teresa stared straight at Nora, her gaze unwavering under the accusation. "Am I to assume your comment is directed to me?"

"You can assume all your little heart desires." Nora was building up a full head of verbal steam and was in her conversational element. "In fact, I have a question for you. Been doing any 'gardening' lately?" She quirked her fingers in air quotes, and I groaned inwardly. This was turning into a full-blown war.

"*How* could you—*when* did you—? Chuckles, take care of them. *Now.*" Teresa's face twisted into an ugly version of itself, two bright red circles high on her cheeks. "Get these two out of my sight."

Chuckles sprang to his feet and motioned for Nora and me to stand as well. "You heard her. Move it."

"Fine by me." Nora tossed her head and pointed one manicured finger at Teresa. "This isn't over by a long shot, chica."

"Ha." Teresa gave a short laugh that sounded anything but amused. "I'd say for you it's already over. Right, Chuckles?"

"Whatever you say, Teresa. You're the boss."

I didn't like the way this was going. We were herded down the stairs and to the door that led to the basement, and my heart sank, all rumba syncopation replaced with the slow rhythm of a dirge.

My funeral dirge.

I remembered the basement's layout from Teresa's house tour and knew there was no way to escape, at least not for me. Nora, with her much slimmer figure, could probably shimmy out one of the tiny windows that encircled the top of the basement walls, but I certainly couldn't. It was enough to make me swear off all carbs for the rest of my life.

If I had a life after this.

With a loud slam, the door was closed behind us and securely locked. Chuckles lived up to his nickname, laughing as he walked away from the door and back down the hallway.

"Well, if this isn't just cozy." Nora and I stood at the top of steep basement stairs, the cement below our bare feet rough and cold. "She could have at least put some carpet in this place."

"We're locked in the basement of a madwoman and all you can think about is the décor? Really, Nora."

I stepped around her and cautiously made my way down the aforementioned uncarpeted stairs, holding tightly to the railing. If I fell and hurt myself, there would be no one to come to my rescue, of that I was fairly certain. Before I gave in to a full-blown panic attack, I wanted to get the lay of the land. There might be options, an as-yet-undiscovered way out of here. I said as much to my partner in crime.

"Oh, yeah. And pigs might fly." It was Nora's turn to be sardonic. "Face it. We're down here until we starve to death or Chuckles, the overgrown imbecile, decides to kill the two of us." She walked over to where I stood, and a shudder passed through her.

Between leaving my earthly life, due to lack of food and water, and being dispatched at the large hands of Teresa's sidekick, I knew which one I'd choose.

"Sounds fine by me." I reached out and gave one of her arms a shake. "Buck up, buttercup. All we need is a plan of distraction to get him to open the door. He can only deal with one of us at a time, right?"

She stared at me, nodding slightly.

"Okay, then. I'll be the one to handle him, and you get out of here as quickly as you can." When she didn't answer, I shook her again. "Nora, say something. The last thing we need is for one of us to get catatonic."

To my relief, she jerked away from my grasp. At least she could hear me. When she began scrabbling at the front of her top, though, I started to get worried. Was this a sign of a nervous breakdown?

"And score one for the girls," she crowed, an extremely thin cell phone hanging from her fingers. "Seems they missed one."

I could've kissed her. I settled for throwing my arms around her and performing an impromptu dance.

"If I've ever said anything mean about the way you carry your phone, I'm sorry." I gave her one more squeeze and stepped away, eyeing the tiny object "Where in the world did you get that? It looks like a toy."

Nora's smile was smug. "Do you remember what Fern said about used cell phones? That they don't need cell service to dial nine-one-one?"

I nodded slowly. That conversation in Seattle, seated around the table in Fern's house, seemed long ago and far away. From down in this basement, time was beginning to feel oddly out of kilter.

"I found this little gem in the back of a dresser drawer. I think I might've used it a handful of times, if even that. It's one of those Razr phones they used to make, maybe ten or fifteen years ago." She waggled the slim plastic case. "I carved out a space for it, so to speak, in my Wonderbra." She moved the wiggle to her chest. "Trust me. No one could tell it was there. Not even Marcus, and that's saying something, believe me."

"TMI, pal." I shut my eyes as though Marcus was standing right in front of me. "I'm glad you decided to bring it along, though."

She flipped open the phone and pressed the power button. A faint green light emanated from it in the gloom of the basement, and I felt like clapping. Maybe this would work. If it did, we'd be out of here before the two criminals from upstairs knew we were gone.

Nora looked up from the cell. The light gave her face a slight greenish cast, reminding me of *The Wizard of Oz*. "I can't get a signal. Guess now's the time to see if Fern is right about dialing the police without cell service."

Chapter 21

I turned around and surveyed our prison. The windows were there, as I remembered them, almost ten feet above the floor, the late-afternoon sun giving them a faint glow. There was no way we'd be able to reach them. We'd need a ladder.

Like the one I saw leaning behind a stack of boxes marked CHRISTMAS DÉCOR.

"Do you think you might be able to get a signal if you were higher?" I pointed toward the window directly above us.

Nora snorted. "Probably. Got an idea of how I might get up there?" She sounded defeated, unlike her normally upbeat self.

Well, I knew how to rally the troops, so to speak. Teaching an "A hour" high school class, long before the sun appeared, had taught me how to motivate the half-asleep teens that drooped over their desks. I drew in a deep breath, cupped my hands around my mouth, and aimed my voice toward my equally drooping best friend's ear.

"This is your captain speaking. Get your rear in gear, and make that frown go upside down, sunshine."

"If you do that one more time, you're gonna think twice about calling me 'sunshine.'" She glared at me, one finger in the offended ear. "What's wrong with you? The 'men's paws' acting up again?"

I laughed. Marcus's definition of that most wonderful time of any woman's life, menopause, had made me laugh then, and it did now. He'd called it the time when a woman didn't want any "men's paws" on her, and I'd almost fallen out of my chair laughing.

The tension was disappearing from my neck and shoulders now. This was going to work. I *knew* it from the bottom of my post-menopausal brain. Or heart. Whichever.

"You, my good buddy, are going to take a trip right up that ladder"—I pointed to the pile of boxes—"to that window. And if I'm not mistaken, I see a latch on it. That means it'll open. You can stick your hand right out of the window and get a signal."

We wrestled the ladder out from behind the boxes with minimal noise, if I didn't count Nora's shriek when I accidently set it down on her bare toes.

"Mind the pedicure, please." This was said through gritted teeth as she leaned down to rub the offended digits. "Who knows when I'll be able to get another one." She looked at the window and frowned. "Are you sure this ladder is tall enough?"

I craned my neck to peer at the rectangle of freedom, its glass opaque from a layer of dirt. The ladder, once we'd moved it below the window, was at least four feet short of the goal.

"It'll be tall enough if you stand on the very top." I pointed to the ladder's topmost rung. "Don't worry. I'll hold onto it and keep it steady."

Nora didn't appear thrilled. Crossing her arms and looking from the ladder to me, she gave her head a small shake and sighed. "Fine. I'll do it. But if I fall, you've gotta catch me."

"Just don't fall." I grasped the sides of the ladder, from the side without the rungs, and nodded at her encouragingly. "Let's get out of here."

Nora placed one foot on the first rung and grimaced. "Ugh. They could've at least had a warmer ladder. This metal is cold as ice."

"Just focus, Nora. *Focus.*"

She climbed to the last rung, stretching up one arm to test the reach. My heart sank as I realized the ladder wasn't tall enough. Unless...

"Can't you stand on the very top?" I watched her slightly wobbling feet with trepidation. "You usually have good balance."

"The top? As on this?" She pointed to where the very top of the ladder was pressed against her legs. "Are you absolutely insane?"

"I've been called worse. Come on, Nora. I believe in you." I used my best cajoling tone, the one I used whenever Herc decided to go rogue during a walk. "If you get on the top, you'll be able to flip open the latch and get your arm out for a signal."

"You owe me huge, girlfriend. *Huge.*"

She placed her right foot on the very top of the ladder. With one smooth motion, she brought the other up and stood balanced as gracefully as a bird on a wire.

"Now what, genius?" She was standing as still as a statue, gaze fixed straight ahead on the wall. Great. Now was not the time to freeze.

"The window is directly above you," I said encouragingly. "Reach up with your right hand—yes, that's it. The latch is just to the left of your hand. Yes, right there. Now, I think you can pull it toward you, and that should pop the lock."

I watched, holding my breath, as she followed my instructions. When the lock moved, I wanted to jump up and down. With Nora posing on the top of a six-foot ladder, though, that wasn't a good idea. I settled for a silent fist pump.

"Hey, you know what? I think I can get out," Nora called down, sounding more like her sure self. "Just make sure you're holding on tight, okay?"

Before I could say anything, she bent her knees, gave a little hop, and grabbed onto the windowsill. I closed my eyes and then popped them open. If she fell, I needed to be ready to catch her. Or to throw my body on the ground for a soft landing.

When I dared to peer up once more, Nora had managed to get the top half of her body out of the window, leaving her Lycra-encased legs dangling behind.

"Give me a lift, Sis." Nora's feet scrabbled against the wall, trying to find a toehold and failing. "Hurry. This is cutting off my circulation."

Give her a lift? And how was I supposed to do that from down here? I said as much, knowing as soon as the words came out exactly what she was implying.

"Wait. You want me to climb up this thing? Who's going to hold it for me?"

"Get a move on. I can hear someone coming up the driveway." Nora gave her bottom an impatient wiggle.

I had to hand it to her. She took body language to a whole new level.

"Keep your wig on." I grasped the rung just above my head and began the slow climb upward. Mount Everest wasn't this tough. One rung at a time, I made it to the top. "Okay, I'm right behind you. Let me get settled, and then I'll give you a boost." I bent my knees and wedged them beneath one of the rungs. It was a false sense of security, and I was well aware of that, but it was amazing how one could convince oneself otherwise. The power of the mind was amazing.

"What's taking you so long?" Nora hissed. "Give me a hand already."

"Okay, okay, miss impatient. I was getting set, if it's all the same to you." Reaching up, I interlaced my fingers into a foothold and nudged one of her bare feet. "I'm ready."

Nora's slim figure belied her weight as I pushed her upward and out of the window. The woman must've had rocks secreted somewhere in her clothes. She'd probably stuffed them in that Wonderbra of hers, along with the lifesaving flip phone. I was still contemplating the miracles of physics when the door at the top of the basement stairs flew open. I didn't wait to see who it was.

I screamed as loudly as I could. "Run, Nora, run!"

The hands that fastened around my ankles weren't those of Chuckles, however. Looking down, my heart in my throat, I stared straight into Martin's upturned face.

"Martin!" I gasped. "Where—how—what in the Sam Hill is going on?"

His grin was wide on a noticeably thinner face. Wherever he'd been, he hadn't eaten much.

"I've already called the cops." He held up a hand to me, and I grasped it as I dismounted the ladder. He looked around, a puzzled expression on his face. "Where's my stepmom?"

I pointed at the open window. "Out there, presumably calling for help as well. And what about Teresa and Chuckles? Are they still here?"

"You mean my loving wife and her stooge?" His voice was loaded with disgust. "I assume they're on the run. I saw the Navigator spin out of here as I arrived."

"You're kidding." I stared at him in disbelief. "You mean they locked us in here and then left?"

Martin grimaced. "Looks like it. What a pair of sweethearts, right?" He motioned to the door at the top of the stairs. "Let's get out of here."

"My pleasure." I followed him out of the basement.

I'd never been so happy or willing to climb a set of stairs. In fact, I would have skipped up them if I hadn't been afraid of losing my balance.

The Seattle Police Department arrived with sirens blaring. Nora, Martin, and I welcomed the cavalry with open arms. Actually, we greeted them with our hands up, assuring the guys and gals in blue that we were the victims and they could find the criminals in Teresa's Lincoln Navigator.

"I've got the vehicle registration, Officer." Martin pointed to the open door behind us. "If you want to come with me, I can give you all the info you'll need to make an arrest for kidnapping, murder, and all-around idiocy."

"Don't forget theft." Nora sounded indignant. "They stole my brand-new Jimmy Choos."

"And my Birkenstocks," I reminded her. She hadn't been the only one to lose her footwear.

"Good riddance, I say." She smiled at me and placed one arm around my shoulders. "I'm teasing. And if they can't find them, I'll even buy you another pair."

"Ladies, if you give us a moment, someone will take your statements about your stolen shoes." The officer spoke in a competent tone, but I sensed amusement lurking just beneath his words.

"Don't forget we were kidnapped as well. In fact, all of us"—I nodded at Nora and Martin—"were held against our will."

"Were you now." It was a statement rather than a question, delivered in the driest tone possible. He turned to follow Martin into the house, but Nora stopped him in his tracks.

"I'll thank you to keep a civil tongue in that mouth of yours." As he turned around slowly and faced her, she added in a rather spiteful tone, "We'd hate for this little exchange to get leaked to the public, wouldn't we now?" With a sweet smile, she reached into her bra and produced the Razr phone.

"Look, ma'am," he began, but she cut him short.

"Get Martin's information. My friend and I will be waiting for you in the living room."

With that pronouncement, Nora grabbed my arm and walked us around the stunned officer and into the house. It was difficult to walk gracefully in bare feet, but Nora managed it beautifully. I did my best, only tripping slightly over a shoe as we entered the wide foyer.

My shoe.

"Look what I found." I bent down to retrieve the battered sandal, waving it triumphantly at Nora. "And I see yours just behind that chair."

I looked at Nora. She appeared as flummoxed as I was. How had they ended up back in the hallway? That was one puzzle too many for now, however, and I was glad to see my sandals had come through relatively unscathed.

Both of Nora's neon-pink stilettos had been tossed in back of one of the chairs that sat in the hall. The other Birkenstock lay underneath them, looking like an inflatable raft holding a pair of exotic animals.

"Oh, my poor heels. Just *look* at the way they treated them." Nora wasted no time in snatching the bedraggled pair from the floor where they lay. "They're missing some of the crystals." She held the shoes closer as she inspected them. "And look—the bow on this one is ripped." Scowling, she slipped her feet into the heels and gave them a dismayed look. "Good thing I got insurance on them. I'm still pressing charges, though."

I gaped at her, one foot still bare. "You bought insurance on a pair of *shoes*?"

She nodded, a smug smile beginning to crowd out the irritation. "Pretty smart, right?"

I had to shake my head. I'd heard it all now. I slipped my foot into the other sandal and followed her into the living room. Did anyone ever insure Birkenstocks?

The living room was much the same as I recalled it from the times I'd been inside the house. What was different, however, was the bankers box that sat in the middle of the low coffee table, its contents spilling across a stack of fashion magazines and a handcrafted crystal bowl. Bending over it, I lifted out the first thing I saw, scanning what was written there.

And gasped. I wordlessly thrust it at Nora and waited for her reaction. I wasn't disappointed.

"You've got to be joshing me." She looked up from the document, her expression one of shock. Finding out that one was the owner of the house in which one had recently been held prisoner was quite the jolt. "And I was only pulling her chain when I said I was her landlord."

"Congratulations are in order, I presume." I gestured to the deed. "I suppose Teresa knew all about this."

"I'm sure she did." Nora smiled wryly, nodding at the box. "I'd say that had something to do with trying to get rid of me."

"Us," I pointed out. "She tried to get rid of both of us. And who helped you escape out the window?"

"Oh, that." She waved off my heroic balancing act as though it had been nothing more than offering to do the dishes. "Martin would've saved us anyway."

"Well. That's a fine way to thank a pal." I glared at her from across the table. "What am I? Chopped liver?"

"Of course not, silly. I see you more as—as the best pâté money can buy."

Her sudden grin was contagious, and I smiled as well. Chopped goose liver with a high price tag? I'd take it.

"You don't need another house, Nora. Maybe you can sell it. Or give it to Martin."

She nodded. "My thoughts exactly. The giving bit, I mean. Who wants another money guzzler?" She gave a mock shiver. "The taxes on this heap plus the upkeep would be enough to give my poor CPA nightmares."

"And here I thought that being locked in a basement was the scary part. *Pardon moi, mon ami.*" I smiled.

It actually hadn't been that bad down there. I'd spotted the shelves of canned and packaged food along one wall. We wouldn't have starved before someone rescued us. Thank goodness Martin had been able to escape his own prison, wherever that had been.

As if my thoughts had conjured him out of thin air, Martin walked into the living room, hands casually thrust into his pockets. Or he might have been holding up his pants. They hung loosely on him, and even the polo shirt looked like he'd borrowed it from a much larger man, but his expression was much happier than I'd ever seen it.

Maybe he'd lost something besides physical weight.

"So, Nora, what's the story with you two?" He included me with a jerk of his chin. "How'd you manage to get locked up?"

"I think the question is how did *you* get locked up, and where did they keep you?" Nora looked him over from top to toe. "Looks like they kept you at a fat farm, if you don't mind me saying so." She reached out one finger and prodded him in the belly. "You've lost a ton of weight."

He laughed, and I realized I'd never heard him laugh before. It was a pleasant sound, not pitched too high or too low. Martin might be on his way to becoming a nice man.

"It was a fat farm, all right." He rubbed his face with one hand as he shook his head. "They kept me in the basement of the restaurant across the street from the cleaners." He smiled across at us, and I could clearly see the lines around his eyes. "Smelling all that Chinese food while being kept on water and an occasional bowl of stale rice did a number on me, that's for sure."

"The restaurant?" Nora and I said in unison, both of us sounding stunned.

"We were there just two days ago." I tried to wrap my mind around the idea of Martin being that close to us all the time. And wasn't that what Nora had said? That he was most likely right under our noses? I pointed this out, and both Nora and Martin chuckled.

"Well, I know I've never said this before, stepmama—oops, *ex-*stepmama—but you were right. For once," he added with a wry smile. "Don't quote me, though. I'll deny it."

Two kidnappings (three, if you counted the failed attempt Martin had ordered on me and Nora before his own abduction) and two criminals on the run, and life still went on as normal. It was mind-boggling, to say the least.

Standing here now with our kidnapper turned kidnap victim, I faced Martin squarely, my hands on my hips, scowling. "Would you care to explain the reason you wanted Nora and me held against our will?"

"Yeah, Marty." Nora reached out and prodded him none too gently in the chest. "What was *that* all about?"

His face reddened, and he hung his head, staring at his feet. Finally, he cleared his throat and looked up. "It was like this," he began in a small voice. "I thought you two were out to close down my business." He lifted his chin defiantly. "It's not my fault my employees were running an illegal betting shop. I had no idea what was going on."

Nora snorted, and Martin shot her an injured look.

"I felt sorry for that new kid, though. He got duped into working there."

"Caleb Greene?" I knew who he meant, but I needed to hear it from him.

"Yeah, that kid from Portland. He was hired to act as the lookout when someone came in to place a bet." He shook his head sorrowfully. "Hopefully this won't ruin his life."

"I don't think it will." Caleb was already home with his parents, working diligently on his community service hours at the local pet shelter. He'd be all right, especially with a girl like Hannah by his side.

Nora was still staring at Martin, her eyes wide with disbelief. "Don't tell me you really thought that's why we drove all the way from Portland, kid. You're still as thick as a brick wall, just like that good-for-nothing father of yours."

Martin flinched at Nora's words, and I felt a sudden sympathy for him. Good old Gwen Franklin, always on the side of the underdog.

"If you can just explain why you felt that way," I said gently, "we might be able to forgive and forget." I looked at my partner in crime, noting that a frown had corrugated her forehead. She must have missed her last Botox appointment. "Nora, tell the nice man you'll forgive him."

"Nice man, my shiny hiney." Still, the wrinkles began to ease as she stared intently at her ex-stepson. "Okay, buster. Who told you we were here to shut down your business?"

Martin mumbled an answer, and Nora gave his chest another poke.

"Speak up. Some of us around here are hard of hearing." She darted a mischievous smile at me, and so help me, I wanted to give *her* chest a poke.

I didn't dare, however. I wasn't sure whether that Wonderbra was holding any other surprises besides that tiny phone.

"I said, Teresa told me. And so did Chuckles. Even Zeke made sure I thought like that." He returned Nora's glare with one of his own, and it occurred to me that being mothered by Nora must have been quite an experience for the younger Martin. "And I wasn't going to hurt you two or anything. I just wanted to scare you away."

Nora threw up her hands in mock surprise. "Well, there you go, chum. Taking the word of a steroid addict and someone with a clown name sounds perfect to me. Right, Sis?" She cocked her head to one side. "So, it wasn't because you thought we knew you'd killed your dad?"

Martin's mouth fell open, his eyebrows shooting up like a pair of inverted commas. "You think I killed my father? You're loonier than I thought, woman."

I didn't like the color that was rushing into his face. With the enforced diet and lack of care he'd been through, I was afraid he'd drop dead of a heart attack before we found out what had happened to the Bottomless Pitt.

"So if you didn't kill him—and I'll give you the benefit of the doubt here—who did? Not that wimpy sister of yours, that's for sure." Nora crossed her arms, tapping one foot impatiently.

The three of us were quiet for a moment, and then I spoke up. "Do you think Teresa might've had something to do with it?" When Nora and Martin stared at me, I added, "Well, maybe not her personally, but those knuckleheads she has working for her." I waved one hand in the general direction of Puget Sound. "There's a lot of water out there where a body can be hidden."

"You know, it just might be possible," began Martin slowly, one finger tapping his newly defined chin. "In fact, I wouldn't put it past her." He smiled at me, his anger dissipated. "I'll mention it to the police, if that's okay with you." This last comment was directed at Nora, who nodded in agreement. "We might never find him, but at least someone will be held responsible."

We stood there in silence for a moment, the only sound that of the landscapers trimming the shrubs that delineated the front walk.

"At least the yard will look nice," I said, apropos of nothing, and gave a hiccupy giggle. I hid my face in my hands, feeling abruptly overwhelmed by the whole situation. It was all too much for one retired teacher who only wanted to relax and read.

"There, there," Nora crooned, her arm around me. "I say we get back to Fern's and decompress with a lovely white wine. We can let the cops figure out this mess by themselves, and they can come to us when they need a statement." She gave me a slight shake. "Sound good?"

I nodded, my face still covered. Roger was either never going to believe this or he was going to insist on coming with me whenever I left my house. Or, and here my face grew warm, he'd move in with me so he could keep an eye on me at all times.

Nora abruptly pulled away from me, her arm dropping from my shoulders. "Sis, are you having one of those flashes from Hades again? Your ears just got as red as a clown's nose."

I peered out from between my fingers. "That's exactly it," I replied, not wanting to explain. "And you know how I am when I get an attack of the 'men's paws.'"

From the corner of my eye, I saw Martin gaping at the two of us, and I bit back a laugh. Better to let him think I was as nutty as a fruitcake and needed someone to watch me twenty-four/seven. That way he wouldn't insist on making this into a long-time-coming family reunion between him and Nora at the present moment. They could work on that on their own time.

What I wanted more than anything at this moment, besides being in my own bed with Herc curled beside me, was to get out of this house.

Chapter 22

Nora, bless her heart, could be a mind reader as well as the best friend any woman ever had. With a gentle tug on my arm, she began guiding me to the living room door.

"We're going to head on out, Martin," she called over her shoulder as we reached the front door. "You can reach us at—" and she rattled off Fern's address. "Come on, Gwennie girl. Time to get you home." She gave me a critical once-over and added, "And you're in no condition to drive. We'll get the car later."

With a minimum of protest from the officer left to watch over the front porch, we were taken away in an Uber driven by the sweetest old man I'd ever met. He must've been eighty if he was a day, and he must've been sitting on a cushion in order to see over the steering wheel, but he was chatty and quite the tour guide. By the time we arrived at Fern's bungalow, Nora and I had heard all about the history of Puget Sound and why it was the best place to kayak and paddleboard.

"You two girls give me a shout when you want a kayaking lesson. I'm the best around, or so I'm told." He gave a short cackle of laughter and a wink over his shoulder, making me wonder exactly what it was he was talking about.

Still, he'd kept my mind on something besides being tossed into a basement like a pile of unwashed laundry. With a cheery wave and a promise to give him a call, Nora and I headed toward Fern's front door.

"You weren't serious, were you?" Nora lifted one eyebrow in question. Her waterproof brow pencil had smeared. I decided to ignore it.

"Of course I wasn't." I stepped to the front door ahead of Nora, smiling to myself. "Besides, I had my fingers crossed, so it didn't count."

Fern answered the door with a pair of knitting needles in one hand and a skein of magenta yarn tucked under her arm. "Welcome back, welcome back." She stood aside to allow us to walk in ahead of her. "You're just in time for some spearmint tea. Just picked it from the garden."

"That sounds absolutely perfect," I said sincerely. "Do you mind if I have my cup while soaking in a hot tub?"

Fern's expression was as passive as ever. "Not a problem. In fact, if you want to get the water started, I'll make a tray for you and carry it up."

"Thank you. That sounds lovely, Fern." I was abruptly close to tears again and turned my head away so she couldn't see.

I wasn't ready to talk about our latest adventure, although I had no doubt Nora would fill her in once I was safely upstairs.

Besides, we'd need to explain the appearance of Seattle's finest. I was certain they'd be showing up soon. With an inward sigh, I headed toward a relaxing bath and a few moments of much-needed peace.

* * * *

As I had anticipated, later that evening, Fern's small living room was host to three detectives and one uniformed officer. After the usual offering of coffee or herbal tea to her guests, Fern disappeared into the kitchen, leaving Nora and me to make our statements.

"Let's begin with your relationship with Martin and Teresa Pitt." A woman with short dark hair and brilliant blue eyes looked directly at Nora. "We'll be recording this, if you don't mind, and will have a copy of it available tomorrow for you to sign."

"And what if I do mind," snapped Nora, "what'll you do about it?"

I looked at her with concern. This was quite unlike my friend. Sass, okay. Sarcasm, certainly. But outright hostility, especially without provocation, was not one of Nora's default settings. I chalked it up to a delayed reaction.

"Nora," I said softly, "if you want to do this tomorrow, that's your choice." I glanced over at the dark-haired detective for confirmation and got a small shrug in return. "In fact, I think tomorrow is a much better time for all of this." Standing, I motioned to the living room door. "I'll walk out with you."

"Ma'am, we'd prefer to do this now. A salient point might be forgotten between now and tomorrow." This was a plumpish young man whose black-rimmed glasses made him look like Clark Kent in need of a gym. "It's a well-known fact that most victims will rearrange their thoughts to match their coping skills. This is why it's better to get a statement while it's fresh in the mind."

"When one has gone through what we experienced today, young man, one does not forget anything about it, salient or not." I looked at him steadily, arms folded, not offering anything else.

"We'll see you two tomorrow, say about ten?" The dark-haired detective motioned her fellow officers toward the door. "Can I send someone to pick you up?"

I shook my head. "We'll call for a ride with Uber. That is, if Nora's okay with that." I smiled at the officer. "Let's just say we've had quite the experience with Uber drivers lately. Besides, I'll need to get my car from the house." I offered my hand and smiled. "But thanks for taking the time to come out, Detective. I'm sure we'll be able to give you the full account tomorrow."

I directed this final comment to the spectacled detective. He ignored me and walked outside, his nose held high. My granny had a saying for that sort of person: if it rains, they'll drown. With a quick peek at the sky, I closed the front door.

"Nora? Want some coffee?" I came back into the living room. Maybe a cup of Fern's excellent blend would put some pep in her step.

There was no reply, however. Nora was lying back on the worn sofa, one arm flung over her eyes, her mouth emitting soft snores. She was plainly exhausted, in both body and mind. I tiptoed out of the room and walked into the kitchen, inhaling the spicy scent of something baking.

"Cake?" I smiled at Fern as I sat down across from her. "And if there's any more coffee, I'll take some."

"Help yourself." Fern nodded toward a stack of clean mugs that sat in a bamboo dish drainer. "And it's my version of zucchini muffins. I add a dash of nutmeg and cinnamon."

"Sounds absolutely delicious." I sipped the steaming brew slowly, savoring the smoothness of the organic beans. There was something to be said for buying the best, and the proof was in the taste.

"Sounds like you two had quite the morning." Fern's gaze flicked at me briefly before returning to the job at hand. With the knitting needles moving at warp speed, she was every inch the self-sufficient woman, and I had a brief moment of envy. It must be nice to know you could care for yourself and not depend on someone else.

It was very brief, though. I liked my life, even the parts of it that Nora had taken over and stirred into craziness. I gave Fern a lopsided smile and nodded. "If you call being locked in a basement as 'quite the morning,' then I have to agree." I took another sip of coffee and placed the mug on the table. "Mind you, they took our shoes first before marching us to the basement door."

"They took your shoes?" The knitting needles paused a moment, Fern's eyes rounded in befuddlement. "Why in the world would they do that?"

"Because Nora's heels make great weapons." I mimed hitting something with the heel, and Fern's expression cleared. "She used them before on one of Martin's employees—long story—and I think Teresa must've heard about it." I gave a slight hitch of one shoulder. "So, Chuckles took off our shoes. I'm not sure what he thought my sandals could do, though."

We sat quietly while the muffins baked, the soft clicking of the knitting needles providing a metronome to my thoughts. I needed a plan of action, especially since it was clear Nora wasn't up to making decisions at the moment.

* * * *

As soon as we made our statements at the police department the next morning, I wanted nothing more than to get my car and load it up. Getting out of this town was the best idea I'd had in a while.

Soon after I spoke with Clark Kent's look-alike and Nora gave her statement to the dark-haired woman, we picked up my car. We loaded it as quickly as we could and waved a final goodbye to Seattle as we hit the road for home. I was never so glad to get behind the wheel of my old car than I was at that moment. One thing was still bugging me, though, and I said as much.

"Do you think there will ever be any closure for Martin and his sister? I know the detectives said that they'll be doing everything they can to find their dad, but…" I gave a tiny shrug and concentrated on the road.

"I sure hope so." Nora shifted in her seat, crossing and recrossing her legs. "I made a point of telling them to take a good look at Teresa and her two stooges. Something tells me they know exactly where my ex is."

It was a quiet ride back to Portland as we contemplated this latest adventure. I made a note to never again get involved in anything that included a dead body, especially if said body can't be found. With great effort, I pushed all thoughts of murder from my mind and focused on getting home.

Roger and Marcus had phoned the night before. My call was brief but pleasant, with Roger assuring me Herc had been well cared for and they'd both see me soon. "Be safe coming home, please. We want to see you again in one piece."

I assured him that yes, indeed, I'd drive safely, said goodbye, and handed my phone off to Nora.

Her conversation with the plaid-wearing private eye was punctuated with laughter and whispers. I didn't want to know what they'd said to one another, and I firmly told my best friend so after we'd both concluded our calls.

"You keep your secrets. Trust me, it won't offend me not to know every detail," I said after she'd hung up with her Romeo, cheeks flushed, eyes shining. Was that how I looked after talking with Roger?

My conversation centered around Herc and assuring Roger that yes, I'd tell him the entire sordid tale once I was safely back in my own little house in Portland.

"It's best told with the doors locked and a cup of tea nearby." I heard Roger's chuckle and was relieved I was able to play down the situation. Once he'd heard the details, I might gain a permanent bodyguard.

Not a bad idea.

After leaving Nora off at her luxury apartment building, I drove on to my little house. Herc would be there, I knew, because I'd called Brent and asked him to pick up my dog before I arrived. Roger had already done enough for me and Herc, and it did Brent good to stay busy.

"You can put him in the backyard," I told Brent. "He knows how to use the doggy door, and I'll be there around three."

"Not a prob, Miss F. Me and Aggie know how to use it too, don't we, girl?"

I heard Aggie's answering yips and Herc's muffled barking in the background. I hoped Brent's long-suffering mother hadn't minded having another animal around the house. At least this one was housebroken.

It was no surprise to find Brent sitting in the middle of my front yard with the two dogs running happily around him. I'd anticipated as much and had gone through a fast-food drive-thru for some instant nourishment. I knew the boy would be starving, per usual, and I could do with a little something myself.

As I handed him the bag, he gave me a wide grin. "You got more company inside, Miss F."

I stopped, momentarily taken aback. I wasn't expecting anyone else until the evening, when I'd promised to give Roger the details.

"Who is it?" When Brent's grin grew even wider, my cheeks grew warm. "I tell you what. I'll go and see for myself. Please don't give the dogs any of that," I nodded toward the bag. "It'll upset their stomachs."

Roger, bless his heart, had come by early in order to start coffee, always a staple on a Portland afternoon, and arrange an offering of Voodoo Doughnuts on one of my Goodwill platters. Max and Doc lay on the living room rug snoring softly in unison, and the man himself sat on the couch.

"I hope you don't mind me arriving early. It was such a pleasant day, so we walked over." He stood to greet me, kissing one cheek and taking my small suitcase from my hand. "Brent had a key, so he was able to let the boys and me inside."

I snorted. "His key is also known as a 'doggy door,' but never mind that now." I stood on tiptop and returned the kiss, inhaling the scent of the sandalwood and patchouli aftershave he wore. "It's good to see you." I peered around him and gave an appreciative sniff. "Give me a moment to settle in, and I'll be ready for a cup of that coffee."

I quickly visited the bathroom before going to my bedroom and changing into a less-wrinkled pair of capris and a loose shirt. The capris were a recent find at a garage sale and a departure from my typical choices in fabric. The plaid pattern was growing on me, though, and I knew Marcus would approve. Unless there was such a thing as plaid Lycra, though, I couldn't see Nora in this pattern.

The maple-bacon doughnut was amazing, per usual, and the coffee was just the way I liked it: smooth and medium roast. The man responsible for the treat was just my style as well.

"If you're ready to hear about my latest adventure, I'll give you the distilled version." I wiped my fingers on a paper towel thoughtfully provided by Roger and went to refill my coffee mug. "More for you?"

He shook his head. "I had one while I was waiting for you to get home." He stood and motioned toward the couch. "Bring your coffee in the living room, and then I'm all yours."

Oh, yes, you are.

Settling myself back against the cushions, I gave a little sigh of contentment and took a sip of coffee. Time to give Roger the play-by-play and hope he didn't go ballistic.

"It all began with Nora's nutty ex-husband and his will." I stared at the ceiling, my inner eye seeing every step we'd taken, every turn we'd made. Drawing in a slow breath, I told Roger every little bit, not leaving one thing or person out.

"I was well and truly fooled by Martin's wife." I shook my head at my own stupidity. "I saw and heard exactly what she wanted me to see and hear, that she was a wife whose husband was abusive, and his bodyguards would be happy to do the same at the drop of a hat. She even had the local police department believing her. Martin's record didn't help him, and she knew it."

"That's too bad." Roger laid one arm along the back of the couch and turned slightly so he could look at me. "That makes it difficult for women who are truly being abused to get help."

"Exactly my thoughts. I've had plenty of time to think this entire thing through, and I don't think I would've done anything differently." I gave a small shrug and reached out for my coffee. "I tend to believe what folks tell me, and when I see someone who I think needs help, I give it."

"And that's what made you such a wonderful teacher." Roger's arm slipped off the couch, hugging me to him. "And speaking of believing what someone tells you, what if I told you that I loved you?"

I'd heard others claim that "time stood still" and "the earth shook" when they finally met the one who made them the happiest. I didn't experience anything like that, but an incredible joy filled me. I looked into Roger's eyes, the kindest eyes I'd ever seen, and I knew I'd finally found my happy place. With a smile that trembled slightly, I leaned into him and took his hand in both of mine.

Acknowledgments

For a book to come to life, it takes more than an idea for a plot. It also requires the guiding hand of an editor, and I'd like to thank Shannon Plackis for her unending patience and gracious guidance. Without you, my characters might still be dangling from quite a few loose ends. Thank you.

If you enjoyed PLAYING POSSUM
by
Dane McCaslin
Go back to where it all began…

The 2 Sisters Pet Valet Mysteries
DOGGONE DEAD
Turn the page for a quick peek at
DOGGONE DEAD
Enjoy!

Chapter 1

What woke me wasn't the insistent ringing of my alarm clock or the sound of the wind that blew in from the Willamette River. Instead, the first official day of my retirement began with an early morning phone call from my best friend, Nora Goldstein.

"What do you want?" I sounded as surly as I felt. I'd been looking forward to this first late morning from the moment I'd announced my intention to retire early from a wonderful but exhausting career as a high school teacher. I wanted to sleep in, get up and have coffee, and go right back to bed, preferably with a book. "This had better be really good."

"And a good morning to you, too, Gwen." She gave a short bark of a laugh that echoed in my ear in the most irritating way. "What's better than two besties spending some time together?"

Besties? *Besties*? This woman was way too awake for my liking.

"Nora, you sound like a geriatric teenager—and, in case you didn't notice, I'm not hanging out with that particular age group anymore."

"Oh, poo on you, spoilsport." Again that laugh. Maybe she was on something.

I'd heard stories of seniors baking brownies with marijuana in them and passing them around to their pals. I made a mental note to check up on Nora's latest whereabouts.

"Besides, I've got a great idea I want to share."

I groaned at her words. "Fabulous. As great as the last one? Please say no."

I could almost hear her disdainful expression.

"It's not my fault the city wouldn't let me start a fish pedicure salon. You'd think it'd be a slam dunk, what with all the fish we've got around here."

What Nora lacked in common sense, she made up for in dollar bills. As in millions of them, all tucked securely away in various banks, thanks to a rather extensive lineup of ex-husbands.

"I'm pretty sure the fish used in those types of salons aren't of the largemouth bass variety." My tone was as dry as a lecture on the finer points of comma usage. "Look, I don't want to spend my first real morning of no more school talking on the phone, even with my best friend."

Sometimes Nora could be as thick as the pea soup fog that rolled in from the rivers. Plain talking was the only way to get through to her. To my surprise, this morning it worked on the first try.

"My thoughts exactly." She spoke briskly, as if suddenly noticing the time. "Get yourself up and meet me at The Friendly Bean in one hour sharp."

And with that, the phone went dead. I let it fall out of my hand onto the fluffy comforter, one arm slung across my eyes. I loved that gal like a sister—I really did—but occasionally her timing could make me crazy.

There was no going back to dreamland now. I was wide awake and, knowing Nora, she'd probably march over here and drag me out of bed if I didn't show up. Sighing deeply, I flung the covers back and shuffled toward the bathroom.

Living in Portland suited me. I liked the climate, the surrounding mountains, the rivers. I liked hiking at Multnomah Falls, even when it was full of selfie-taking tourists. I even liked the rain—as long as I was indoors, preferably with a mug of coffee and a good book.

Being retired suited me as well. I'd planned on reading through my extensive collection of mysteries, beginning with the dame herself, Agatha Christie. Why Nora thought I needed anything else to do was as nebulous as she was, hard to pin down and always changing. It was a good thing that we were as close as we were, better than real life sisters, as Nora had said more than once. She'd even taken to calling me "Sis" when we were much younger, something that could confuse those who didn't know us and put a smile on my face whenever I heard it.

Except, of course, when I got pulled into one of her nutty ideas.

Within the prescribed hour, I was showered, dressed, and walking toward The Friendly Bean, our neighborhood coffee spot with some of the best blends around town. And it was a coffee kind of day, no doubt about it, but most of them were here in the great Northwest. Clouds that had earlier looked like soft pillows were now turning bruised faces towards the darkening Columbia River. Rain had already begun its daily drizzle shortly before I left my small bungalow, a soft prelude to a larger battering to come.

True to their promise, the skies opened up as I walked, drenching me and every other unfortunate person who happened to be outdoors. We were in for a day of what we called "weather" here in Portland. I yanked up the hood on my jacket and scurried for cover, my Birkenstocks flapping on the wet pavement like a pair of stranded fish.

Nora was sitting near the rear of the small café, one arm draped in a proprietary fashion around the back of the only empty chair in the place. Ignoring the frowns of those having to drink their coffee standing at the various tall tables that dotted the room, I hurried toward her, flinging raindrops as I did.

"It's already getting messy out there." I hung my wet jacket on the back of the saved chair and slipped damply into it.

The coffee shop was full of the sound of hissing espresso machines and baristas calling out orders, almost masking the noise of the rain as it hurled itself against the windows that streamed with condensation. Portland, I'd heard one tourist say, tended to rain both inside as well as out.

"I'm glad I Ubered here." Nora reached up to pat her hair, a smug expression on her thin face. "Rain and hairspray aren't a good mix." She inclined her head at the two mugs already sitting in front of me. "I got you the usual, Sis."

"Thanks. Some days I feel like I need coffee more than food." I took an exploratory sip and winced. The coffee was hovering somewhere near molten. "And why in the world did you use a taxi? You live closer than I do."

"Because I didn't want to get my new shoes wet."

I leaned over to stare at a pair of bright pink sky-high heels, each one sporting a lacey bow on top. Typical Nora. Ostentatious and girly in one fell swoop.

"And you do know, don't you, that fifty is the new thirty?" Taking a sip of her drink, a chocolatey concoction that could have doubled as a dessert, Nora dropped one frosted eyelid in a wink. "I mean, just look at Julia Roberts. And me."

I couldn't unsee her if I wanted to. Her hair, what was left of it after a recent disastrous bout with perming rods and an overzealous hairdresser, was teased to within an inch of its blonded life and tucked underneath a hefty "fall" of fake hair. She favored clothes a few decades too young, especially the type made from the stretchy, tight material that would have been at home in a yoga studio. It always amazed me I couldn't read the care tag stitched into the seams of her clothes. Her makeup routine was based on the "more is better" mindset, and her shoes were usually of the stiletto heeled variety. Altogether, Nora was a conglomerate of styles that defied age and common sense, in my humble opinion.

I, on the other hand, favored a bare face and shoes as flat as I wished my stomach was. I made up in real estate what Nora lacked. I was wide where she was thin and rounded where she was angled. Life, as far as I was concerned, had been so much better before the advent of irritants such as cholesterol and calories, back when a little puppy fat never did a girl any harm.

I sighed, shook my head, and took another tentative taste of my coffee. Good to go. It was a real woman's drink: dark roast, black as ink, and guaranteed to put hair on my chest. As if that would even matter. I glanced at my unshaven legs, where they poked out from a pair of old denim capris, scratchy with stubble and white enough to use as nighttime beacons in the harbor. Retirement chic in all its glory.

But if I was honest, I'd preferred a slap-dash approach to fashion my entire life. Nora, in contrast to my choices, had been a fashionista even in kindergarten.

"Oh, come on, you. Cheer up already. Just think, no more grading papers, no more whining parents, no more doing anything you don't want to do." Nora held her mug out and clinked it against mine, causing a small tidal wave of coffee to spill on the table. "Here's to a whole new Gwen Franklin!" She gave my current ensemble a critical look, sweeping her gaze from stem to stern. "And we've got to do something about that wardrobe of yours."

I cautiously waved my mug in her direction, careful to keep the dripping coffee away from my lap. On top of everything else, I didn't want to walk around town looking like I had an issue with incontinence.

"Just because you've got the wherewithal to do whatever you'd like doesn't mean I can. Really, Nora. Have you seen the size of a teacher's paycheck these days? How big do you think my retirement checks will be?" I leaned in, catching an enticing whiff of chocolate. "And when it comes to choosing between having the lights on and buying clothes, well, let's just say I prefer to see what I'm doing."

Although, running around sans garments in a lighted house might not improve my standing with the neighbors. We had children in the neighborhood, for goodness sake.

"Whatever." She brushed my comment aside as if it was a troublesome fly. "Look, I've been thinking, Gwen. What you need is a hobby."

I snorted, earning a frown from Nora.

"And no, I don't mean doing the daily crossword. I mean a *real* hobby. One that'll make you some money."

I had to laugh. Sometimes Nora's thought processes were difficult to follow. And sometimes they were downright comical, like now.

"I'm pretty sure that's called a 'job.'" I set my still-dripping mug on the table. "And I didn't retire from one only to get another." I slumped back against my chair. "Besides, I can only work a few hours a week anyway before they start docking my monthly check."

"Not if they don't know you're working." Nora's smile could have given the Cheshire Cat a run for its money. "The way I see it, we could do a few things around this place that you don't need to report."

That last statement had me worried. Not the fact I wouldn't be reporting the income of whatever it was she had in mind, but the "we" part of it. Clearing my throat, I leaned in closer, crooking one finger at her.

"And who's this 'we,' if you don't mind sharing?" My voice was a shade above a whisper, a little teacher trick I'd used whenever I needed someone's attention. "Are you talking 'we' like the queen, or 'we' as in you and me?"

"As in us, of course." She tossed her head, sending the faux ponytail bouncing.

I watched, fascinated, as it settled back into place, this time a good inch lower than it had been.

"I've been doing some thinking," she began, and I cringed inwardly. Nora had her manicured fingers in a lot of financial pies, mostly from an investor's standpoint, but she'd recently begun a one-woman dog walking service for some of the residents in her luxury apartment building, just to "help out the poor dears," as she liked to say. I'd noticed, however, that her idea of "help" came with a price tag. So much for being altruistic.

If she thought that I was going to join her—well, she had another think coming.

And of course she did. My throat began itching as I listened to her enthusiastically describing our new partnership. I was allergic to all things furred and feathered, and not just a little bit. It was a full-fledged reaction to any type of dander that could begin with a runny nose and end with my eyes swollen almost shut. Benadryl was my friend, and I made sure to steer clear of anyone with a pooch or a cat. Working with them was completely out of the question.

"Nora, has it slipped that mind of yours that I'm horribly allergic to animals, especially those of the pet variety? Cats make me sneeze, dogs are worse, and even rabbits can make me break out in hives."

"Oh. That's right. Dang." She looked down, tapping a long fingernail—fake, of course—against her chin and then straightened with a bright smile. "Well, you'll just have to wear one of those mask things, the kind doctors wear when they're getting ready to operate. Besides, it'll keep your face hidden in case the folks from the state come looking for you. Just kidding."

I glared at her. "Not funny." My momentum plunged as I recalled all the dire warnings we'd been given. In every one of the pre-retirement meetings I'd attended, we'd been cautioned about The State, capitals implied, and what might happen to our annuity if we got caught working outside of the prescribed limitations. I was pretty sure that one of Dante's infamous circles in you-know-where had been reserved for all retired teachers who tried to beat the system.

"Oh, get a sense of humor, girl. Who's really going to check to see what you do with your time? They don't own you anymore." The fake hair slid another inch as she shook her head. "And besides meeting me for coffee, what else were you planning to do today?"

She had a point. And I did need something to do with all the time I'd have on my hands, besides rearranging my bookcases.

I gave a small shrug and tipped my head back, emptying the cooling coffee in one gulp. Placing the thick white mug back on the table, I looked at Nora and lifted my chin. Chins. All right, I lifted my chins. I was ready. "Okay, let's hear it. I guess I'm in."

The exaggerated whoop of delight Nora let fly was just this side of a sonic boom. Before I could say "boo," she leaned across and wrapped me in her arms, rocking me back and forth like a crazed wind-up toy.

I managed to catch her ponytail as it slid from its pins, holding it in place with one hand and attempting to free myself from her grasp with the other. I'd never had a problem when thirty pairs of juvenile eyes stared at me in the classroom, but there was something uncomfortable about having a dozen grown people in a coffee shop gawking at the sight that was Nora with her arms wrapped around me, especially when I had one hand on the back of her head while she was hugging me like a long-lost friend.

"Nora, get a grip," I hissed in her ear, a line of tiny gold loops nearly catching in my teeth. "You've lost your, uh, your hair, and everyone is staring at us."

By the time we left, Nora's hair was somewhat back in order. I'd never seen a ponytail look like that before, and, judging by the expressions on the other faces, nobody else had either. If this was going to be the start of something big, at least we were going to do it in unforgettable style.

At Nora's insistence, we took an Uber for the short ride from The Friendly Bean to her apartment building. We needed to head for her place first, she'd decided, so we could talk about our plans for our newly hatched partnership.

"The way I see it, there are at least three pets per floor in my building, not to mention the ones I see every day at the dog park. I've been walking one or two a day, tops, but between the two of us, we can double that." Nora grabbed at the sissy bar above her door as our driver took a sharp turn in front of a rather large logging truck. "If we live, that is. Young man, if you want me to give you a tip, I wouldn't drive like that. Besides, you might give my friend here a relapse, and trust me when I say you don't want that to happen."

Just what it was I was supposed to relapse back into, I had no idea, but I played along, letting my eyelids hang at half-mast while I collapsed against the seat and clutched feebly at the front of my jacket. Nora looked back at me approvingly, reaching over to pat my hand as though I was really ailing.

"You hang in there, Gwennie girl. We'll get you home and you can put your feet up if we aren't killed first." She twisted around to frown at the driver.

"I'm not gonna get us killed," he protested, sounding as young as one of my high school students. "Miss Franklin, is that you back there?"

Fabulous. I bolted upright, my eyes now wide open, trying desperately to recall his name. After twenty something years of teaching, though, most faces looked the same. Unless, of course, they'd made some sort of impression on me, usually that of the negative kind.

"Oh, hey you." I spoke weakly, resorting to my tried and true greeting of forgotten students. "How are things?"

"I'm great." He fixed his gaze on the rearview mirror and narrowly missed a bicyclist that had swerved into our lane. "Sorry to hear you aren't feeling so good. Is that why you quit teaching?"

"Something along those lines." I tried to glare at a grinning Nora and smile at the driver simultaneously. I was saved from further conversation by a cacophony of horns as we zipped into the only empty space in front of Nora's luxury apartment building.

"Thanks for the ride. It was really good to see you again."

"Yeah, you too. Gimme a call whenever you need to go somewhere." He reached into the middle console and fished out a grubby card. "Use this number and I'll let you know if I'm available, okay?"

I grabbed it out of his hand before Nora's fingers closed on it. Brent Mayfair. That was his name. Smiling at him as I opened the back door, I waved the card at him.

"Well, thanks again, Brent." I felt smug when I said his name. "Please say hello to your mom for me."

"Will do, Miss F. See ya." And with a screech of tires, he shot back into traffic millimeters ahead of a fully loaded passenger van.

"If that kid makes it to his next birthday without causing an accident, I'll personally bake him a cake." Nora started to shake her head but reached up one hand instead to explore the ponytail. "Well, come on, partner. We've got big plans to make."

The big plans entailed making a pot of coffee, slicing a Danish pastry—cream cheese, my favorite–and thumbing through Instagram and Pinterest. By the time I'd looked at a million videos of cute kittens and puppies and commented on a handful of posts, I was ready to go home. All of that screen time, plus a few bites of pastry, and I was ready for a nap. Nora hadn't even touched her Danish. That probably had something to do with why I was a bit broader in the beam than she was.

"Nora, it's been a blast, but I need to get going." I stood and stretched, stiff from sitting curled up on one of Nora's overstuffed linen-covered sofas. "So much for our business planning session." I stifled a yawn, glad I could fall back into bed if the spirit moved me. Maybe I did need to get a hobby.

Nora looked at me, one eyebrow lifted in that half-questioning, half-mocking way she'd perfected over the years.

"What do you mean, 'so much for our business yadda yadda'? I got most of it done while you were playing on your phone." Holding her iPad up so I could see the screen, she gave me a smug smile. "And here's what I'm calling it. Two Sisters Private Services. Whaddya think?"

"Nora, that 'private services' bit makes us sound, I don't know, a tad sleazy, don't you think?" I held out one hand for the iPad, visions of what our uniform might entail nearly giving me the heart attack I'd feigned in the Uber.

She leaned over and poked me in the arm, a mischievous glint in her eyes. "I'm just kidding, Sis. How about Two Sisters Pet Valet Services? I think that has a classy ring to it, don't you?"

I sat back down with a relieved thump, rubbing my arm where she'd hit it. "Much better. I don't think it would be good for my reputation to be part of a 'private services' gig anyway." I glanced at the iPad, noting she'd listed her name first. Fair enough. "Any idea how we might start rounding up a few takers?"

She gave a nonchalant shrug, a too-casual dip of one shoulder that had me instantly on high alert.

"Easy enough. I'll print up a few business cards and slide them underneath the doors in this building while you canvas the dog park across the street." She started walking toward the desk that peeked out from behind a Japanese silk screen in one corner of the room, the latest in desktop computers and printers sitting primly side by side on its polished surface.

"Hold up." I stared at her, my hands lifted and eyes narrowed. "How come you get to stay inside and I have to go out? It's raining cats and dogs out there, in case you didn't notice."

"All the better to snag a few clients."

"Oh, hardee har har. I'm serious."

"So we both go. Gwen, if we're going to be successful pet sitters, we've got to get used to being outside."

She had a point. Just as sure as God made those little green apples, Portland skies would always be ready to dump something on our heads.

I was ready to give in gracefully when another thought crossed my mind. I bounced to my feet, hands on my hips, a suspicious expression on my face.

"Nora, exactly how much experience have you had in, uh, dealing with animal waste? I mean, you do realize that we have to clean up after the little darlings, right?" I pointed to her stilettos, one eyebrow lifted in question. I could practically see the steaming ooze left behind by one of our clients. The pets, not the owners. And definitely *not* a pleasant visual, I can tell you that.

"Me?" She gave a laugh as she quickly tapped on the keyboard, glancing at the computer's wafer-thin monitor as she typed. "I'm not the poop scooping type. Not one bit. My last husband, or was it the one before, always employed someone to clean up after his precious yappy dogs." She glanced over at me. "And my parents were too busy for me to have any pets of my own."

"I hate to break it to you, but that someone is going to be *us* in this little business venture." A thought occurred to me and I said, "You haven't been picking up after the dogs you've been walking, have you?"

She stopped typing and stared across the room at me, eyebrows drawn together in consternation.

"Well, no, but..." Her voice trailed off and then her face brightened, the lines smoothing out. "But we can hire someone to do that part of it. Easy peasy. How about that kid that drove us here? He needs something else to do besides trying to cause a wreck."

I let my hands drop to my thighs, wincing as I hit a bruise I'd collected from a recent round with the lawn edger. That was Nora's answer to everything. Hire someone. Throw money at them. How we were going to pay for all of this and still make any money was beyond me. Before I could get any further with these rather dismal thoughts, Nora looked at me, smiling and waving a handful of newly printed business cards.

"Aaand here we go, Sis! It's time to get this show on the road to fame and fortune."

Two hours and fifteen floors later, plus a brief jaunt across the street to the Portland Pooch Park during a break in the rain, we had collected four new clients.

And a few other souvenirs as well.

I examined the bottoms of my Birkenstocks before wiping them on a patch of grass outside of the apartment building. I'd have to hose them off before I could wear them again in polite company.

Nora, of course, had managed to navigate the puppy pitfalls in her sky-high heels.

"This could really turn into something big, Gwen. Really big." She tossed the leftover cards onto the concierge's desk as we walked back into the luxury apartment building, ignoring the irritated expression on the woman's face. I walked behind Nora and scooped the cards up again with an apologetic smile. Sometimes going places with Nora made me feel like a pet owner in training: I always had to clean up her messes. And judging by the way the woman's face wrinkled in revulsion, she thought so as well.

Or maybe it was my shoes.

"So, what's the schedule?" I hurried to catch up with Nora, shoving the cards into my jacket pocket. "Did we say I'd be starting tomorrow?"

"Tomorrow?" Nora snorted, giving her head a hair-wrecking toss. "You're starting today, hon." She looked at me with a critical eye, her nose wrinkling as her glance swept over my sandaled feet. "I guess I'll have to loan you something to wear."

I looked down and saw the dark streak that stretched from the bottom of the shoe to the side of my sock. It was pretty repugnant. I really hoped I wouldn't have to toss out the shoes. They'd been faithful companions for at least ten years. Maybe more. And were much less critical than some folks, that was certain. They never uttered a peep, no matter the weather, and were always ready to roll for any occasion. Sigh. Maybe it was time to retire them. Kind of like me, come to think of it. Was that how an old teacher was viewed? As a worn-out shoe with disgusting things stuck all over the bottom?

"Gwen? You all right?" Nora was leaning toward me, a concerned expression on her face. "I didn't mean I don't like your sandals, I really didn't. It's that they've got, well…" She let her words trail off into midair as the elevator came to a juddering halt.

Forcing myself to smile, I straightened my shoulders, hopefully adding an inch or three to my height and subtracting a few unnecessary pounds from around my middle. "Not a problem. I'll take them off before we go inside."

"And I know just the place you can leave them, too." Nora giggled, pointing down the carpeted hallway. "That snotty Linda Fletcher needs a surprise package, wouldn't you say?"

Dealing with Nora was like handling a roomful of hormone-crazed teens. The best way to do that, I'd always found, was to respond firmly but kindly and to redirect their risk-taking brains in another direction.

"Why don't we leave her a business card instead?" I pulled one out of my pocket. "She can give it to someone who has a pet." Or not. She'd probably tear it up and sprinkle the pieces in front of Nora's door.

The ongoing feud between Nora and Linda was something out of a soap opera. Or an elementary playground. I didn't know the entire story, but I did know there was something to do with a man, of course, and maybe a few mean-spirited tricks or two that Nora might have played on her.

"You're no fun. How'd you ever survive teaching high school?"

"Because I wasn't any fun." I said it solemnly, only half in jest, and she began laughing, pulling me inside behind her.

"Oh, you. You probably had them falling out of their desks. And kick off those sandals," she called over her shoulder as she headed to the kitchen. "I think there's an extra pair of house slippers under the couch. Coffee? Or hot tea?"

"Tea, please." I bent down to fish out the slippers. I'd taken my socks off for good measure, holding them by the cuff before tucking them inside the sandals. Might as well go whole hog and dump the lot. Maybe I could have a farewell, a send-off, Viking style. It might smell pretty bad, though. Tossing them in the nearest dumpster was probably the best bet. Sighing morosely, I slipped my bare feet inside the pair of fuzzy shoes and shuffled toward the kitchen.

And froze.

Nora was standing in the middle of the room, both hands covering her mouth, eyes opened as wide as they'd go. Stretched out on the floor, a large knife protruding from her chest, was Linda Fletcher. And, judging by the pool of blood on the floor surrounding her, this was no joke.

About the Author

Dane McCaslin, *USA Today* bestselling author of the Proverbial Crime Mysteries series, is a lifelong writer whose love of mysteries was formed early in life. At age eight, she discovered Agatha Christie—much to her mother's dismay—and began devouring any and all books she could find that featured murder and mayhem. After retiring from her career as a high school and community college English teacher, Dane now devotes her newly found freedom to writing mystery novels…and reading for pleasure.

Printed in the United States
by Baker & Taylor Publisher Services